D. R. Meredith's first book,
MURDER BY IMPULSE

"The crime is imaginative, the characters memorable, the West Texas locale evocative and the story hair-raising. In four increasingly suspenseful novels ... Meredith has developed into a fresh, snappy voice of crime fiction."

Newsday

"Meredith, in *Murder by Impulse*, is continuously testing the limits of the crime novel genre. Her intricate plot is smoothly and ingeniously stitched together. ... There are now some excellent mystery writers living and working in Texas, and D.R. Meredith is one of the best."

Dallas Times Herald

"Fans who liked Meredith's sheriff stories are sure to be charmed with her new detective, John Lloyd Branson, and members of the quirky supporting cast who make their bows in *Murder by Impulse*."

Amarillo Sunday News-Globe

"A bright combination of mystery, character study and old-fashioned romance ... Meredith, creator of the prize-winning 'Sheriff' mystery series, is a skilled professional who knows how to pull the wool over the reader's eyes."

Rave Reviews

Also by D. R. Meredith
Published by Ballantine Books:

MURDER BY IMPULSE
MURDER BY MASQUERADE
MURDER BY REFERENCE
THE SHERIFF AND THE PANHANDLE
    MURDERS

MURDER BY DECEPTION

D.R. Meredith

BALLANTINE BOOKS • NEW YORK

Copyright © 1989 by D. R. Meredith

All rights reserved under International and Pan-American Copyright Conventions. Published in the United States of America by Ballantine Books, a division of Random House, Inc., New York, and simultaneously in Canada by Random House of Canada Limited, Toronto.

Library of Congress Catalog Card Number: 89-90726

ISBN 0-345-35243-2

Printed in Canada

First Edition: August 1989
Third Printing: July 1992

TO GEORGE AND SHARON DRAIN,
TO S.T.A.N.D. AND THE NUCLEAR WASTE TASK FORCE,
TO THE EMBATTLED FARMERS OF DEAF SMITH COUNTY,
THIS BOOK IS DEDICATED.
FOR THE THOUSAND GENERATIONS YET UNBORN,
MAY GOD GRANT US THE STRENGTH TO SAVE THE LAND.

The characters and events in this story are fictitious.
The nuclear waste repository and the threat it poses are not.

CHAPTER ONE

Amarillo, Texas—late August

HE WAS GETTING OLD, HE GUESSED, AS HE CLIMBED OFF HIS tractor to close the gate. Time was when he was in the fields by five o'clock. He'd turn off the tractor, smoke his first cigarette, and enjoy the orangy sunrise. The wind would hardly be stirring, like it was taking a deep breath, preparing itself to blow the rest of the day and half the night. It was his favorite time: the cool stillness before the day heated up and the wind tried to pick up his topsoil and carry it into the next county.

No time for that kind of lollygagging this morning. He'd missed the sunrise by a good four hours. It was late in the day, and late in the season. He should've burrned off the wheat stubble a month ago, and by mid-August he should've plowed under the charred stalks and planted his winter wheat. But he hadn't, and trying to get the soil ready for planting this late in the year was pure foolishness. Or more likely,

1

pure habit. Plant, harvest, plant again. For forty years he'd lived by that cycle; he reckoned he'd go on living that way. Long as he could anyway.

He climbed back on the tractor and put it in gear. That might not be much longer, he thought, as he glanced to the east, where tall buildings shimmered above the horizon. Amarillo was pushing closer every day, annexing land in big gulps, spitting it out in the form of housing developments where a man could live ten feet away from his neighbor. It wasn't decent, folks living jammed together like cattle in a pen. All kinds of meanness and disease could breed under conditions like that.

He twisted around on the high tractor seat to make sure the plow blades were slicing into the earth, leaving furrows in the rich soil. Facing front again, he noticed a black-and-white police car turning into the driveway of one of the houses in the development just across the road. Meanness already, he thought. Those folks didn't even have a good stand of grass in their front yard, and already the police were paying them a visit. Well, it wasn't any of his business—as long the meanness didn't cross his fence. If it did, he knew how to take care of his own. A twelve-gauge shotgun would cure a lot of meanness.

He turned down the fencerow and stopped the tractor. It was a long time before he stopped looking at the white cloth hanging on the fence, and at what was lying twenty-five or so feet in front of it.

Meanness had crossed the road and crept through the fence.

At first glance, he was a fine figure of a man: tall, broad-shouldered, slim-hipped, with curly black hair and blue eyes. Even the butcher knife buried in the middle of his chest didn't seriously detract from his good looks. Of course, that was at first glance, thought Sergeant Larry Jenner. After that, your eyes kept returning to the brown plastic handle pointing toward the sky like some kind of obscene lightning rod, and you didn't notice anything else.

"We ought to cover him up."

Jenner jerked at the sound of the farmer's voice. He'd forgotten the old man was there. "Can't," he replied. "This is what we call a crime scene and I have to preserve it just as it is. I can't move anything, touch anything, damn near can't breathe. Can't contaminate the evidence, you see. I just watch over the body and its bedsheet"—he nodded over his shoulder toward the white material hanging on the fence—"until the Special Crimes Unit shows up. They investigate all suspicious deaths, and that gentleman over there sure didn't die of natural causes."

The farmer rubbed his gnarled hand over his face. "Don't seem decent, him just lyin' there nekkid as a jaybird."

Jenner grinned nervously. "He does have on socks."

The old man tightened his lips in disapproval. "Disrespectful," he muttered, and Jenner couldn't decide if the farmer was referring to the victim's nudity, or to his choice of fluorescent footwear.

There was silence and Jenner hoped his companion had run out of conversation about the corpse. It was bad enough to have to stand guard over it, even from twenty-five feet away, without having to talk about it. Let the Special Crimes Unit listen to the old man. That was their job. He was a plain vanilla cop, not a murder investigator. All he was responsible for was securing the crime scene until he was relieved, and then writing up an incident report explaining how he happened to be the first officer on the scene.

"Why'd they dump him in my field?" demanded the farmer.

Jenner sighed. Evidently the old man was going to worry the whole incident like a dog worrying a bone. "You don't recognize him?"

"Don't know him. It's not right to drop him in my field. Man could have a heart attack seeing a thing like that. At first I thought he was a drunk or one of them perverts, and I was gonna tell him to get his nekkid ass off my property. Nearly fell off my tractor when I saw that knife a-stickin' out of his chest.'' The farmer wiped his hand over his face again. ''I seen dead men before—I was in the war—but I don't expect to see 'em in the middle of my field. It ain't right.'' Again he bore that tight-lipped look of disapproval. ''And it ain't decent. It just ain't decent.''

Jenner wondered what the old man's definition of a decent murder was. One where the victim kept his clothes on? He shifted his feet and wished the Special Crimes Unit would hurry. It was hotter than the hinges of hell and he wanted to get back in his air-conditioned patrol car. It was supposed to be a hundred and five in the shade. Except there wasn't any shade around, just fence posts and stubble and a dead body, which in the heat would start to smell before long.

He swallowed quickly. He wished he hadn't thought about the smell. And as long as he was wishing, he wished he hadn't been driving down this particular back road on the western edge of Amarillo, wished the farmer hadn't flagged him down, wished some inconsiderate bastard hadn't dumped the body inside the city limits. He even wished he'd never climbed out of bed this morning. Damn, but he hated murder.

''These must be the folks you're waitin' on,'' observed the farmer, cupping his hands around a match to protect it from the wind while he lit a cigarette. ''The way they're using them sirens, a man would think the corpse was fixin' to get away.''

Jenner didn't answer. And he wasn't watching the caravan of black-and-white cars from the Amarillo Police Department, nor the chocolate-and-white units from the Potter County Sheriff's Office. He wasn't paying attention to the big cream-colored van that carried the personnel of the Special Crimes Unit along with the hundred and one pieces of equipment needed to investigate a crime scene. In fact, reflecting on it later, Jenner wasn't sure if he'd seen any vehicles other than the ten-year-old battered green Ford (with one red door) braking to a halt, spewing a cloud of black smoke from its exhaust that would have earned any other driver a citation for faulty pollution control. Not that particular driver, though. There wasn't a cop in Amarillo, or maybe the entire Texas Panhandle, who was man enough to issue a traffic citation to the owner of that car. Not even if he ran over the mayor's gray-haired mother.

"Jenner!"

The voice rumbled from the barrel-chested man climbing out of the Ford.

The sergeant considered his options. He could make a break for his patrol car, or cower behind the bedsheet and hope the stocky man lumbering toward the fence would think he'd vanished down a prairie dog hole.

"Jenner!"

Jenner capitulated. Anyway, he'd heard prairie dogs carried rabies. "For God's sake, Schroder, I heard you the first time, and so did half of west Amarillo."

Sergeant Ed Schroder, investigator for Special Crimes, matched his car, right down to the cloud of smoke, which in his case spiraled up from the unfiltered cigarette poking out of one side of his mouth. The collar, cuffs, and seams of his shirt were frayed; his sport coat was missing a button; and the Salvation Army donation drive would screech to a halt if he offered them his necktie. In short, his clothes didn't look slept in; they looked *camped* in.

Schroder rolled his cigarette to the other side of his mouth, focused washed-out blue eyes on Jenner, and grunted, "Step on that bottom strand of barbed wire."

"What!"

"The fence," said Schroder impatiently. "Not as limber as I used to be."

Jenner put his size eleven boot on the strand of barbed wire. "Hell, Schroder, I thought you'd just look at this fence and it would part like the Red Sea.'' Schroder glared at him and the sergeant remembered the investigator had the sense of humor of a clod of dirt.

Schroder slipped between the strands of barbed wire with all the finesse of Peter Rabbit escaping Farmer Brown. He left his jacket hanging from the top strand, and a three-cornered piece of his trousers on the bottom one. Anyone else would've felt ridiculous, thought Jenner, retrieving the jacket and handing it to the investigator. But not Schroder.

''Background,'' said Schroder, putting on his jacket and fishing in one sagging pocket for a tiny notebook. His eyes flickered from the corpse to the old farmer standing where Jenner had left him.

''At approximately 9:20 on August 26, I was proceeding down Soncy Road after answering a domestic disturbance call when Mr. Leroy MacPhearson, self-employed as a farmer in Potter County, flagged me down to report a possible homicide. I asked the location of this alleged homicide and Mr. MacPhearson—''

Schroder's eyebrows drew together until they formed a solid line. ''When I want to hear an incident report, I'll read one aloud, Jenner. Do you think you can tell me what else happened without sounding like your underwear's full of official crap, or shall I kick your ass up between your shoulder blades?''

''I'm going by the book, Schroder!''

''I don't read that book. Besides, you're just trying to make me mad. You think if you sound like you've got mush between your ears, I'll kick you off this case and you can get back to handing out tickets for running stop signs.''

''Damn it to hell, Schroder! I'm not on this case. I just caught the squeal, discovered it was a D.R.T.—Dead Right There—and called Special Crimes just like I'm supposed to. Then I secured the scene until you got here. Since I'm not a homicide investigator, I'll just get back on duty. I'll write up my incident report before I go off shift and send it over to your office tomorrow.'' He raised his hand. ''Nice to see you again, Schroder.''

He was two steps away when he heard a sound like an avalanche rumbling down a rocky mountainside. Except the nearest mountain was at least two hundred miles away in New Mexico. Besides, he'd heard that sound before. Wearily he turned around. ''All right, Schroder, want to tell me what's so goddamn funny.''

''You are, son. Walking away with your shoulders all hunched up like you were expecting somebody to stab you in the back.''

Jenner straightened his shoulders. ''Maybe that's because I don't trust you, Schroder. Maybe that's because every time I turn my back, you go running to the chief with some bullshit about how you need my help and could you borrow me for the investigation.'' He heard himself yelling and stopped to take a breath. ''It's not gonna work this time. There is no way, N-O W-A-Y,''—he spelled the words—''you can twist the facts to convince the chief to reassign me to Special Crimes.''

Schroder fired up another cigarette with a lighter that looked as old and battered as his car. He squinted at Jenner through the smoke. ''Already have, son. The chief was real understanding, seeing as how it's vacation time and I'm shorthanded. I told him how you helped break that case up in Canadian, told him I couldn't have done it without you. What's the matter? Your face is turning red and swelling up like a toad. You ought to wear a hat in weather like this. A man can get sunstroke before he knows what's happening.''

''You son of a bitch!''

Schroder shook his head in disapproval. ''You want to watch your language in front of civilians, son,'' he said, nodding toward the old farmer. ''Gives them a bad impression of the police department.''

Jenner felt himself turn even redder and he swallowed his next words, which dealt with where Schroder could stuff his investigation. The burly detective was right. It was unprofessional to be cursing another officer in public. Even when the other officer deserved it. "I'm *not* your son," he finally said between clenched teeth.

Schroder grinned and Jenner wanted to gag. Schroder's smile would spoil a cannibal's appetite for a week.

The investigator slapped Jenner's back. "Just wishful thinking, Sergeant. Told the chief just before I came out here that I couldn't be prouder of you if you were my own son. Told him you got a real gut instinct for homicide investigation."

"I damn sure do! It makes me want to throw up!"

Schroder ignored him. Selective deafness was one of the investigator's less endearing personality traits. "Let's take a look at the deceased."

"I've already seen him," protested Jenner. "He's not going to look any different now than he did thirty minutes ago. That's the way it is with corpses: they just don't improve with age." The glare from Schroder made him wish he'd kept his mouth shut. Reluctantly he trailed after the detective.

One of the female investigators was busily photographing two sets of footprints. After snapping each picture, she leaned down and moved a ruler to the next footprint. Routine, thought Jenner numbly. Everything at a crime scene was photographed, measured, tagged, and carried away to be examined, weighed, poked at, and discussed. Including the corpse. Especially the corpse.

Schroder stopped a few feet from the body and squatted down. A good trick, Jenner decided, since the detective was shaped like a barrel. He could see freckled scalp through the thinning hair on the top of Schroder's head and thought about a hat. A man going bald needed to wear a hat when he was out in the sun. Shit, he thought. Must be suffering from sunstroke myself if I'm worried about Schroder. Let the bastard get a sunburned head. Jenner reconsidered. On the other hand, Schroder with a sunburn might be an even bigger bastard to get along with. He wondered what kind of hat the old fart would like.

"Either set of footprints yours?" asked Schroder, getting to his feet.

Jenner blinked and stopped thinking of haberdashery. "Yeah, that set to the left of the body."

Schroder rubbed a bristly patch of chin whiskers that his razor had missed. "What's the old man's name again?" he asked, jerking his head toward the farmer.

"MacPhearson. Leroy MacPhearson. Seems like a nice old guy. He's really upset about someone dumping a body here."

"Is he color-blind?"

"How the hell would I know?"

"Either he is or the victim was. Why else would the corpse be dressed in one pink sock and one yellow sock?"

Jenner felt the sweat running down his spine turn icy. "What are you saying, Schroder?"

The investigator rolled his cigarette to the other side of his mouth. "There ain't but two sets of footprints, and one set is yours. Now unless we want to believe someone dropped a dead body from an airplane or helicopter or some other kind of flying machine, which doesn't fit the facts, then the other set belongs to the murderer. I looked kinda close at those footprints, and they appear to be made by someone wearing thick-soled workboots. And there's something else about those prints: they're deep like maybe the man who made them was carrying something heavy. Like a body."

"And maybe the guy was fat. Did you ever think of that, Schroder? Maybe he weighed three hundred pounds all by himself."

Schroder nodded approval. "Now you're thinking like a homicide investigator. You consider all possible explanations, then you see which one fits the facts. Now the fact is whoever made those footprints wore a boot on his left foot that had a heel two inches higher than the one on the right.

That farmer over there, looking like butter won't melt in his mouth, wears an orthopedic workboot on his left foot that ought to match our footprints.''

Jenner involuntarily glanced at Mr. MacPhearson's foot. Schroder was right about the boot, but that didn't make him right about everything else. ''If you think Mr. MacPhearson is a murderer, then you're as full of crap as a Christmas turkey. He's an old man.''

''Then he's a tough old man, tough as shoe leather, because he's sure as hell the murderer.'' He made a circling motion with one thick, stubby finger. ''Look at the footprints, Jenner. You don't have to be an Indian tracker to figure out what they're telling us. Deep prints lead from the tractor to the body. Shallower prints lead from the body to the fence where that sheet is hanging, and from there back to the tractor. All the prints are made by the same pair of workboots.''

Jenner raked his fingers through his hair and glanced at Leroy MacPhearson placidly smoking a cigarette, then back at the investigator who was also placidly smoking. He hoped Schroder choked on the smoke. He hoped his head sunburned a bright cherry red. ''For Christ's sake, Schroder, maybe he just walked over to look at the body, make sure he wasn't seeing things, then went over to look at the sheet. Maybe he thought someone was hanging their wash on his fence.''

''With a bloodstain the size of Potter County in the middle of it?''

Jenner looked at the sheet and swallowed hastily. It wasn't merely stained; it was stiff with blood. ''There's another explanation, Schroder. There's got to be. Why would that old man dump a body in his own field?''

''Maybe he didn't want it cluttering up his house. Or maybe he thought nobody would believe he was stupid enough to leave it on his own property.'' An inch-long cigarette ash fell onto Schroder's tie, hung indecisively, then disintegrated into a gray smudge. "One thing for sure, though. The John Doe didn't walk into this field."

Jenner resisted the impulse to brush off Schroder's tie. "How can you tell?"

The investigator shrugged. "No footprints and his socks are clean."

"So maybe he put his socks on after he got here," suggested Jenner.

"That's right. Except someone else put those socks on his feet after he was dead."

"Come on, Schroder, there's no way you can know that." Jenner rubbed his arms. The idea of someone pulling socks on a dead man's feet gave him goose bumps.

Schroder rubbed out his cigarette on the bottom of his shoe and dropped the butt in his coat pocket. "Mr. Doe lying over there bled like a stuck pig. His body is smeared with blood, probably from being wrapped in that sheet. But there's not a speck of blood on his socks."

Jenner wished he hadn't eaten breakfast. In fact, he wished he hadn't eaten dinner the night before. The murder was beginning to sound like a ritualistic nightmare, the kind you read about in a book about Jack the Ripper. But that kind of nightmare didn't happen in a wheat field in the middle of the Texas Panhandle. But it had, and he was involved, and it made him sick to his stomach. And it was all Schroder's fault. He hoped the investigator's head not only turned cherry red, but blistered, too.

"But why, Schroder? Why the socks?"

CHAPTER TWO

Canadian, Texas—late August

"MISS FAIRCHILD!"

"That's me. According to my driver's license, which will probably be suspended. I collected six speeding tickets driving up here from Dallas. Now, what's the emergency, Mrs. Dinwittie?" asked Lydia. "Is John Lloyd ill? Is he hurt?"

"Oh, my, no. Dear Mr. Branson is healthy as a horse," said the older woman, springing to her feet. "He will be as pleased as punch to see you. He was saying the other day that this dusty old law office just wasn't the same without your cheerful face."

"I'd gladly have sent him a photograph."

"Oh, no, that wouldn't have done at all."

Lydia sighed. Getting gold out of Fort Knox was easier than extracting information from Mrs. Dinwittie. "What am I supposed to do?"

"Talk to dear Mr. Branson, of course."

Mrs. Dinwittie looked like a Kewpie doll, wore glasses with pink lenses shaped like cat's eyes, sprinkled clichés through her sentences, and worshipped the ground upon which lawyer John Lloyd Branson walked. Lydia could forgive her every fault but the last one.

"Is the deity in?" she asked.

Mrs. Dinwittie giggled. "Miss Fairchild, you're such a card. I know you'll be able to cheer up Mr. Branson. He's been so down in the dumps lately. Goodness knows, I've tried, but I'm only his secretary." She patted her wavy hair, which to Lydia always looked as if it had been carved out of wood and painted with several coats of black varnish. "That's when I decided to call you."

"Are you saying John Lloyd's depressed? I drove over four hundred miles because you think John Lloyd's depressed? That's impossible. He doesn't believe in depression, and when he doesn't believe in something, it simply doesn't exist." Lydia felt a warm spot begin to spread through her midriff. "Or are you saying the old curmudgeon missed me?"

"Oh, I don't think so, Miss Fairchild."

The warm spot shrank. "That figures," Lydia said in disgust. "You work with a man every hour of the day for three months, and he doesn't even have the decency to miss you."

"But you've only been gone a week . . ."

"That's beside the point."

". . . and he's been worried about this latest murder case. He's not been himself; he's been acting odd."

"John Lloyd Branson doesn't act odd; he *is* odd. Why else would he decorate his entire office in Victorian antiques, including the bathroom. I bet he has the first flush toilet ever invented. As for that couch in his office, it ought to be in a museum. I can feel myself sprouting a bustle every time I sit on it. And the way he talks. My God, he doesn't believe in using contractions. And he signs legal documents with a quill pen. I know; I've seen him do it. The man doesn't live in the twentieth century. What on earth could he be doing that is any odder than usual?''

Mrs. Dinwittie glanced at the door that led into John Lloyd's private office. ''Yesterday he was pacing up and down in his office, so I went to see if he wanted coffee, and Miss Fairchild''—Mrs. Dinwittie lowered her voice to a conspiratorial whisper—''he had taken off his jacket and loosened his tie.''

''His jacket *and* his tie?'' asked Lydia with a sense of unease.

Mrs. Dinwittie nodded. ''I haven't seen him so bothered since he helped me with my little''—she cleared her throat delicately—''problem.''

Only Mrs. Dinwittie could refer to chopping her husband into bite-size pieces with an ax as a little problem, thought Lydia. ''Can't have the great man bothered, can we?'' she asked dryly as she opened the door and silently stepped into the lair of John Lloyd Branson, Attorney at Law.

The lair was just as Lydia remembered it, but then she'd only been gone a week. Besides, change and John Lloyd Branson were a contradiction in terms. The couch, two armchairs with hassocks, occasional tables, marble-topped, of course, and the bookcase-lined walls were unchanged. At the other end of the room were more bookcases, her own small table, a door into the law library, a hat rack holding a Stetson and a silver-headed cane, and center stage: a gigantic rolltop desk with the great man himself, all six feet, four inches of gaunt body and thin, ascetic face, sitting behind it and looking anything but depressed.

In fact, thought Lydia, tiptoeing across the Persian carpet and stopping a few feet short of his desk, he looked damn pleased about something. Eyes closed, he was resting his head against the back of his chair, his hands folded comfortably over his belly. She couldn't see a hair out of place, or a button unfastened. He looked as he always had, or at least as he had for the three months she'd known him. In his black three-piece suits, hand-tooled boots, and Stetson, he looked either alternately like a nineteenth-century undertaker or a riverboat gambler—depending on whether he wore a string tie or a bolero. Today it was a string tie.

Lydia always felt as if she should be clad in black crepe and a veil on string tie days. She tilted her head to one side. As for black crepe—with his eyes closed and his hands folded, John Lloyd looked as if he were laid out for a funeral.

She brought her palms together, closed her eyes, and raised her face heavenward. "Dearly beloved, we are here to pay final tribute to our departed friend in Christ, John Lloyd Branson . . ."

"Miss Fairchild." His voice was exactly the same: a deep, slow drawl.

". . . whose passing will be mourned by all who knew him . . ."

"I am flattered, Miss Fairchild, but your eulogy is positively premature."

Lydia opened one eye. He was amused! She opened her other eye and glared balefully at him. "I wouldn't make book on that, John Lloyd, because in about five seconds I'm going to bludgeon you with the first blunt instrument I see."

He chuckled. "Miss Fairchild, your propensity for settling disputes with physical violence is a character trait you must learn to control."

"This is not a dispute! It's a fight to the death!"

He rose awkwardly from his chair and stepped toward her. "My choice of weapons, I believe?"

"What do you mean?" she demanded suspiciously.

One blond eyebrow arched. "Miss Fairchild, I am disappointed in you. For a reader of graphic historical romances, you should certainly be familiar with the protocol governing a duel. As the challenged party, I have the privilege of choosing the weapon."

Lydia stared at him, trying to decide if he had finally slipped into outright insanity. His obsidian black eyes, always so startling with his blond hair and fair skin, gave no hint of what he was thinking. But then, John Lloyd had refined being poker-faced to an art.

"Are you subject to petit mal seizures, Miss Fairchild?"

"W-what?"

John Lloyd took her arm and led her toward the couch. "You have been staring blankly at me for several minutes. In silence. In the course of our brief acquaintance, I have never known you to be speechless, so I quite naturally assumed you were in the throes of an epileptic seizure. A cerebral hemorrhage could also account for your silence, but I eliminated that diagnosis upon observing no other paralysis except that afflicting your tongue."

Lydia jerked her arm away. "Go to hell, John Lloyd."

"While I abhor your phraseology, I am delighted that your speech centers are not impaired."

"I don't have epilepsy, I haven't had a stroke, and my speech centers are fine," she heard herself shouting. "It's my judgement that's impaired! Otherwise I wouldn't be here."

He gestured at the couch. "Please sit down, Miss Fairchild. I believe you are in what my grandmother called 'a state.' The preferred remedy is to loosen your stays, assist you to a fainting couch, and serve you a cup of tea or a glass of sherry . . ."

"I'm not in a state!"

". . . however, given your propensity for shunning foundation garments—whether stays or their modern equivalent—loosening your clothes would result in an immodest condition that might scandalize Mrs. Dinwittie . . ."

"How can you scandalize someone who ended her marriage with the blade of an ax?"

"With the exception of that one regrettable lapse, Mrs. Dinwittie has been a perfect lady, one you would do well to imitate."

"I'd rather imitate her when she was swinging her ax."

She put her hands on her hips and glared at him. "Do you know what I think?"

"No, but I am certain you will enlighten me. Wait!" He lifted up his hand in an imperial gesture that made her grit her teeth. "It has been an exhausting week. If you would permit me to sit down without accusing me of a breach of manners, I would prefer to be comfortable while you deliver your opinions of my character."

"By all means, sit." She pointed to one of the chairs. "It's easier to talk when you're not looming over me."

His black eyes glittered. "Even at my height, it is difficult to loom over five feet, ten inches of enraged womanhood."

He turned and limped toward the chair. Lydia wondered if his disability was worse than when she had last seen him. Of course it was late in the day, and his limp was always more noticeable in the afternoon, particularly if he was tired. And he had been asleep when she walked in. He was probably in pain, she decided, and she was being a first-class bitch, yelling at him like a shrew.

She trailed after him and perched on the arm of his chair. "Are you all right, John Lloyd? Does your le—?"

She swallowed the last consonant sound as she met his eyes. "I do not need your pity, Miss Fairchild," he said, snapping out each word with no trace of a drawl.

Whoever said dark eyes were warm had never met John Lloyd Branson, she thought. It was her own fault, of course. No one mentioned John Lloyd's bad leg in his presence. Or in his absence either. It was a forbidden subject.

She licked her lips. "I meant, does your head hurt?"

"In view of your stated intention of, uh, bludgeoning me, your extraordinary concern with my health seems a bit illogical, Miss Fairchild," he drawled. "Unless, of course, you have some compunction against harming a sick man. Or does this concern have something to do with Mrs. Dinwittie's phone call?"

She twisted around to stare at him. "You knew?"

He touched the tips of his fingers together. "I had every reason to believe that my behavior would precipitate a response from Mrs. Dinwittie. My casual mention of your name on several occasions determined the direction of that response."

"You bastard! Manipulating poor Mrs. Dinwittie! Manipulating me! To think I drove all the way up here, collecting six speeding tickets on the way, because I was terrified you'd been in some terrible accident, or you were about to die from some unspeakable disease." She sprang off the chair and paced up and down. "Then, when I drag my exhausted body up those stairs . . ."

"You could have used the elevator," he commented quietly.

". . . Mrs. Dinwittie tells me you've slipped a cog worrying about this murder case. I rush into this office . . ."

"You tiptoed," he interjected.

". . . ready to save you from a nervous breakdown, and what do I find? You! Asleep in your chair, looking your usual pristine, stuffed-shirt self, and with a smirk on your face."

"It was necessary," he said, his black eyes studying her intently.

"Why?" she demanded. "Why couldn't you just pick up the phone and ask me to come up? Are you too macho to admit you were worried and needed moral support? For God's sake, John Lloyd, Mrs. Dinwittie's call even scared the dean into missing his breakfast so he could track me down."

"Ah, yes, the dean," he said in a peculiar tone.

"You remember? The dean? Your old buddy, the Dean of the Southern Methodist University School of Law . . ."

"And a very astute man," remarked John Lloyd. "You had best hope he accepts the rather flimsy alibi I concocted for you."

"Alibi?" she squeaked.

He pushed the hassock out of his way and rose from his

chair. "Because I offered you a position with this firm after your graduation next year, I have a proprietary interest in your academic progress." He took a step toward her.

She took a step backward. "Now, John Lloyd."

"I spoke to the dean the second day of classes; the *second* day, Miss Fairchild, and learned that you had already been in his office inquiring as to how many days you might be absent without losing your scholarship. Adding that fact to other facts, such as your not arranging for the utilities to be shut off in your apartment and failing to pick up your cleaning, I concluded you were planning an unscheduled vacation, quite probably next week." He took another step toward her.

She backed up another step. "I can explain."

"And I am sure your explanation would be both elaborate and imaginative. However, you are an abysmal liar, Miss Fairchild. Your cheeks flush, your eyes dart about the room like a horsefly in a stable, and you stutter. In short, you have the poise of a grammar school pupil caught placing a garter snake in her teacher's desk. You would not have fooled the dean, and you would have found yourself minus a scholarship—and quite possibly suspended." He took another step. "I could not permit that to happen. So I engaged in that undignified charade that resulted in Mrs. Dinwittie's calling the dean, thus saving you from the consequences of your emotional impulsiveness."

Lydia waltzed backward until she bumped into the wall. She gazed openmouthed at John Lloyd as he stalked toward her, marking off the distance one slow step at a time, his eyes as black and expressionless as a rattlesnake's just before striking at its prey. Not that he would actually touch her, not John Lloyd, the world's most self-controlled man. But then he didn't need to, not with those black eyes skewering her to the wall. Besides, he had already verbally flayed her alive. Without his exaggerated Texas drawl, his tongue could draw blood.

She straightened her shoulders and advanced. She might

be bloodied, but she wasn't beaten. "All right, I admit it. I'm guilty."

John Lloyd inclined his head like a king accepting tribute. "Most commendable of you to accept responsibility for your actions," he drawled.

Lydia advanced another step and poked him in the chest. "You, however," she said, mimicking his drawl, "are not entirely innocent, either. So climb down off your high horse, Mr. Branson, and join the rest of us emotionally impulsive humans."

A surge of blood stained John Lloyd's high cheekbones. "I pride myself on never acting on an emotional impulse."

Lydia noticed his drawl had disappeared again, a sure sign she'd struck a nerve. "Then why did you lie for me, John Lloyd? Why didn't you wait for me to turn up on your doorstep and kick my buns back to Dallas?"

His eyes blinked once, then he chuckled. "Congratulations, Miss Fairchild. If this were a courtroom, you would have impressed a jury with your spirited rebuttal. A remarkable recovery from ignominious defeat." He chuckled again as he turned and walked toward his desk, his limp barely perceptible.

She stalked after him. "Are you going to answer my question or not?"

"In order to kick your, uh, buns back to Dallas, I first had to insure their proximity to my boot. There was a possibility, remote perhaps, but still a possibility, that you were planning an assignation with some unsuitable male companion . . ."

"I was!" she injected. "You!"

". . . on the other end of the state. By arranging Mrs. Dinwittie's phone call, I morally obligated you to come to Canadian. Now that you are here . . ." He grasped her shoulders.

She twisted. "There's no need to manhandle me, John Lloyd; I'll go quietly. I'll explain to the dean that you had a miraculous recovery. An experimental drug or something.

Hey, what are you doing?'' she cried as he twirled her around and steered her toward the small library table adjacent to his desk.

''Miss Fairchild,'' he drawled as he pushed her down in her chair. ''At most you will miss five days of very boring lectures given by very boring men who have been too long away from the courtroom. You have the blessings of the dean who believes you to be giving me aid and comfort.'' He leaned over and whispered, ''My dear young woman, you should never disappoint a dean.''

When he released her shoulders and turned to his desk, Lydia sagged back in her chair. She had a feeling she'd been outmaneuvered. First he climbed her frame for planning to cut classes, then provided her with an ironclad alibi for doing so. When she offered to return to school, he insisted she stay. ''John Lloyd, you are a devious bastard.''

''I assure you I am quite legitimate.'' He picked up a thick accordion file from his desk and handed it to her. ''Peruse this, Miss Fairchild. While I am allowing you a respite from lectures, I am not excusing you from educational pursuits. This is constitutional law and criminal procedure in practice. This is the law in the flesh, human beings in crisis. This is murder. Read it.''

She tucked her long blonde hair behind her ears, kicked off her shoes, and proceeded to read. At the end of an hour, she leaned over and tapped John Lloyd's shoulder. ''You have a dog of a case. No footprints other than the defendant's. The body found on his property. Fibers consistent with those from his shirt found on the bloody sheet. Defendant's head hair found on body. God himself couldn't help this man.''

''God is not the attorney of record, Miss Fairchild. I am.'' He swiveled his chair around to face her, stretched out his long legs, and crossed them at the ankles. ''Read the autopsy protocol, analyze it, weigh it against the other evidence, and decide: is Mr. MacPhearson guilty or innocent?''

Lydia read the opening page, absently noting that Sergeants Jenner and Schroder observed the autopsy, and decided that she was going to buy a basic anatomy textbook at the very next bookstore she saw. As it was, she had to keep referring to the enclosed diagram to correlate what she was reading with what had happened. Maybe a medical dictionary wasn't such a bad idea either. She didn't know the meanings of several terms used. She did, however, recognize heart, stomach, liver.

She slammed the paper down and swallowed several times. "My God, John Lloyd, I vaguely knew what went on at an autopsy, but reading about the pathologist weighing the heart and the stomach—just cutting them right out and slapping them on a scale! Ugh!" She pressed her hands over her stomach, which was waging a protest of its own.

John Lloyd placed his palms together in a oddly prayerful gesture. With his thin, austere face and somber black suit, there was something almost monkish about him. Except for his eyes. They were not the eyes of a man living a life of peaceful contemplation, but those of a man who embraces the world and finds it wanting. Lydia found herself holding her breath when he began to speak.

"Miss Fairchild, unless you wish to spend your life writing contracts or searching property titles, the practice of law—particularly criminal law—is one harsh experience after another. Most of your clients will not be individuals you would want to invite home for dinner. You would not be wise to turn your back on many of them. They will lie to you, curse you, and confess—*if* they confess—to acts of depravity that will sicken you. The mildest transgression they will commit against you is to steal your fountain pen should you be foolish enough to leave it on your desk. Do not believe that as a defense attorney, we will be defending the innocent. We will not. The majority of our clients will be guilty. Moreover, they will be unrepentant, uncooperative, and resentful of having been arrested."

"Then why, John Lloyd? Why do you defend them?" Lydia whispered. "And why do I want to?"

His eyes had a feverish gleam, a martyr explaining his cause. His voice was slow and deep, an evangelist's voice, persuasive in a terrible calling. "Because the State is impersonal and the sinners all too human. Would you have a man judged by an abstract? No! He may be measured *against* that abstract, but he must be judged by men. It is our duty, our destiny if you will, to defend that man as if he were the only innocent client we might ever have. Because, Miss Fairchild, he might be as guilty as Satan himself, but *not* of the crime of which he stands accused. To judge a man is a terrible thing. It falls to us to insure that he is judged fairly, and that means judged on the evidence. He is not to be found guilty because he is black or brown or white or poor. Or because we don't like him, or his neighbors don't like him, or his reputation is bad. He must be judged guilty because the evidence, fairly collected and fairly presented, *proves* him guilty beyond a reasonable doubt in the eyes of other men."

He rested his head against the back of his chair and closed his eyes. Lydia drew a shallow breath, then a deeper one. She felt almost embarrassed, as if she had seen John Lloyd nude. And in a certain way she had. But she would never call him cold again. John Lloyd Branson was the most intensely passionate man she'd ever met.

He turned his head toward her. "Guilty or innocent, Miss Fairchild?"

"Who?" she asked in confusion.

He sat up to lean over and tap the file case. "Mr. Mac-Phearson."

"Oh, guilty. I told you that before."

"Of what is he guilty, Miss Fairchild?"

"He stabbed this guy in the heart and dumped his body, for God's sake."

John Lloyd put his hands on his knees and leaned forward. "Exactly, Miss Fairchild. Mr. MacPhearson is not guilty of murder, only of abusing a corpse and unlawfully disposing of same.''

"But it was his field, his footprints, and his butcher knife."

John Lloyd shook his head impatiently and picked up the autopsy protocol. "Miss Fairchild, the single most important piece of evidence in a homicide investigation is the victim. You must overcome your squeamishness and pay closer attention to details revealed by an autopsy. The victim's heart was pierced twice by two different fixed-blade knives. According to the pathologist's finding, the attacks occurred from six to eight hours apart. Mr. MacPhearson stabbed a corpse."

CHAPTER
THREE

Amarillo, Texas

SERGEANT LARRY JENNER WAS FEELING SORRY FOR HIMSELF.
He knew it and he wasn't ashamed. He supposed he ought
to be, but damn it, even a grown man had a right to feel sorry
for himself sometimes. And today was one of those times. It
had been a piss-poor day from the moment the alarm clock
didn't go off. He'd cut himself shaving. He'd pulled a button
off his last clean uniform shirt—and the only safety pin in
the house was a diaper pin, one with a pink plastic end. When
he got to work, his black-and-white wouldn't start and he had
to check out another one.

Then, as if enough hadn't gone wrong, there was a wreck
on the Canyon Expressway that left two motorists dead and
traffic backed up for a mile. There were at least ten witnesses
and every damn one of them had a different story. He'd barely
cleaned up that mess when the dispatcher called. Get over to
the D.A.'s office; one of the assistants was having a shitfit

over the MacPhearson case. It was enough to make a cop consider a career change.

He parked his borrowed black-and-white in the only va-cant space in the parking lot behind the Potter County Courts Building. He slid out of his unit into the blistering August heat, slammed the door, and stood looking at the Courts Building, one foot resting in a chuckhole. That building and this parking lot were as screwed up as his day. Fred, the wino who lived in the Dempster Dumpster behind the Shrin-ers' building across the street, had told Jenner the Courts Building would be marble-faced rubble in five years. Fred was an optimist, Jenner decided. Within a year the roof leaked, the elevators worked only intermittently, the air-conditioning blew hot air into the windowless jury rooms, and the fire alarm in the District Attorney's suite had mal-functioned three times in as many weeks, bringing in droves of firemen and sending the district attorney into gibbering fits.

Jenner lifted his foot out of the chuckhole and walked across the parking lot, nimbly avoiding deep ruts left from the last rain three months ago. Actually, the parking lot wasn't a parking lot; it was the location for the new jail. Which hadn't been built yet because the county commissioners who voted to spend 5.2 million dollars were defeated or didn't run in the last election, and the new commissioners decided fiscal responsibility (and their chance for reelection) man-dated putting the project on hold. And strictly speaking, the jail wasn't going to be a jail, but a holding facility where prisoners were retained overnight, or until they could be transferred to the county correctional facility at the old air force base.

He climbed the ramp of stairs to the brick-surfaced terrace outside the back entrance of the Courts Building. All the glass doors were propped open with boxes of toilet tissue. Great, he thought; the goddamn air-conditioning broke down again. Now he could sit in a hot airless cubicle while some assistant

D.A. chewed his ass over a damn case he didn't have any business being involved with in the first place. And not just any assistant D.A. Hell, no. It had to be Cleetus Miller, Maximum Miller—so-called because he always asked the jury for the maximum sentence allowed by law. And got it. Defense attorneys developed ulcers if they didn't already have them when they found out Maximum Miller would be prosecuting their clients. He ate cops for a snack. Sucked all the information on a case out of them, grilled them harder than the worst cop-hating defense attorney, then tossed them aside liked used-up condoms. And Sergeant Larry Jenner was next on his menu. All because that overweight, sloppy, chain-smoking asshole Schroder had served him up on a platter.

Stepping around a box of toilet paper, he walked down the hall past the District Clerk's office and the bathrooms to the other side of the building. As he passed the elevators he noticed an out-of-order sign hanging on both of them. Just like my life, he thought, as he pulled open the door of the D.A.'s suite: out-of-order and the repairman's out to lunch.

He could hear Miller's voice coming from the number three cubicle before he got past the receptionist's desk. "Goddamn it, Schroder, I never saw a case turn to shit so fast. What are you people at Special Crimes doing: sitting around with your heads up your butts?" As Jenner stepped into the office, he roared at him, "What the hell do you want?"

"Larry Jenner, Sergeant Jenner, Amarillo Police Department Traffic Division."

"What's a traffic cop doing on a homicide investigation?" Miller demanded.

Jenner opened his mouth to say it damn sure wasn't his idea when Schroder interrupted. "Temporary assignment. I asked for him. He's got good instincts."

Miller grunted. "I don't give a damn about instincts. I want evidence!" He slammed a beefy fist on the top of his desk. "And we ain't got it. This case's got a hole big enough to drive my suburban through."

Jenner sat down on one of the gray contoured chairs in front of Miller's desk and tried to find a comfortable position. It was impossible. The chair was contoured to fit a long-legged dwarf with middle-age spread. He crossed his legs and watched Maximum Miller's histrionics instead.

Cleetus Miller was built like a fullback gone to seed. His hair was mostly gray, what there was of it, and his skin was so black it had blue highlights. He was raised in the Flats, Amarillo's first black enclave, before it was an area of substandard housing and decaying businesses. He went to law school on a scholarship, graduated at the top of his class, and went to work in the D.A.'s office before the federal government began pushing racial quotas. He allowed no one to forget the latter. A handprinted sign hung on his office wall: I'M NOT ONE OF THE QUOTA; I'M HERE BECAUSE I'M GOOD. He was, too.

He demanded absolute racial equality, and allowed no familiarity from whites. One of Jenner's favorites among the stories about Miller concerned his comment to a young, snot-nosed white attorney who made the mistake of condescending to the black assistant. "Now you listen here, son," Miller had roared. "You quit acting like you white Southern folks won the Civil War and let's get our business done, or get your skinny ass back over to your office and tell your boss I said you ought to be fired for being stupid." The young attorney resigned and left town.

"He wasn't no great loss," said Miller later. "He must have been a Yankee anyway, 'cause he didn't correct me when I said Civil War. Every white Texan knows it was the War Between the States, or the War of the Southern Secession."

He didn't allow any familiarity from blacks either. Jenner's other favorite story concerned a black pimp Miller was trying. The pimp accosted the assistant D.A. outside the courtroom and asked him to go easy on a soul brother. Miller grabbed a handful of the pimp's chartreuse shirt and lifted him six inches off the floor. "The only thing we got in common, motherfucker, is the fact both our mamas was black." Miller then walked into the courtroom. The pimp got twenty years.

". . . the best thing I can say about your incident report, Jenner, is that you didn't misspell any words."

"Huh?" asked Jenner, aware he hadn't been listening and was going to catch hell for it.

Schroder stuck a fresh cigarette in the corner of his mouth. "Now, Cleetus, you're getting riled. Not doing anybody's blood pressure any hurt but your own. Why don't you just tell us what's got your bowels in an uproar."

Cleetus leaned back in his chair, not a contoured one, Jenner noticed, and looked morose. "Goddamn it, Schroder, this case looked so good when you brought it to me," he said plaintively. "Wasn't no doubt in my mind but what I was going to send that man to the pen for the rest of his natural-born life. He was going to do his farming for the State of Texas. We had evidence, Schroder, evidence I could show the jury. We had fiber, we had hair, we had footprints. I was going to hang that bloody sheet over the rail in front of the jury box for the duration of the trial; leastways until the defense objected. I even started jotting down a few notes for my closing argument. Had my quotes from the Bible all ready. I started working up my re-creation of the crime. He looked at Jenner. "I always kind of act out the crime in story form for the jury. Makes it easier for them to understand what a real motherfucker the defendant is. But my story was missing a few details, like where the murder happened. It wasn't in that field. No sound of disturbance around that body, no sign of blood. Wasn't no blood anywhere on that farm 'cept where ole Farmer MacPhearson killed a chicken for his Sunday dinner. That's when I really began to see we needed some more investigation. But I wasn't worried. Even the Lord took seven days to create the earth. Sergeant Schroder of Special Crimes was in charge, and he's the best.

He's just like an old coonhound; he just keeps following the scent until he trees that coon. You treed him yet, Schroder?'' Miller was pulling his black sharecropper act and Jenner considered snickering. Cleetus Miller was a born and bred Amarilloan. His definition of rural was setting out tomato plants in his flowerbed.

Schroder blew out a cloud of cigarette smoke. "That farm's a sizable piece of real estate, Cleetus. Takes a long time to go over the ground, but we ought to be finished today."

Miller nodded. "I can understand that, Schroder. And 'course maybe I can just open my story with MacPhearson dumping the body. We *know* he did that because of the footprints. And we know that butcher knife's from his kitchen. He sharpened his knives on an old whetstone out in the barn and the FBI can positively identify the patterns made in the steel by the whetstone. So I'm okay there. But there's another little detail missing. Who the hell is this buckass-naked honkie, and what does he have to do with MacPhearson? Juries want to know little things like that. They like a little flashback in their stories. Who is he, Schroder?'' The black assistant was beginning to snap like a dog with distemper.

Schroder ground out his cigarette in the ashtray. "We don't have a record on him and neither does Texas Department of Public Safety. We sent his prints to the FBI, but that'll take a while."

"You're telling me he's still a John Doe?"

Schroder was beginning to look a tad bad-tempered himself, or Jenner guessed he was. Schroder always wore an expression like a bear with an abscessed paw. "Cleetus, you know an investigation always goes faster after we make the victim. And we'll make this one. He ain't a down-and-outer. He's got a fancy haircut and manicured nails. Somebody's gonna miss him. We're still working the case. Like you said, the Lord didn't make the world in a day."

"The Lord didn't have John Lloyd Branson on his ass, Schroder!" yelled Miller. "Mr. Branson sashayed in here yesterday morning like he could walk on water, sat in the library, read the case file like he's entitled to, all the time looking wiser than Solomon. He was still sitting here when the pathologist sent over the autopsy protocol. He grabbed it right out of the messenger's hands, photocopied it, and had it digested before I got my reading glasses on. That's when the shit hit the fan, Schroder.''

Miller was standing up now, his eyes ready to bulge out of his head. Jenner scooted down in the chair and crossed his legs. It was nice to see somebody chewing Schroder's ass for a change. ''Why didn't you tell me about that autopsy, Schroder? Weren't you and the traffic cop there observing? Your names are on the protocol. I checked just so I'd know whose asses to kick.''

Schroder glanced at Jenner and the younger man knew his ass was grass just as soon as Schroder could get him outside. The investigator lit another cigarette, inhaled, then let the smoke trickle out of one side of his mouth. ''I was out of the room for a few minutes.''

Miller started to breathe heavily, like a bull about to charge. ''Out of the room! You aren't supposed to leave the autopsy.'' He turned to Jenner. ''What about you?''

Jenner stuttered. ''I—I was out, sir.'' He had been, too. Out cold on the floor. Schroder had dragged him into the hall, brought him around with a glass of water in the face, and left him leaning against the wall, puking into a bedpan. God, but he hated autopsies.

''What was in the autopsy protocol that let Branson pin your ears back, Cleetus?'' asked Schroder. Miller told him. Then the investigator gave Jenner a look that told him he was chin-deep in shit, and Schroder was personally going to push his head under.

Miller sat down and wiped a handkerchief over his sweating bald head. ''Branson sat right here in this office and told me he might let his client plead to abuse of a corpse. Then he folded his hands over that silver-headed cane of his, and allowed that on reconsideration, he wouldn't do that either. Said it was questionable whether we could prove abuse since there weren't any fingerprints on the knife and juries always liked fingerprints. All the goddamn TV they watch. Before I could argue that point, the son of a bitch said he was filing a motion with the judge to reduce bond—seeing as how we had mischarged his client. He bonded MacPhearson out an hour later.''

He slammed his fist on his desk again. "I don't like feeling dumb, Schroder. In my fifteen years as a prosecutor I've lost five murder cases, every damn one of them to John Lloyd Branson. I'm not going to lose this one. He asked the judge for an examining trial, because he felt His Honor would agree that the prosecution—that's me, Schroder—didn't have enough evidence to support asking the grand jury for a murder indictment. He said an examining trial would save both his client and the prosecution the embarrassment of an unjustified murder charge. I told the bastard I'd protect my own reputation. But I was lying. Lawyer Branson is going to kick my ass all over the courtroom come Monday morning. But MacPhearson is implicated in this murder right up to his eyebrows. My gut tells me that, and so does yours. And I think Branson's says so, too. That's why he's pushing for an examining trial. Catch us with our pants down, get a quick dismissal, then scream harassment every time we look sideways at his client.''

"You sure don't like Mr. Branson, do you?" asked Jenner involuntarily.

"You young idiot!" roared Miller. "John Lloyd Branson is the only white man I've ever met that I'd let my sister marry. That's because he's the only man I ever met, black or white, who's as smart as I am." The black prosecutor sat down and wiped his face. "Schroder, you take this fool traffic cop, and the two of you get out on the streets, or down on old MacPhearson's farm, and get me some evidence, or I'm going to make chitlins out of your balls.''

CHAPTER FOUR

LYDIA STOOD AT THE WINDOW LOOKING DOWN AT THE TOWN of Canadian. Dusty pickups were clattering down its uneven red brick streets, stopping at corners to discharge wives in a hurry to begin Saturday morning shopping. With a wave of the hand and a vague remark about errands to run, their drivers sped off in search of farming cronies at the feed store, or the farm equipment store, or the hardware store, or maybe the local café. They'd gossip about one thing or another: who was in trouble with the bank, or with his wife; whether to sell cattle or feed them over the winter; the chances of the Canadian High School football team winning the conference.

Sooner or later, Lydia knew, the conversation turned to the IQ, parentage, and sex habits of politicians—the natural predators of farmers. They all agreed the first was low, the second doubtful, and the third indiscreet. Farmers held politicians in about as much esteem as green bugs in the wheat. Maybe less.

33

After wishing the politicians, individually as well as collectively, all the prosperity of a chicken farmer with one sterile rooster, they would choose up sides and argue farm policy: higher farm subsidies, lower farm subsidies, no farm subsidies; lower production by letting land lay fallow to force prices up, raise production and export more, sell wheat to the Russians, don't sell wheat to the Russians. They never all agreed on any one policy, but it was a way to pass the time until they picked up Mama and the kids for lunch.

But there was one subject about which every farmer agreed: the dump. In Deaf Smith County just southwest of Amarillo lay one of the three test sites for America's only underground, high-level, nuclear waste repository. The dump. An ecological disaster in the making, a radioactive time bomb with a ten-thousand-year fuse ticking away underground. Also underground lay another kind of repository: the Ogallala Aquifer, the water supply for eight states. Eight *agricultural* states, the breadbasket of America. One leak, one bit of seepage, an unexpected shift in the earth's crust, for whatever reason, that endangered the integrity of the dump, and the aquifer would be contaminated—forever. From productive land to nuclear waste in a single generation. America would no longer worry about selling wheat to the Russians; America would be buying wheat from them.

Whenever Lydia thought of the proposed dump, she added a few curses of her own. She wanted to shake somebody, to scream at every member of the Department of Energy. How could those idiots risk *eight* states, for God's sake? Very little chance of an accident, said the DOE. Lydia would rather depend on a fortune-teller to predict the future. Tarot cards were more reliable than the assurances of the DOE.

"Miss Fairchild, much as I commend you for your concern over the survival of the Panhandle, clenching your fists and scowling will not stop the robots from the Department of Energy. They have been programmed, and any constructive comment or exhibition of opposition is met with an automatic response: it does not compute. One must approach their masters, who, being politicians, are much more likely to melt in the heat of adverse publicity and organized opposition.''

"How did you know I was thinking of the dump?'' asked Lydia. "Have you taken up mind reading?''

He snapped his watch closed and tucked it back in his vest pocket. "Miss Fairchild, I am a man of logic. I do not indulge in the mumbo jumbo of carnival fortune-tellers. Moreover, in the case of your mind''—he bowed, and she had the urge to kick him in the shins—"extrasensory perception is not necessary. Excluding myself, the repository is the only entity that causes you to clench your fists. I pity any Department of Energy spokesman who should happen to be within grasp.''

Lydia flopped down in the chair behind her table. "I'd like to poke one of them in the nose.''

John Lloyd slipped a yellow legal pad into a briefcase. "So would eighty-seven percent of the population if the latest poll is at all accurate. However, I advise against it. There are other avenues of resistance. Remember Gandhi brought down an empire by nonviolent protest.''

"Three cheers for Gandhi,'' said Lydia sarcastically. "He wasn't fighting the DOE.''

John Lloyd cocked one eyebrow. "That is true, Miss Fairchild. The British government boasted a few men of intelligence. I am not sure the same can be said of the Department of Energy.'' He rose to his feet, surreptitiously putting most of his weight on his good leg. "However, the repository has nothing to do with our task for this morning, which is that of persuading Mr. MacPhearson to divulge more information than his insistence that he can afford my fee. While that fact is gratifying, it is hardly the basis upon which to build a defense.'' He picked up his briefcase and reached for his hat and cane. "Do not dawdle, Miss Fairchild. Mr. MacPhearson is waiting.''

Lydia grabbed her shoulder bag and trotted after him, wondering how anybody with a gimpy leg could move so fast. "I thought you had a defense. Abuse of a corpse, et cetera."

He hurried her through the reception area. "Miss Fairchild," he said in a voice so slow there was practically a heartbeat between each word. "Like a good novel, a murder has a beginning, a middle, and an end. We know the end, and so does our adversary, Sergeant Schroder. But it is the beginning and the middle that concern me. When they are known, they might well prove that Mr. MacPhearson was both the last and the first to stab our corpse."

"Do you think he'll tell you, John Lloyd?"

"Occasionally I find it necessary to resort to subterfuge, Miss Fairchild. Set the cat among the pigeons, so to speak."

Lydia grabbed his arm. "The last time you did that, you used me as the cat, without telling me, I might add, and I ended up with kitty litter all over my face. I refuse to be a party to any sneaky, underhanded charade you have in mind."

"You are clenching your fists again, Miss Fairchild. If that means you are preparing to assault me, please wait until we reach the bottom of the stairs. Blood might stain the wood."

Lydia unclenched her fists and walked down the stairs, promising herself that one day she'd win an argument with John Lloyd, even if she had to resort to subterfuge to do it.

"Old MacPhearson had a farm," sang Lydia as they parked in front of a two-story farmhouse with gingerbread trim and a porch that ran its length. "Look, John Lloyd, there are chickens and pigs, and I can see some cows in a pasture behind the barn. There's a tractor and a—what is that big thing?"

"I believe you are referring to a combine, Miss Fairchild," he replied dryly. "It is used to harvest wheat."

"I know what it's used for. I've just never seen one in real life. I grew up in Dallas, remember. You don't exactly find combines on every street corner."

She climbed out of John Lloyd's black Lincoln and discovered several things at once. The first: that there is a very good reason for animal pens to be built at some distance from a farmer's home. The combined waste products of pigs, chickens, and cattle produce an odor far removed from the Romantics' odes to rustic life. Her second discovery was that every farmer has at least one dog, sometimes more. Leroy MacPhearson had three snarling dogs of indeterminate breed, all vying for the first sizable chunk out of Lydia's anatomy.

"Help!" she screamed, vaulting onto the hood of the car with the agility of a track star.

John Lloyd was showing agility of his own as he bounded out of the car waving his cane. "Down, you blasted mutts!"

Crouched against the windshield with her arms crossed over her face, Lydia heard the animals' snarls change to whines. She peeked over her arm to watch each dog roll onto his back in a wiggling, fur-covered posture of subservience. John Lloyd had that effect on some people, too.

A screen door slammed behind a wiry old man in overalls. "Them dogs botherin' you, Mr. Branson?"

John Lloyd knelt down, his left leg stretched stiffly to one side, and scratched each dog's belly. "Not at all, Mr. MacPhearson. They were merely extending an exuberant welcome."

"Looks to me like they treed that young lady," MacPhearson said, peering at Lydia perched on the hood.

John Lloyd looked up at Lydia, and she almost thought she saw an expression of concern in his black eyes. Almost. "The young lady misinterpreted your dogs' intent."

"The hell I did," muttered Lydia, scrambling down only to be pinned against the car door by a panting, tail-wagging, black-and-white dog the size of a small horse. "Good doggie—ugh!" she yelped as the creature, excited by a kind word from this nice-smelling human, licked her face from chin to forehead.

"Down, Spot," commanded his owner, slapping his hands. "You dogs git to the barn." The three animals raced away, the black-and-white one bearing a sappy grin on his face. "You all right, young lady?" he asked.

"I'm fine," said Lydia, looking down at her white blouse and contemplating the third thing she'd learned about rural life: farm dogs generally have muddy paws.

"Miss Fairchild is muddied but unbowed," observed John Lloyd with a snicker. "However, to prevent further damage to her pride by errant livestock, I suggest we retire to your living room, Mr. MacPhearson, before indulging in further discussion."

The old man looked blank for a minute before he grinned and clapped John Lloyd across the shoulders. "Mr. Branson, you probably know more words than the dictionary. Fellow can't always figure out just what you're sayin', but that's why I hired you. If I don't know what you're talking about half the time, that jury won't know their hindquarters from a hole in the ground either. They'll let me go 'cause they'll be scared maybe you proved I didn't do it and they were too dumb to understand what you was sayin'."

It was Lydia's turn to snicker.

John Lloyd took her elbow, his obsidian eyes glittering as if they had bits of crystal buried in them, and turned her toward the car. "Get my briefcase, if you please." He released her arm and his voice dropped to a low murmur. "One more thing, Miss Fairchild. I do not object to one's laughing at my expense. However, I do object when that laughter resembles the nickering of a bloated horse."

"Better than sounding like a pompous ass," she retorted under her breath as she retrieved the briefcase from the car and trailed after the two men.

"Dad, what's going on? Who are those people?" demanded a feminine voice from behind the screen door.

"It's Lawyer Branson," MacPhearson answered.

"Thank God it's not the police again." The sound of footsteps on wooden floors receded into the shadowy interior of the house.

"That's my daughter, Frances," said the old man, lurching up the two steps to the porch. Lydia noticed for the first time the extraordinarily thick heel on his left boot. "Frances and her husband, Willis, drove up from Hereford today. She's been in kind of a state since this happened."

"Wonder what your grandmother would advise," Lydia murmured to John Lloyd, but other than a sharp glance he didn't answer.

John Lloyd's grandmother would definitely not advise loosening Frances Whitley's clothes, thought Lydia ten minutes later as she sat on an afghan-covered couch in the living room. The woman's walking shorts and striped tank top were so tight that nudity would have been an understatement. Her bust reminded Lydia of two sofa pillows stuffed in one pillowcase. Furthermore, she looked like a goat—with hair bleached white and cut in shaggy wisps around her face, and dark brown eyes that bulged just enough to make one wonder if she suffered from an undiagnosed goiter. She was short, not much more than five feet, lean, tanned to the color of shoe leather, and twitchy. When she wasn't tapping her long red nails (false, thought Lydia) against the chair arms, she was crossing and recrossing her legs to swing one foot or the other in jerky circles.

John Lloyd seemed to find Frances fascinating, but then big boobs usually fascinated males, thought Lydia resentfully. She gave him ten points for subtlety; other than one quick glance and a raised eyebrow, he had kept his eyes above Frances's neckline.

"You have to help me," Frances bleated, putting her hand over her cleavage. "I haven't been able to sleep since it happened."

"Shut up, Frances," Willis Whitley said gruffly. "You

aren't the one in a fix; your daddy is.'' If Frances was a goat, Lydia thought, her husband was a bull: thick neck, massive shoulders, huge hands that completely swallowed the can of beer he was holding.

Frances ignored him. ''Police asking questions, showing us awful pictures . . .''

''Similar to these?'' asked John Lloyd, whipping a set of photographs from his briefcase and fanning them out like a hand of cards in front of her.

''Oh, God!'' cried Frances, and sank her fingernails into the upholstery of the chair.

''There's no need for that, Mr. Branson,'' said Willis. ''That sergeant from Amarillo's already been after us. We told him we didn't know nothing about any dead man in Leroy's field. Frances got so upset she fainted, and I kicked them fellers off the place.''

John Lloyd ignored him. ''Look closely, Mrs. Whitley. These are only head and shoulder shots of the deceased. There is nothing about them to distress a lady of delicate sensibilities. The deceased appears to be asleep.''

Lydia choked on her Coors beer. She'd seen those pictures. The deceased didn't look asleep; he looked dead.

Frances shrank back and closed her eyes. ''I don't want to. Please leave me alone.''

''Quit whining, Frances. You sound like you're talking through your nose.'' The voice was husky, controlled, disgusted, and belonged to the most beautiful woman Lydia had ever seen. Long and lean and fortyish, she stood poised gracefully in the doorway, green eyes focused on the other woman. Lydia immediately felt young, callow, and unkempt. She crossed her arms over the muddy paw prints on her blouse.

Frances clawed the upholstery. ''Get out of here. This is family business.''

The woman glided into the room like a swan over water, although how someone wearing Levi's, a faded blue shirt,

and boots could glide was beyond Lydia's comprehension.
"My brother married you. That makes me family. Good
morning, Leroy. Glad to see you back home. Makes it much
easier to wring your neck. In the name of God, why didn't
you leave that body where it was?"

The old man set his beer on the floor by his rocking chair,
and took a can of chewing tobacco out of his pocket. "I had
my reasons."

"That Department of Energy idiot, Rory Tinsdale—God,
what a name—is making noises to the newspaper already.
Something to the effect that anyone opposed to the dump is
violent, perverted, and I quote: *unworthy of the public trust.*
He hasn't mentioned you by name yet, but he's sniffing
around the idea."

"The dump!" Frances cried. "My father's been arrested
for murder, and all you can talk about is the dump!" Her
hands curled into claws. "You don't care about anyone."

"I care about our grandchildren, Frances. I don't want
them to glow in the dark."

"Grandchildren! Do you think you'll ever have any? Your
only child dyed his hair *pink*!"

Elizabeth shrugged her shoulders. "Beats shaving his head
and joining the Moonies. Every boy has to rebel. It's a sort
of puberty rite. He can't be his own man without it. I'm just
cutting David enough slack to let him tell me to go to hell.
However, I don't intend to pay for the privilege of being told.
He'll find out he's out of slack the next time he tries to cash
a check."

"Bravo, Elizabeth." John Lloyd applauded. "You have
always been an eminently practical woman." His black eyes
expressed admiration, approval, appreciation, and something else Lydia didn't like at all: sexual awareness.

"Good morning, John Lloyd." She shook her head and a
sleek mane of chestnut hair brushed her shoulders. "No,
don't get up. Save your leg and manners for a more appropriate occasion." Green eyes gleamed with sexual awareness

of their own, and Lydia wondered what a more appropriate occasion might be. She didn't care for the idea that occurred to her.

John Lloyd rose with an almost imperceptible lurch, and walked over to kiss Elizabeth's hand. "What could be more appropriate than greeting a lovely lady?" he said, his voice as smooth as honey.

Lydia gritted her teeth. If *she'd* made a remark about his leg, he would have bitten off her head, not kissed her hand.

"And you must be Lydia Fairchild," Elizabeth said, gliding to the couch and shaking hands like a man. "I'm Elizabeth Thornton. John Lloyd and I are old friends."

I bet you are, thought Lydia, glaring at the lawyer over Elizabeth's shoulder. "Hello," she mumbled.

"And this"—Elizabeth gestured to someone behind her— "is my niece, Rachel Whitley."

"Why did you bring her?" screeched Frances. "Why? I told you to keep her."

"She's not a stray puppy, Frances," snapped her sister-in-law. "She's your daughter, and that makes her family, too. However, I realize you have the mothering instinct of a guppy, so that fact might have slipped your mind."

"That's not true!"

A delicate girl in her late teens with honey-colored hair stepped around Elizabeth. Like a fawn, thought Lydia, smothering a giggle. Fawns, swans, goats, and bulls; Old MacPhearson had a farm in his living room.

"Don't panic, Mother. I wouldn't share the same house with you." Unlike a fawn, there was nothing timid or shy about Rachel. "I'm staying with Grandpa. Hap's bringing my clothes in . . ."

"He's not family! He's not staying!"

"He's a consultant to the committee," said Elizabeth coolly. "He's staying."

"Somebody please make a decision. Am I going or staying?"

Lydia looked toward the door, and felt a little sexual awareness of her own. She didn't normally like redheaded men. But this one was a six-foot hunk with auburn hair and iridescent blue eyes. She wasn't sure what animal he reminded her of, but whatever breed, he was best of show.

He stepped inside the room, and deposited two suitcases on the floor. "I can take a walk if you're uncomfortable, Frances." A beautiful body, gorgeous face, and he's kind, too, thought Lydia.

Frances jumped up, and Lydia was reminded not of a goat, but a cornered rat. "I'm sick of you, and sick of her, and sick of the committee! STAD—Stand Together Against the Dump. What a laugh! My father stood with you; in fact, he started the committee. Now he's in trouble, and all you and that vulture Elizabeth can think of is how to get rid of him so he won't embarrass STAD. Well, you both can get out. This is family business. It has nothing to do with the dump."

"Exactly." John Lloyd's voice echoed across the room like a pistol shot. He stood with his legs apart, his cane little more than a prop, as his gaze shifted from face to face. "The motive for the murder has nothing to do with the dump."

"But John Lloyd," began Elizabeth.

John Lloyd held up his hand. "But the effects of that murder may very well cripple our war against the repository."

"John Lloyd, talking out of both sides of your mouth may confuse the hell out of a jury, but I've never liked it. You just said the murder had nothing to do with the dump, and now you say it does. Now which is it?" demanded Elizabeth.

"I said the *motive* for the murder had nothing to do with the dump. The fact that this particular murder was committed, does."

"What's so special about this murder?" asked Elizabeth suspiciously.

"Miss Fairchild." John Lloyd beckoned at Lydia. She approached him warily.

He pulled the victim's photographs from his pocket. "If you would display these on the coffee table for our three late arrivals, please." There was the sound of a sharply indrawn breath, and John Lloyd's eyebrows snapped together in a frown as he searched for the source.

Lydia stood frozen, the photographs in her outstretched hand, but she heard nothing but the buzzing of a fly against the window. John Lloyd brusquely motioned her away, and turning, she walked to the coffee table. A pall of tension hung over the room. Lydia quickly spread the pictures on the table and stepped back as the three crowded in.

Elizabeth picked up a photograph, then dropped it as if it had scorched her fingers. "Holy shit!" she exclaimed.

CHAPTER
FIVE

SCHRODER'S OFFICE HADN'T CHANGED IN THE TWO MONTHS since he'd last seen it, thought Jenner, waving his hand through the several layers of cigarette smoke in an attempt to find breathable air. Probably hadn't been cleaned either. He was sure he recognized a cigarette butt lying on the corner of Schroder's desk.

"You trying to swat a fly?" asked Schroder out of one corner of his mouth. The other corner was occupied holding a cigarette.

"I'm trying to breathe," said Jenner. He could feel his eyes start to water, and his sinuses swell.

"Use your nose," said Schroder with a grunt, his thick fingers ripping open a manila envelope.

"Very funny, Schroder. You ever thought of going on Johnny Carson?"

"That crooked son of a bitch knew! I'd bet my last dollar on it!" Schroder exclaimed, leaping out of his chair and slamming the desk with his fist, sending the overflowing ash-

45

tray skittering across its surface, over the edge and onto the floor, bouncing off Jenner's knee on the way.

"Goddamn it, Schroder!" yelled the younger man, grabbing his knee with one hand, and brushing cigarette butts and ash off his uniform with the other. "What the hell was that all about? Did something bite you on the ass? Whatever it was, is probably poisonous. Have to be, living in this office."

The overweight investigator waved a document in Jenner's face. "Shut your mouth and look at this. It's the FBI report on our John Doe's fingerprints."

Jenner sneezed. His knee was pounding like a drum, sending waves of pain up his thigh and down his ash-covered shin. He took the document out of Schroder's hand and focused his watery eyes. "Charlton Price-Leigh III from Virginia." He looked up at Schroder. "How the hell did a dude from Virginia with a fancy-assed name like that end up in a Texas wheat field?"

Schroder shoved another document under his nose. "Charlton Price-Leigh III worked for the DOE. He was a public information officer, and he was on assignment in Hereford."

"Hereford, Texas?"

"Of course, Hereford, Texas!" roared Schroder. "Where else are those DOE people thicker than ticks on a hound dog? He was the one responsible for handing out the government's official line of bull about how the dump's not gonna leak. That damn fool MacPhearson's gonna spend twenty years to life for killing him." Schroder's blue eyes seemed to be bulging from his head.

"Sit down before you have a stroke. You've got so many blood vessels popping up, the whites of your eyes look pink," said Jenner. "I don't know why you're so upset. According to Maximum Miller, we don't have any proof MacPhearson murdered anybody."

"We'll get it. Now that we know who the victim is, we'll

backtrack until we find the murder scene. Then we've got MacPhearson hooked. There's no way a man can commit murder without leaving trace evidence at the scene. That just happens in storybooks. In real life, a good police lab can find hair, fiber, metal filing, tire tracks, footprints, finger-prints, blood, even spit. All you need is a suspect to match all them things up to, and we've got a suspect."

"Maybe he's innocent."

"Don't act dumber than you are, son. Innocent people don't dump dead bodies in their fields. *Nude*, dead bodies. Innocent people don't call John Lloyd Branson!" finished Schroder in a shout as he looked around for an ashtray. Giv-ing up, he ground out his cigarette on the edge of his desk and dropped the butt in his wastebasket. "That old man's next address will be Huntsville."

"Maybe not, Schroder. Those DOE people are about as popular as a blood donor with AIDS. I don't think you need to stay awake nights with a guilty conscience about sending an old man to the pen. People around here'll see it as a public service killing. The jury'll probably give MacPhearson a sus-pended sentence if Branson doesn't get him acquitted in-stead." Jenner swallowed the rest of his words. Schroder's eyes had the same mean look that a bull's have just before it gores a matador.

"Guilty conscience! God almighty, Jenner, if I weren't a cop, I'd strangle that old man *and* his shyster lawyer myself!"

Jenner decided that his swollen sinuses must be affecting his hearing. "What?"

Schroder shook his finger in the younger man's face. "Even without the beard, they'd recognize him."

"Beard?" asked Jenner. "What beard?"

"Price-Leigh had a beard. I thought he looked familiar, but I'd only seen him a couple of times on TV. But Mac-Phearson and Branson are up to their armpits in the anti-dump movement. They go to all the public hearings. They

probably knew Charlton Price-Leigh III better than his own
mother did. Everyone we've talked to knew the bastard.''

"And you're pissed because Branson and the old man
withheld information?''

Schroder sat down and gazed at Jenner like a teacher whose
best pupil had just flunked an exam. "That was a stupid
question. I ought to send you back to traffic detail.''

Jenner tried to look as dumb as possible. "That's a good
idea, Schroder.''

Schroder ignored him. "MacPhearson's under arrest, and
the law says he doesn't have to tell me shit. And Branson
wouldn't give God Himself any information about a case of
his. No point in wasting my time getting mad about it.''

"Then what *are* you so mad about, Schroder?''

"Because MacPhearson couldn't take on a load in a bar
and shoot somebody over a floozie, or poker debt, or some
other respectable reason. He has to kill a DOE employee,
give the whole anti-dump movement a black eye. But does
Branson try to downplay the whole thing, maybe keep the
media from circling around like a bunch of vultures? Hell,
no! He demands an examining trial, makes us and the D.A.'s
office look like a bunch of idiots.'' He stared gloomily at
Jenner. "But that ain't the worst.''

"It's not?''

Schroder shook his head, and Jenner was prepared to swear
the investigator was scared. "The worst thing is Maximum
Miller. He's gonna be after our balls with a butcher knife and
a pan of hot grease.''

Jenner felt a twinge of pain between his legs. "But it's not
our fault.''

Schroder pulled a handkerchief out of his pocket and wiped
his forehead and the back of his neck. "Let's go let you
explain it to him.''

"So you see, Mr. Miller, the identity of the victim will
attract some media attention . . .''

"Is that right?" asked Miller, raising one eyebrow as he stared blandly across a large butcher block table at the two sergeants. An electric wok stood on the counter behind him, and Jenner could smell meat stock simmering in a saucepan. Standing in his own immaculate kitchen and clad in jeans, sweatshirt, and a bright red apron with the words BIG CHIEF stenciled across the front, Maximum Miller looked anything but dangerous.

Jenner relaxed. The assistant D.A.'s voice resembled the purr of a large black tomcat. And he looked so damn domestic standing at that table chopping vegetables with a large cleaver. "Sergeant Schroder and myself immediately drove over here to inform you, as you demonstrated an interest in the progress of the investigation . . ."

"Drove over immediately, huh?" asked the assistant D.A., reducing a carrot to uniformly sized slices almost faster than the eye could follow the motions of the cleaver.

"Sergeant Schroder did take the time to call the DOE office in Hereford to obtain the victim's local address." Jenner grinned at Miller. "Sergeant Schroder and I will proceed directly to that location upon leaving here . . ."

"Proceed directly there, huh?" The thud of the cleaver as Miller chopped a stalk of celery into pale green slivers sounded louder to Jenner than a minute ago. He decided his ears were unstopping in the smoke-free atmosphere.

"Yes, sir," said Jenner. "Upon arriving there, the sergeant and I will secure the scene and—"

"Secure the scene?"

"And search for clues," finished Jenner, wishing the assistant D.A. would stop interrupting.

"And search for clues," repeated Miller, halving an onion with a downward flick of his wrist.

"Yes, sir," said Jenner, wondering if there was an echo in here.

"Just like one of them fancy dudes"—he quartered the onion with a resounding thud—"in a detective story."

Jenner winced as the cleaver struck the table. "Well, I guess so."

Miller waved the cleaver at Schroder. "Where the hell did you say you picked up this boy? From some damn TV police show?" The purr was gone from his voice. Jenner wished he were somewhere safe—like the other side of the moon.

"Searching for clues, my ass!" shouted Miller, swinging his cleaver like a saber and splitting a head of cabbage. "Evidence, boy, evidence, not clues."

"Ease up, Cleetus," said Schroder. "You're getting excited. Not good for your blood pressure."

"Excited?" Miller swung at the cabbage again, missed it, and sank the cleaver an inch into the table. "I was excited yesterday. Today I'm pissed off. That goddamn examining trial is gonna bring the FBI, the federal district attorney, the national media, the DOE, and probably some damn Congressional committee with nothing better to do, flying into Potter County and landing on my ass. The TV people'll make some cracks about violent Texans, the FBI'll scream conspiracy, the federal D.A. will slap subpoenas on everybody in sight, the congressional committee will try to pin the whole thing on the president, and run around looking for the smoking revolver. If those idiots ever found a smoking revolver, they'd shoot their toes off with it."

He bared his teeth in a feral grin. "And the DOE? You know what the DOE will do? They'll use this murder to discredit the groups opposing the dump. They'll push a bill through Congress authorizing them to kick the farmers off the land and start drilling. The Panhandle will end up with radioactive isotopes buried underground, and we can all watch our balls rot off with radiation sickness."

Jenner wished Miller would stop mentioning balls. "Maybe MacPhearson was trying to keep his land from being confiscated."

Miller swung his head toward Jenner. "I keep up with the anti-dump movement on the sly. As a county employee, I can't get involved with political action groups. How do you like that?'' He laughed bitterly. ''We're talking about survival, and I'm worried about losing my job. When that dump leaks, there won't be a county left to employ me. Anyway, I keep up the best I can, and I know the names of all the farmers in danger of losing their homes. MacPhearson isn't one of them. He killed that DOE guy just because he *was* DOE.''

He gripped the ends of the table and glared at Schroder. ''It's all your fault, Schroder.''

''Wait a minute!'' protested Jenner, then wished he'd kept his mouth shut. Miller's eyes looked madder than a rabid dog's.

''That's just about what you got, boy: one minute before I start kicking ass.''

''Sergeant Schroder and I didn't have anything to do with MacPhearson murdering that guy.''

''No, but you arrested him, then screwed up the investigation and left me hanging by the heels like a butchered steer so John Lloyd Branson could come along and slice off a few cuts of meat. You know what he's gonna do with those cuts? Come Monday morning he's gonna roast them over an open fire in that courtroom in front of the whole damn country.'' He tilted his head and waggled a hand in the air. ''But that's all right. I'm a fighter. Now that I know MacPhearson's connection with the victim, I can maybe persuade the judge we ought to take the case to the grand jury, let them decide whether or not to indict. I can paint MacPhearson as a gun-toting anti-dump fanatic, insinuate that maybe there's a hit list and what's-his-ass is just the first. Oh, I can do a lot a damage to Mr. Branson while he's trying to gut me. But I don't want to do that. I don't want to damage the anti-dump people. But I'm not gonna let a murderer go free.''

Miller's skin was glistening with sweat and he stopped to wipe his face on the tail of his red apron. ''Schroder, you and this overage Hardy boy get down to Hereford and you find me some evidence that'll tie this case up in a blue ribbon. I want MacPhearson cold so I can persuade Branson to drop this examining trial idea, maybe even get him to plead his client guilty. After I explain who the victim was, I'll appeal to Branson's better nature, if the son of a bitch has one, to keep this case as quiet as possible.''

''Branson already knows,'' Jenner blurted, then remembered that no good ever came to the messenger bearing bad news.

Miller's head turned to Schroder. ''He knows?'' the assistant D.A. asked ominously.

Schroder looked uncomfortable. ''Branson's the legal advisor to STAD and several other groups. I'm always reading about him meeting with the DOE people and giving them hell. It'd be a real coincidence if he didn't recognize the victim from the autopsy pictures.''

''And he demanded the examining trial *after* he saw that autopsy protocol?'' Miller's skin had lost its polished ebony look. ''What in the hell is that bastard trying to do, Schroder?''

''What do you think, Schroder?'' asked Jenner as he braced his feet on the floorboard and tried not to think about how fast the rusty old Ford was traveling toward Hereford.

''About what?'' grunted the investigator, plucking a cigarette out of a battered pack and tucking it securely in one corner of his mouth. He lit it with his museum-vintage Zippo lighter and puffed contentedly until gray smoke circled his head.

Jenner rolled down the window and took a breath of manure-scented air, courtesy of Hereford's feedyards. It smelled better than Schroder's cigarette smoke. ''What's Branson trying to do?''

Schroder gazed out the window and Jenner gripped his shoulder harness and closed his eyes. ''He's slicker than a grass lizard. Catch him by the tail and he'll just shed it and run off. No limit to the number of new tails a lizard can grow. I think that no matter what we find in Hereford, and no matter how many times he grabs Branson, Maximum Miller's gonna be left holding a lizard's tail.''

Jenner peeked at Schroder. The investigator had his eyes on the road and Jenner let go of his seat belt. "In other words, you don't know."

"No idea, and I can't worry about it. We've got to concentrate on finding Maximum Miller's blue ribbon. That means who, why, when, where, and how. We know who and when. We know the how of the thing even if we don't have the exact weapon. What we don't have is the where, and without that we can't tie MacPhearson up with anything but disposal of the body.''

"You left out the why," said Jenner.

"MacPhearson strike you as a crazy man?''

"He's a nice old man. I told you that before you arrested him.''

Schroder shook his head. "Get your head out of the sand. MacPhearson's a killer, but I don't think he's a cold-blooded killer. Been around enough of those to know the difference. Some of the things they do to their victims make a man sick to his stomach. But they aren't men; they're animals. You can see the wildness in their eyes. Just ask any cop who's been around for a while. They'll tell you.''

Jenner grabbed the armrest as Schroder squealed around a corner. "That's not very scientific. I thought you Special Crimes types depended on lab work.''

"We didn't turn in our instincts when the county issued us a microscope and argon laser, and my instinct tells me that there's more to the why than Miller thinks. That's the reason Branson wants an examining trial. He knows it, too.''

Schroder slammed on the brakes and the car rocked to a stop. Debris slid off the dash and showered on the laps of the two investigators. "We're here.''

Jenner tried to breathe. His body had kept traveling forward after the Ford stopped and his shoulder harness had cut off his breath. "Where?" he gasped.

Schroder brushed scraps of paper, a paperback book, a flashlight, several rags, and an empty cigarette carton off his lap. Then he unbuckled his seat belt. "Charlton Price-Leigh's house, the scene of the crime."

"How do you know that?" demanded Jenner, while releasing his harness and rubbing a sore shoulder.

"Logical," said Schroder, heaving his two hundred plus pounds out of the car. "Man was nude. Most folks only take their clothes off in their own house. Could be wrong. There's the Special Crimes van now. I'll turn everybody loose on the place and we'll see."

He tucked in his shirt and ambled toward a Hereford PD patrol car that pulled in behind the Special Crimes van. Jenner trailed after him, swearing to himself that Schroder's shirts had lives of their own. They'd wiggle out of his pants even if the square-bodied detective stood absolutely still.

Schroder shook hands with a tall man blessed with a magnificent head of curly black hair and middle-age spread. "Lockhart, figured you'd beat us here."

Allen Lockhart, chief of police for Hereford, Texas, lifted his hat, ran his fingers through his hair, and replaced the hat. "Didn't see any need in waiting around here for you to show up. I sure didn't want to go inside, maybe mess up any evidence, so I stationed a patrol car at the edge of town to watch for you. The officer radioed in when you passed. At least, he guessed it was you. He said all he really saw was a blur. You're gonna kill yourself one of these days driving like that, Schroder. I just hope you don't take anybody with you."

Schroder ignored the admonition, which didn't surprise Jenner. Schroder always ignored criticism. "You ready to go in?"

Lockhart adjusted his hat again. "To tell you the truth, I'm not real interested. It's your case, and I've got troubles of my own. I don't want to be mixed up with the DOE. It's real hard to be polite to those folks, dead or alive." He heaved a long-suffering sigh. "I'll follow you in the house so I can testify that the city of Hereford cooperated in the solving of a heinous crime. Then I'm going to sit in my patrol car and drink coffee."

"Suit yourself, Chief," said Schroder, turning toward the house.

"I intend to," answered Lockhart, lifting up his hat and scratching his head.

Jenner looked at the house. Medium, he thought. Medium size, medium price range, medium porch screened by medium tall trees and shrubs. Even the neighborhood was medium with kids, dogs, bikes, skateboards, and station wagons. Typical, average, run-of-the-mill small town America.

There was nothing average or run-of-the-mill about Charlton Price-Leigh III's bedroom. Small town America master bedroom decor doesn't ordinarily include a circular bed, mirrored ceiling complete with spotlights, ankle-deep plush carpet, and a pornographic fountain. Neither does it often include a bloodstained mattress.

Jenner felt his stomach muscles tense and swallowed rapidly. God, but he hated homicide, hated even breathing around a homicide, particularly when the air smelled of decayed blood. "My God, Schroder, it looks like somebody dumped a gallon of brown paint on the bed. It even dripped on the floor. Whoever inherits this house is sure going to have to replace the carpet."

"I came, I seen, and I'm leaving," said Lockhart. "I'll be outside if you need me." He left the room faster than he'd entered it.

Jenner kept staring and swallowing. "Have to do something about that fountain, too. Can't have a thing like that in the house if you have kids."

Schroder grabbed his shoulders and shook him. "Quit babbling, son. I've seen worse and so have you."

Jenner swallowed again. "Good Lord, Schroder, it's obscene!"

Schroder glanced at the fountain. "It sure ain't great art."

"I wasn't talking about the fountain, for heaven's sake; I was talking about the room and that bloody mattress. This isn't some cheap motel where a pimp carved up one of his girls for skimming money off the top, and it isn't a flophouse where two dopers got in a fight over a bindle—you know, one of those paper bags of heroin, or cocaine, or whatever crap they happen to be shooting up or snorting. This is middle America! There are kids riding bikes, running through sprinklers, girls playing with Barbie dolls. I even saw a woman cutting roses. I'll bet somebody's baking an apple pie. And in here"—he waved his arm—"in here we've got a room that looks like a porno movie set."

"He's not too far off the mark, Sergeant," said a female investigator for Special Crimes, the one who always reminded Jenner of his son's kindergarten teacher. Except he hoped his son's kindergarten teacher didn't act so nonchalant around dried blood. She pointed to a walk-in closet she had opened after carefully dusting its door for prints. "There's enough cameras in there to film a movie."

"And here are the props," said another investigator, standing by a seven-foot-tall cabinet full of what are euphemistically called sexual aids by the more sedate girlie magazines.

Jenner identified the functions of a few of the objects, guessed the uses of others, and felt the bile rise in his throat. First the corpse in the field, then the autopsy, then the bloody mattress, now this. It was too much. He wasn't any tough-as-nails homicide cop, and to hell with the propaganda that said a cop was a professional always in control of himself. "I'm gonna puke," he said, rushing toward a closed door he hoped led to the bathroom.

"Not on the crime scene, goddamn it!" shouted Schroder.

Jenner yanked open the door and took two steps toward

the toilet when he saw the face of the man in the shower. ''Holy shit!'' he screamed and backpedaled into Schroder.

Schroder stumbled backward. ''What the hell . . . ?'' he started.

''There's somebody in there!'' shouted Jenner.

Schroder's .357 revolver was out of its holster, and he was plastered against the wall next to the bathroom door before Jenner could get his own gun out. ''Police!'' he bellowed. ''Get your hands in the air and step out here!''

There was a click as the shower door opened. There were answering clicks as the entire Special Crimes team cocked their revolvers and drew a bead on the bathroom from behind whatever cover they'd managed to find. Reality was different from TV, thought Jenner, as he stood against the wall on the other side of Schroder. On TV the cops would have rushed the bathroom, a good way to be walking a beat in front of the pearly gates. Real cops took cover and hoped like hell the guy would come out with his hands up.

''Don't shoot. I'm unarmed,'' said a high-pitched voice from inside the bathroom.

''Come out and let's see,'' commanded Schroder.

A tall, thin man with thinning brown hair and a prominent Adam's apple stepped out of the bathroom, his hands high in the air. Five Special Crimes men and one woman stood up, their guns trained on him. ''This is uncalled for,'' he said, his voice changing into a squeak as he stared at the gun barrels.

Schroder holstered his gun, stepped away from the wall and to one side. ''Is that so?'' he asked. ''Turn around, put your hands against the wall, and spread your legs, and we'll talk about it while I frisk you.''

Pale brown eyes blinked behind wire-rim frames. ''This is a violation of my civil rights. I demand a lawyer.''

''You ain't been arrested. Yet,'' added Schroder, grabbing the man's shoulders and whirling him around to face the wall.

"This is police brutality," the man protested as Schroder patted him down. "Your superiors will be hearing from me."

"I got maybe a supervisor," said Schroder, lifting the man's wallet from his back pocket and opening it. "I don't have a superior." Several of the Special Crimes Unit snickered and Schroder frowned at them. "Get on with the investigation. This guy's clean."

The man turned around and pulled on his cuffs until they were at the precise spot on his wrists dictated by *Gentleman's Quarterly*. "I should think so," he said. He straightened his tie and fastened one button on his sport coat. "That was an entirely unnecessary demonstration of police power." He pushed his glasses up and looked at Schroder. "Is that my wallet?"

Schroder was peering at a driver's license. "It was in your pocket, at least."

The man grabbed for the wallet. Snatching something from Schroder was about as safe as snatching a honeycomb from a grizzly bear, thought Jenner. A man had to be either brave or stupid to try it. He figured this yahoo for stupid.

"Give that back, you yokel." His voice ended in a soft *poof* of air as he bounced off Schroder's elbow as the burly detective turned sideways.

"Try that again, and you'll find yourself charged with assaulting a police officer." Schroder's voice was soft. So was granite when compared with a diamond, thought Jenner.

"I refuse to be treated as a criminal. I have a perfect right to be here."

Schroder's face wore an expression of long-suffering patience, which Jenner knew was false as hell. Schroder was never long-suffering and seldom patient. "You are Mr. Rory Tinsdale?"

"That's correct," Tinsdale said, patting his receding hairline with a white handkerchief.

"Senior man for the DOE's got a right to be in his office, Mr. Tinsdale." He lumbered toward the man and Jenner braced himself for the explosion. "He's got no right at all to be standing in the shower at a murder scene. *Now you tell me what the hell you're doing here!*"

Tinsdale's glasses fogged up from Schroder's breath. He backed up a few steps and looked nervously through his misted-over lenses toward the bathroom. "Waiting for you."

"In the shower?" asked Schroder in disbelief.

"I was afraid you might be the murderer returning. Don't they often return to the scene of the crime?"

"Not unless they're stupid . . ."

"Schroder, there's a box full of papers and documents in the shower," yelled one of the Special Crimes investigators from the bathroom.

". . . or trying to destroy evidence," said Schroder, baring his nicotine-stained teeth in a grin.

CHAPTER
SIX

"IT'S THE BEARD," SAID ELIZABETH THORNTON, TAPPING
the photo Lydia had given her. "The son of a bitch shaved
his beard."

"Or had it shaved. Postmortem," drawled John Lloyd,
looking at Leroy MacPhearson rocking slowly in his chair.

Lydia felt the hair stiffen on the back of her neck at the
image John Lloyd conjured up. It was one thing for a mortician to shave the dead. It was another for the ordinary,
average person, someone like old Mr. MacPhearson, to do
it.

"Oh, my God!" exclaimed Elizabeth.

"I am not absolutely certain, of course," John Lloyd continued in that same slow drawl. "But logic tells me that the
possibility of my being wrong is quite remote."

"No, no," Frances moaned, and rocked her body back
and forth on the chair.

"Shut up, Frances," said Elizabeth automatically. "What

insane reason would anyone have for shaving someone he'd just killed?''

"Motivation for a particular act, when understood, is never insane, Elizabeth. Even a serial murderer caught up in his moment of blood lust has a motive consistent with his own logic, if not ours. In this instance, there was a very logical, very sensible, reason for shaving our late, unlamented adversary, Mr. Charlton Price-Leigh III.''

"Oh, God, oh, God," repeated Frances, rocking and commencing to wash her hands like Lady Macbeth. Lydia expected her to deliver a soliloquy at any moment.

Other than a sharp look Elizabeth ignored her. "So what's the reason?''

John Lloyd's obsidian eyes examined each person in the room before coming back to rest on MacPhearson. "Even though Mr. Price-Leigh received media coverage commensurate to his ego—and in excess of his worth—during his corporeal existence, without the beard, and without clothes, and deposited in a stubble field some distance from his usual environment, it is doubtful any of the law enforcement officers or other officials viewing his early remains would recognize him. As for the general public, a published description of the deceased without his beard would fit any number of the male species. Given the number of men his approximate age who flee home and hearth each year for whatever reason, it is even remotely possible that he might be misidentified. In any case, shaving Mr. Price-Leigh gained the barber time.''

"Time for what?" demanded Elizabeth.

Again John Lloyd glanced around the room before focusing on MacPhearson. "I do not know.''

MacPhearson lit another unfiltered cigarette and puffed without speaking.

"I do not know," repeated John Lloyd, holding the old farmer's gaze. "But I must know, or I will be ineffectual as your counsel. A blindfolded man is at the mercy of those with sight, and the prosecuting attorney, Mr. Miller, is a particularly clear-eyed individual.''

MacPhearson removed the cigarette from his mouth and watched the smoke spiral from the end. "Maybe he don't know either."

"Mr. Miller has an annoying habit of rising to the occasion. I must know the answers before he asks the questions."

"You're talking as if Leroy were guilty, Mr. Branson," said Hap.

Lydia jerked around to look at him. The redheaded man had been so unobtrusive, she'd forgotten about him. Maybe he was a member of the barnyard after all: a chameleon, invisible until he chose to move.

Everyone in the room looked from Hap to John Lloyd. Except MacPhearson, who took another puff of his cigarette and gazed absently toward the ceiling. Lydia decided the old farmer must have no nerves at all. He ought to be protesting his innocence. If he *was* innocent. Personally, she doubted it.

John Lloyd hesitated and Lydia felt shivers run up and down her back. John Lloyd never hesitated except for dramatic effect. "Of course he is guilty," he finally said.

Except for the air-conditioner, the room was so quiet Lydia was sure she could hear her own heart beat. Everyone appeared stunned, or shocked, or at least speechless. Except MacPhearson, who slanted a sideways glance at John Lloyd before contemplating the ceiling again.

The silence was only temporary. "Dear God, what are we going to do?" asked Frances.

"Shut up, Frances," snapped Elizabeth. "God had nothing to do with this mess, and I don't think He's going to oblige us by making it go away. Willis, can't you do something with her?"

Willis patted his wife's shoulder with a Virginia ham–sized hand. "It's all right, Frances."

She jerked away from her husband like the skittish goat she resembled. "You're an atheist, Elizabeth."

Judging from the look on Elizabeth's face, Lydia concluded that being called an atheist in the Texas Panhandle was a little more serious than being called one in Dallas. "You overdeveloped sow. At least my sins don't hurt anybody."

Frances came out of her chair with false fingernails extended. Hastily Lydia stepped between the two women. "Ladies, please," she began.

Elizabeth shouldered her aside and Lydia stumbled back and sat down hard on the coffee table. She rubbed her bruised hip and decided John Lloyd could play peacemaker. But other than a mildly concerned look in her direction, John Lloyd stood silent as a statue. Lydia wished he really were a statue and a whole flock of pigeons would relieve themselves on his head.

She looked around the room. Everyone was motionless except Elizabeth and Frances, who were circling each other like two fighting cocks. Or more accurately, two barnyard hens, and the sight of them irked Lydia to the depths of her feminist soul.

"That's enough," she shouted, and staggering to her feet, she stuck her arms between the two women and slammed each in the chest with an elbow. Frances toppled back into her chair, and Elizabeth stumbled backward into John Lloyd.

"Miss Fairchild, I am shocked at your unprofessional behavior," said John Lloyd, steadying Elizabeth with one arm.

Lydia was sure she'd misunderstood. "What?"

"Manhandling a client is not a proper response to a stressful situation."

"Manhandling! Stressful! I get my butt busted, and you're worried about them!"

"Your language is inappropriate for a member of the bar. Please confine yourself to a written record of this meeting. Your notebook, please, Miss Fairchild."

Grabbing a pad and pen out of her purse, Lydia flopped down on the arm of the couch, flinching as her sore hip protested another hard landing. "I'm ready," she said. He inclined his head in that imperial way that always made her grind her expensively straightened teeth together. "I am certain you are, Miss Fairchild."

She was, too, she thought. Ready to scratch out his eyes as soon as they were alone. Doing it in front of an audience would constitute unprofessional behavior.

"Well," announced Elizabeth, brushing her hair out of her eyes. "Now that we've relieved some stress"—she cast an amused look at Lydia—"I think I have an answer for you, John Lloyd."

For the time it took Lydia to draw a breath, she thought John Lloyd looked shocked. Impossible, she thought a second later as he turned a pleased face to Elizabeth. No one could recover that quickly.

"I am gratified," he drawled.

"Leroy is insane," she stated.

Frances was on her feet again. "My father is not insane! Don't you ever say that again!"

"Shaving a dead man and dumping his body in a field aren't exactly the actions of a sane man, Frances."

"He's saner than you are. Nobody's ever been crazy in our family!" shouted Frances, pounding the arm of her chair.

"Then you must be a foundling," remarked Elizabeth, turning back to John Lloyd.

Willis grabbed his wife's shoulders. "It's all right, Frances."

Privately Lydia didn't think so. Something was very wrong if Frances would sit quietly while John Lloyd accused her father of murder, but go berserk because Elizabeth called him insane. Surely it was better to be insane than to be a murderer.

"Don't you see, John Lloyd?" continued Elizabeth without another look at Frances. "Insanity is a defense against murder. Leroy can plead insanity by reason of his inhuman treatment by the DOE. The more I think about it, the better the idea sounds. Leroy doesn't go to prison; no one thinks the anti-dump movement is shooting anyone we don't like; and we get a public forum to warn the country. A courtroom is about the best forum there is. We can spend the weekend writing up a crackerjack confession for Leroy. We'll pass out copies to all the national media. Just think about it for a minute. National television. *Twenty-Twenty*, *Sixty Minutes*, a special news broadcast, maybe even a mini-series. It'll be a chance to stop this insanity before this country has its own Chernobyl. Before we risk a nuclear accident that could kill hundreds of thousands of people because a train carrying that radioactive shit to the dump derails in a metropolitan area. And famine. Won't John Q. Public sit up and take notice when he finds bread might cost ten dollars a loaf and beef twenty-five dollars a pound because the underground water supply for eight states has been contaminated by nuclear waste?"

She spread out her arms, eyes glowing with fervent light. "Earth to earth, ashes to ashes, dust to dust. The DOE will lay waste to the land for ten thousand years."

Lydia shivered and felt tears come to her eyes as Elizabeth intoned the words from the Book of Common Prayer. We should be dressed in black, she thought, looking around the room at the solemn faces. They might be mourners at a funeral if the DOE won. The dump site would become a burial site for hundreds of future generations to wonder at and to ask: why did they do it?

The rocking chair creaked as Leroy MacPhearson shifted his weight. "I ain't insane," he said, a calm expression on his face.

"Maybe not," agreed Elizabeth, fervor fading into persuasiveness. "But isn't a psychiatric ward better than prison?"

"I ain't planning on spending time in either place." He

dropped his cigarette butt in his empty beer can and started rocking again.

"You get out of this house, you cold bitch!" screamed Frances, tugging futilely against Willis's hold. "And leave my father alone! Daddy, don't listen to her! She's the one who's crazy!"

"Damn it, Leroy, can't you see I'm trying to keep your ass out of jail?" demanded Elizabeth, turning her back to Frances.

"I got a lawyer for that, and I sure would appreciate it if everybody'd hush up so I could hear what he has to say. Frances, you keep quiet now, you hear me?"

John Lloyd leaned on his cane and gazed at the floor for a few seconds as if organizing his thoughts. Or reorganizing them, Lydia thought suddenly. Like a politician who goes to a meeting with several prepared speeches but delays deciding between them until he gauges the mood of his audience. And that's what John Lloyd had been doing, she realized. That's why he hadn't taken charge of this conference, why he'd stood by and let Frances and Elizabeth bicker, why he'd been angry when she interfered. She decided there was a touch of the demagogue in John Lloyd Branson.

"I am confident that Mr. Price-Leigh's mortal coil will be identified very soon, and that like the wolf upon the fold, Sergeant Schroder will descend upon you."

"Just a minute, John Lloyd. I'm not involved in this," objected Elizabeth.

Frances laughed, a hysterical sound that made Lydia cringe. "That's not what you said a few minutes ago. What's the matter, Elizabeth? Got a guilty conscience?"

"Shut up, Frances," said Elizabeth, taking a few steps toward the woman.

"Don't touch me!"

"That is enough!" said John Lloyd, his voice sharp and concise with no trace of a drawl. "I have neither the time nor the patience to witness another altercation between the two of you. Elizabeth, as a committee member of STAD who is also related by law to this family, you will not be spared an interrogation. Frances, your statement that you called your father to inquire about his arthritis around eleven o'clock on the evening of the murder was ill-advised.'' He looked at her. ''Long-distance telephone calls can be verified.''

Lydia jerked around to stare at Frances. The woman's lips were as colorless as her hair and her face twitched as if she were suffering from a nervous disorder. Her dilated pupils made her eyes as black as John Lloyd's. ''Oh, God, oh, God,'' Frances chanted until Lydia expected Him to answer if only to shut her up.

''Never lie to Sergeant Schroder,'' said John Lloyd.

''Meaning we should tell the nice policeman everything we know,'' said Rachel in a tone both sullen and defiant. Lydia felt the palm of her hand itch with the urge to smack the young girl's behind.

''Sergeant Schroder lacks charm, has limited diction, and needs the services of a good tailor. In no respect can he be described as nice. However, he is quite intelligent. Too intelligent to play silly games with children.''

''I'm not a child! I'm eighteen.''

''That is unfortunate. As a child, the law would afford you some protection against Sergeant Schroder. As an adult, you are at his mercy.''

''I ain't having my family abused by that sergeant,'' said MacPhearson.

''Just a minute, Branson,'' said Hap suddenly. ''You just said you believed Leroy was guilty, and he's already been charged. So why would this Sergeant Schroder be giving everybody the third degree? You're bluffing for some reason of your own, and I'm calling.''

Lydia jerked and her pen skipped across the notepad. She'd been wrong. Hap wasn't a timid chameleon hiding on the barn wall, satisfied to be overlooked. In fact, he wasn't a lizard at all, but a mignificent ram out to defend his herd.

He was also a pretty stupid sheep, or he'd think twice about accusing John Lloyd of bluffing. In Lydia's opinion, John Lloyd never bluffed; he always played with a stacked deck.

John Lloyd smiled what Lydia privately called his crocodile grin because he always wore it just before he ate someone alive. "Never call a poker player's bluff unless you know what cards he is holding—based on the probability of certain cards being dealt in a certain sequence *and* on the psychology of the person betting the hand. You are calling me based on the faulty psychological assumption that I believe Leroy MacPhearson guilty of murder."

"But you said he was," protested Hap.

"He is guilty of shaving the departed; he is guilty of moving the body; he is guilty of stabbing the corpse. He is not guilty of murder, and I shall prove it Monday morning at the examining trial. Charges will be dismissed, and Sergeant Schroder will be prowling like a very angry, very hungry bear. He will stalk each of you because he knows—and I know—that each of you carries the scent of murder."

"I always knew you had balls, John Lloyd, but standing there like God in a black suit and accusing us of murder takes more than I thought even you had," said Elizabeth, clenching her fists.

"Probability, Elizabeth," he answered. "Leroy MacPhearson disposed of the body. The probability of someone in this room not being involved is, by my estimation, one in ten million."

The rocking chair creaked as MacPhearson got up. "I've heard enough, Lawyer Branson. It's bad enough to have that sergeant after me and my family. I ain't fixing to have you sniffing around like a stray dog, too. I hired you to be my lawyer, not to be no Perry Mason sticking his nose where it don't belong. You just concentrate on getting them charges dismissed."

MacPhearson held out a hand that trembled almost imperceptibly. "I'll see you in court, Lawyer Branson."

John Lloyd stared at the old man's hand for a few seconds before gripping it with his own. "Whom are you protecting, Mr. MacPhearson?"

"I think that was called the bum's rush," remarked Lydia as she and John Lloyd drove away from the farmhouse, chased by MacPhearson's dogs.

"Your description of our leave-taking is colloquial but accurate," said John Lloyd, staring out the windshield at the gravel road.

"And speaking of bums," said Lydia, twisting around on the seat to face him.

He glanced at her, one eyebrow arching. "I infer from your expression that you are speaking of me?"

"Do you see anybody else in the car who owes me a pound of flesh?"

John Lloyd sighed. "You should develop the capacity to look beyond appearances, Miss Fairchild. I took a calculated risk, of course . . ."

"You certainly did. I wanted to strangle you."

". . . but I knew I could depend on your interfering before Elizabeth and Frances indulged themselves to the point of bloodshed."

"What! You counted on my interfering?" Lydia squeezed the end of her seat belt and wished it were John Lloyd's neck. "I thought you were angry because I stopped the fight, but that was just histrionics."

"Please, Miss Fairchild, histrionics more aptly describes my clients' behavior than my own."

"You deliberately goaded those women into a fight. I warned you about using me as part of your strategy again . . ."

"Tactics, Miss Fairchild. You were an admirable tactical weapon."

". . . then you chewed me out in front of those bitches . . ."

"Tsk, tsk, Miss Fairchild, your language is shocking."

"You're doing it again, damn you! You're criticizing me, humiliating me!"

"You will survive a bruised ego."

"It wasn't my ego that was bruised, you cold-blooded, manipulating bastard! It was my—"

He interrupted. "Better a wounded, uh, posterior than a soul sickened unto death, Miss Fairchild."

She stopped in the act of unfastening her seat belt. "What are you talking about?"

"Leroy MacPhearson will not survive in prison. Not that he would die physically, but away from his fields and the endless rotation of seasons, his soul would wither. I simply will not permit that to happen."

"What does my sore behind have to do with Leroy MacPhearson not going to jail?"

"One cannot be an offensive player . . ."

"You were offensive, all right," Lydia said.

". . . and referee at the same time," he finished. "You fulfilled that function, allowing me to analyze the weakness of the defense."

"Allowing you to manipulate people, you mean."

"Although I have occasionally been guilty of manipulation"—he glared at her sniff of disbelief—"I am innocent in this instance. I merely ran a series of plays and anticipated certain responses from the defense. And . . ."

He stopped the car and sat watching the traffic on Soncy Road as if mesmerized. "And?" asked Lydia impatiently.

"Although I scored once in the last quarter, I lost the game, Miss Fairchild."

CHAPTER
SEVEN

"I'LL HAVE YOUR BADGES FOR THIS," SCREAMED TINSDALE as Schroder handcuffed him.

"Wish you civilians would stop watching those TV cops," grunted the investigator as he grabbed Tinsdale's arm and marched him out the front door and down the sidewalk. "Seems like every suspect I arrest quotes me something from one of those shows. Nobody's got any originality anymore."

"At least he didn't say he knew the chief," said Jenner, grabbing Tinsdale's other arm.

"Chief's against the dump. He'd be more likely to give us a medal than take our badges."

"Did you hear that, Tinsdale? Can't use that line."

"I want to call my lawyer," said Tinsdale.

"Worse and worse," said Jenner as he held on to Tinsdale's arm while Schroder opened the old Ford's rear door. "Can't you at least think of a fancier way of asking?"

Tinsdale bent down to slide into the car, then suddenly backed up and straightened. His eyes were round and staring behind the wire-rim glasses, and his mouth was gaping open. Jenner had seen a rookie cop with the same expression after he got too close to the rear end of a horse during the Tri-State Fair parade.

"I'd rather sit in a nuclear waste dump than in that car," announced Tinsdale.

"There's an original statement for you, Schroder," said Jenner, bending over to peer into the backseat. He swallowed and backed up. He wouldn't go so far as to call it a nuclear dump, but personally he'd rather follow a horse.

"Nothing wrong with my car," said Schroder, cleaning off a two-foot space by tossing rags, paper sacks, empty chocolate milk cartons, crumbled potato chips bags, jumper cables, crumpled cigarette packages, candy wrappings, an overdue library book, and a flat tire to the other side of the car. Grabbing a wadded-up blanket out of the floorboard, he spread it over the seat. "Won't even get the seat of your pants dusty. Now sit down."

Tinsdale looked at the blanket. "Is it alive?"

Jenner looked over Tinsdale's shoulder. Given the amount of dog hair, cat hair, and possible body hair of a hitherto unclassified species of mammal clinging to the blanket, the DOE man had asked a legitimate question. "Maybe you ought to shoot it before he gets in, Schroder. It might be carnivorous."

Schroder gave him a look like a hungry cougar and Jenner shut up. The blanket might not be carnivorous, but he wasn't sure about Schroder. "In the car, Tinsdale, before I add obstructing justice to the rest of the charges."

Tinsdale looked at Jenner. "You look like a compassionate man," he whimpered. "Help me."

Jenner patted his shoulder. "I'll see you get a tetanus shot, Mr. Tinsdale. Now just close your eyes and get in. It could be worse."

"How?" asked Tinsdale bitterly as he squatted on the seat like a chimpanzee on a tree limb.

"Schroder could sit back there with you." Jenner leaned in the window and lowered his voice. "Confidentially, though, his breath is carcinogenic."

Tinsdale covered his face and groaned. Jenner whistled as he walked around the car and slid in the front seat. "Don't you think we ought to get Mr. Tinsdale a cup of coffee or glass of water, Schroder? His color looks bad, like he's coming down with something."

"Got a thermos of coffee back there somewhere," said Schroder, turning around to peer over the seat.

"I don't want any coffee," said Tinsdale quickly.

"Suit yourself," said Schroder, sticking a cigarette in the corner of his mouth and lighting it. "Don't claim later we didn't offer."

"Put out that cigarette," ordered Tinsdale. "I don't tolerate smoking in my presence. I don't intend to risk my health to the hazards of tobacco smoke."

Schroder's eyes narrowed and he began breathing rapidly through his nose like a bull preparing to charge. "You're fixing to try to dump seventy million metric tons of nuclear trash in my backyard, and you're bitching about cigarette smoke?"

Tinsdale leaned forward until he was perched precariously on the backseat. "Do you know what percentage of smokers develop lung cancer compared with nonsmokers?"

"A whole hell of a lot smaller percentage than's going to die from your dump. You idiots can't even build packaging to store that crap in that won't corrode in twenty-five or thirty years. That just leaves nine thousand nine hundred seventy or so years for us to worry about."

"We're working on the problem. You can safely leave it in the hands of the Department of Energy," said Tinsdale in the supercilious tone of voice Jenner had heard the DOE project manager use in the public hearings.

"With the safety record you people have, I wouldn't trust

you to build an outhouse," said Schroder, his face turning redder by the minute.

"Hey, Schroder, ease up," said Jenner, alarmed by the burly investigator's florid color. "Murder is the topic, not the dump."

Schroder took a deep drag on his cigarette and blew the smoke toward the backseat. "Yeah, I remember; I just got sidetracked. Now, Mr. Tinsdale, I've charged you with breaking and entering, criminal trespass, interfering with evidence. No law against being a fucking hypocrite, so I can't charge you with that. Listen while I read you your rights." He pulled a soiled, crumbled card out of his pocket.

Jenner listened to Schroder's hoarse voice droning out the Miranda warning. The cops called it Mirandizing a suspect. He supposed it was sort of like sanitizing a case so a confession would be clean enough for the courtroom. Except he'd bet a month's paycheck Tinsdale wouldn't open his mouth, much less confess to anything.

"Do you understand your rights, Mr. Tinsdale?" asked Schroder, pulling out a form and writing in date and time. "If you do, sign here."

"Of course I understand," said Tinsdale, impatiently signing his name. "Shall we get on with the business of clearing up this little misunderstanding? I have more important things to do than waste my time on trivialities."

Jenner felt his mouth drop open and saw the grimace that passed for a sign of confusion on Schroder's face. Tinsdale wasn't screaming for a lawyer. Either he was dumb, or he was innocent, and he damn sure wasn't innocent, so that left dumb.

"In the first place, I wasn't breaking and entering. I had a key."

"Jesus, you mean that guy didn't care if you saw that whorehouse of a bedroom?" asked Jenner.

Tinsdale sniffed. "Charlton's life-style was his own business."

"His and the vice squad's," muttered Jenner.

"What were you doing with a key to Price-Leigh's house?" demanded Schroder.

"Charlton and I were in Washington so frequently that we exchanged keys in case of emergency."

"What kind of emergency?"

Tinsdale waved his cuffed hands in the air. "Oh, a fire, or vandalism, or papers we might have left at home."

"Was he supposed to be in Washington this week?"

Tinsdale shifted his weight and wiped his manacled wrists over his forehead. "Not to my knowledge."

"Then didn't you think something was funny when he didn't show up for work? Didn't you call his house?"

Tinsdale looked triumphantly at Schroder. "No. Because Monday morning I found a note on my desk from Charlton saying he would be out of town for a while."

"Don't play games with me, asshole," said Schroder, lighting another cigarette. "Where's the note?"

"I didn't keep it," answered Tinsdale. "Why should I? How was I to know that some sadistic cop would want to see it?"

Jenner wrote dumb in capital letters in his notebook. Tinsdale would find out it was safer to bait a bear than Sergeant Schroder.

"Who has keys to your office?"

"The staff, Charlton and myself, and a janitorial service."

"When did you last see Price-Leigh?"

"Friday about six. He left before I did. I had several speeches to prepare so I didn't leave until after midnight. I make a lot of speeches trying to educate the public on the waste repository. Sometimes it's difficult."

"You know what they say, Tinsdale. You can fool some of the people some of the time. But folks out here aren't as dumb as you think they are."

Jenner heard the mild tone of Schroder's voice and noticed a frown on the investigator's brow, two sure signs the older man was thinking. And there was a lot to think about, Jenner knew. Charlton Price-Leigh didn't put the note on Tinsdale's desk because Charlton Price-Leigh was dead shortly after midnight.

"Did you check on the house this week, water the lawn, pick up the mail, anything like that?" asked Schroder.

"I drove by a few times," said Tinsdale, shrugging his shoulders. "Naturally I didn't go in."

"Why naturally?"

"I certainly would've notified the police if I had gone in."

"After you carted off a little evidence," said Jenner, looking up from his notepad.

"That box of materials has nothing to do with Charlton's murder. It is government property and my responsibility."

"You aren't responsible for your own shit if you leave it at a murder scene, Tinsdale," said Schroder. "Jenner, run in the house and see if that box of *government property* has been tagged. If it has, bring it out here."

"Sure thing. I could use some fresh air." He slid out of the car. "By the way, Schroder, I've been meaning to ask if you still have your pet bull snake. Might warn Tinsdale if you do. Wouldn't want him to be scared if Oscar crawls up his pants leg." He went whistling up the walk, but not before he saw Tinsdale trying to vault over the seat into Schroder's lap.

"You guys finished with that box Tinsdale was hiding in the shower? Schroder wants it," he called through the front door. He wasn't going near that bedroom again if he could avoid it.

A skinny Special Crimes investigator whose name Jenner couldn't remember handed it over. "It's all dusted and tagged. A few clear prints, but mostly smudges, even on the photographs. Tell you what, buddy, if this stuff belonged to the victim, he was a real sick guy. The only thing some of them pictures and books'll stimulate is the urge to puke."

"They won't make me sick," said Jenner, taking the box. "I've been sitting in Schroder's car."

The investigator looked sympathetic. "Jesus, you want an anti-nausea pill?"

Jenner shook his head. "I got a cast-iron stomach."

A few minutes later, sitting in Schroder's car and examining the contents of the box, he wasn't so sure. "Good God, some of these pictures must be trick photography. I mean, is this position physically possible?" he asked, pointing his finger at one of the snapshots.

Schroder wasn't listening. He was looking at Tinsdale, breathing hard, and had that bull-about-to-charge look on his face again. "Government property," he hissed through clenched, nicotine-stained teeth. His lips jerked and cigarette ash showered over the back of the seat. "If some of this filth is government property, then I'm the president. Who the hell do you think you're messing with, you swellheaded jerk? I'm with the Special Crimes Unit of Amarillo, Texas, and we're the goddamn best. Just ask the FBI. Now you want to back up and tell me your story again, or you want to tell it to the bogeyman?"

"Who's that?" asked Jenner.

"Maximum Miller," said Schroder, grinning at Tinsdale. "He's the biggest, baddest prosecutor in the state of Texas. He eats dope kingpins and serial murderers for dinner. Come to think of it, he won't eat you. He'll just pitch you out in the backyard for his Doberman to maul."

Tinsdale was sweating. "You don't understand . . ."

"Why don't you explain?"

"One has to maintain a certain image in government service."

"Sure as hell ain't honesty if you're any example," interjected Schroder.

Tinsdale cleared his throat. "We have to worry about our personal reputation, particularly in a sensitive area like energy. We even have to take training courses in dealing with the public."

"Yeah, I know," said Schroder. "I heard a rumor about one of those courses. I think it was called How to Deal with the Rural Mind."

"As I was saying, we must maintain a good reputation in the community. Charlton's personal, uh, practices were a little cosmopolitan for the Texas Panhandle. I mean, Charlton's reputation as a ladies' man wasn't quite in line with DOE's public image."

Jenner had heard all he could stand. "Ladies' man! Damn it, that's like calling a child abuser a disciplinarian. I've seen cleaner photos than these in a porno bookshop. The man was a lousy, sick-in-the-head pervert. And if you're interested in my opinion, Charlton Price-Leigh fits the DOE image perfectly."

"What's this mean, Tinsdale?" demanded Schroder, holding up a county map with a large area colored red, surrounded by a smaller blue border.

Tinsdale dived at the map and bumped his nose on the back of the seat as Schroder jerked the map out of his reach. "That's none of your business, you ignorant hick. That's government business."

Schroder spread the map out on his knees. "In these United States, the government is supposed to mean the people, isn't it. Well, I'm one of the people, so I think I'll just take a look at my business."

"That's just a map of the repository . . ."

"Dump, you mean," interrupted Jenner. "Why don't you people use the right word? It's a goddamn dump."

"If this red area is the dumpsite, what's the blue border mean, Tinsdale?" asked Schroder.

Tinsdale glanced around the car while licking his thin lips, and Jenner thought of a lizard looking for a place to hide. "That's an extra safety factor."

"This blue area figures out to a six square mile perimeter.

What kind of safety factor are you talking about that takes six square miles?''

"It's a containment area."

"Containment for what?" demanded Schroder.

"This is difficult to explain to a layman with no specialized training."

"I graduated from high school, and I'm even computer-literate, so why don't you try me? Better use words of one syllable so you don't tax my brain." Schroder looked meaner than Jenner had ever seen him.

"It's a containment area for radiation," said Tinsdale in a rush of words.

Schroder threw his cigarette out the window. "A containment area for radiation, did you say?"

His voice was low and placid-sounding, but Jenner braced himself anyway. The burly investigator smoked his cigarettes down to the last quarter inch. The one he threw out the window was at least three inches long.

Tinsdale nodded. "That's what I said."

Schroder was leaning over the backseat, his face within inches of Tinsdale's. "You sorry son of a bitch! You people damn sure didn't talk much about a radiation containment area, did you? You flapped your mouths about how safe the dump was and about how silly and misinformed we all were to be worrying. DOE isn't so damn sure after all, is it? It's no damn wonder the farmers are pissed off. You're trying to turn the tenth most productive county in the whole United States into a radioactive trash heap. They ought to declare a bounty on your scalps."

Schroder took a deep breath. "Where do you expect the first accident? At the handling facility on the surface? In the mine shaft on the way underground? Are you afraid that shaft might collapse? Are you afraid it might crack where it drills through the aquifer? We're in a pot full of trouble if that happens, aren't we?"

"There might be some unpleasant consequences," said

Tinsdale, his head canted back as far as possible from Schroder's face.

Schroder studied Tinsdale as he would a cockroach trying to climb out of the sewer. "Unpleasant consequences, the man says. You know something, Tinsdale? I arrested a man for chopping a woman into four pieces, and I liked him a lot more than I like you."

"Schroder." Jenner listened to the sound of his own voice and decided he was hearing an echo. Might have something to do with talking around the bile rising in his throat. He swallowed and tried again. "Schroder, look at this. It's a list of landowners who own property in the blue area. Mac-Phearson's name is at the top of the list. We got the who and the where and now we know the why of the murder."

"Let me see that," said Schroder, jerking the list out of Jenner's hands.

"MacPhearson? Did you say MacPhearson?" asked Tinsdale, tugging on Schroder's shoulder.

"Yeah," said Schroder, squinting at the list. "What about it?"

"Charlton had a meeting with MacPhearson the day of the uh . . ."

"Murder," suggested Schroder.

"The DOE hasn't officially notified the landowners in the containment area . . ."

"Slipped your mind?" asked Jenner.

Tinsdale ignored him. "But MacPhearson accused Charlton and the DOE of being thieves. He said Charlton wouldn't live long enough to see MacPhearson land stolen by the government."

CHAPTER EIGHT

LYDIA DUG HER FINGERNAILS INTO THE VELOUR UPHOLSTERY of John Lloyd's Lincoln. She touched the dashboard, then looked through the windshield at the housing development across Soncy Road. Finally, she twisted around and looked back at Leroy MacPhearson's farmhouse.

"Miss Fairchild, if you would please stop twitching," said John Lloyd. "You remind me of Frances."

"I wanted to see if everything was the same, or if the earth had shifted, or maybe we were caught in the twilight zone."

John Lloyd tapped the steering wheel with one long lean finger. "Now you are babbling. Also like Frances. I had not previously noticed your propensity for adopting the personal quirks of those you meet. If this is a new facet of your personality, please either control it, or seek professional treatment."

"Do you know what you just said, John Lloyd?"

"Certainly. I am not the one having difficulty expressing

myself. I told you to correct your behavior or seek out a psychiatrist.''

Lydia dismissed his comment with a wave of the hand. ''Not that one! You said you'd been outplayed. Do you know how frightening that is? I'd sooner expect my preacher to stand in the pulpit on Sunday morning and announce God was dead than to hear you admit a bunch of loony tunes outmaneuvered you.''

''Given the naive social doctrine and the fuzzy political opinions being preached from the modern pulpits by proponents of the left and the right, an announcement of atheism would at least have the benefit of focusing attention on the central issue of religion.''

''Quit changing the subject, John Lloyd, and explain yourself. I'll admit you didn't exactly come on like Clarence Darrow, but you did hazard a couple of lucky guesses that made them squirm. Your comment about shaving the corpse and then asking MacPhearson who he was protecting got some reaction.''

John Lloyd turned his head. His eyes had a cold, hard expression that made Lydia do a little squirming of her own. ''Miss Fairchild, I do not make guesses, lucky or otherwise. I make logical deductions based on observable facts and the psychological proclivities of both victim and client. My relationship with Leroy MacPhearson predates this case by several years. In all those years I have never known him to commit a violent act. While it is possible for him to act out of character, I did not think it probable. Therefore, the most logical explanation for his behavior was that he was protecting someone else. To test my theory, I arranged a family conference and I accused those closest to him. He reacted as I thought he would. He told me to mind my own business.''

''Why didn't you push harder? Why didn't you accuse somebody, like Frances or Rachel?''

''Have you ever known me to be a reckless man, Miss Fairchild?''

"You're a gambler."

His offended expression made her feel as if she were five years old again and had just said a naughty word in Sunday School. "I am *not* a gambler. I occasionally play poker. There is a subtle difference."

"Not that I can see. You're still gambling."

"I play the odds in a game of skill, which usually involves wagering money. In the MacPhearson case the odds were against me. Had I actually accused a frightened, neurotic woman or a helpless young female who happen to be his daughter and granddaughter, Leroy would quite probably have confessed to murder. I do not wager lives."

"At least then we'd know whom he was protecting, and we could break the case, keep Leroy from taking the rap."

He flinched. "Miss Fairchild, not only is your outdated gangland vernacular appalling, but your conclusion is faulty. The only thing we would break would be Frances's delicate psychological balance."

"Then we could use the insanity plea. A jury would come closer to believing Frances is unhinged than that Leroy is. Let's face it, John Lloyd. That woman is so far around the bend, she can't even be seen."

"Where is your sympathy, Miss Fairchild? Be charitable."

"Charitable! Frances strikes me as the type to bite the hand that feeds her, and she might be contagious. Look what she's doing to her own father."

"Have you considered that her erratic behavior might be motivated by her fear for her father rather than by guilt?"

Lydia cleared her throat. "Uh, no."

"Then consider it." He shrugged his shoulders. "It might even be true."

"You mean you don't know?"

"If I knew, do you seriously believe I would permit this conspiracy to continue?"

Lydia reached over and patted his arm. "Don't get paranoid. Two people don't make a conspiracy."

He brushed her hand off. "Did you notice that not one person proclaimed Leroy's innocence, that the charges against him were false? Not one! Why, Miss Fairchild?"

"Maybe they all think he's guilty. Have you considered that, Mr. Branson?" she asked in an imitation of his drawl.

He turned his head to look at her, and she wished she hadn't mimicked him. She'd describe his mood as somewhere between bad and piss-poor. "Use your intelligence, Miss Fairchild. Why would they think that unless they all have some knowledge of the crime? Why else is Leroy MacPhearson afraid of me, so afraid that he instructed me not to question anyone?"

"But when Sergeant Schroder questions the family, he certainly won't be civil about it."

"And you think I would be?" asked John Lloyd.

His fingers curled around the steering wheel as if it were someone's throat and Lydia shivered. Schroder at his worst was Mother Teresa compared with John Lloyd Branson. "What are you going to do, John Lloyd?"

John Lloyd turned north on Soncy Road before answering. "Bring the guilty to justice and protect the innocent."

"Do you suppose that just once in your life you could answer a simple question."

"Are you cross-examining me, Miss Fairchild?"

"Yes!"

"Excellent! If your previous question is an example of your skill at that particular procedure, you need the practice. Ask specific questions."

"John Lloyd, you are the most exasperating man I've ever met. No, that's wrong. You're a real pain in the butt. How's that for being specific?"

"Specific enough for the average judge to consider citing you for contempt of court. You cannot insult a witness, Miss Fairchild."

"Cut the crap, John Lloyd, and tell me how you're going to keep Leroy MacPhearson out of jail."

"That is the question you should have asked in the beginning. Minus the profane introductory remark."

"I did!" yelled Lydia, feeling a little exasperated herself.

"You asked for my goal, not for my methods in achieving that goal, Miss Fairchild."

"Witness is being evasive," she quipped, and glanced at him. He was staring straight ahead again, frowning at something, and Lydia felt sure it wasn't the traffic.

"Miss Fairchild, I find you occasionally irritating, frequently impulsive, but almost always perceptive."

"What?"

"Yes, I am being evasive," he said impatiently. "If you are going to cross-examine a witness successfully, Miss Fairchild, you must keep track of your questions."

"I can keep track of my questions. It's your answers I have problems with."

He pulled onto I-40 going east and stepped on the accelerator. "I have no answers."

"What?"

"Are you losing your hearing, Miss Fairchild?"

"No! But I'll have it checked because I thought I heard you say you didn't have any answers. That's impossible. You'd stand up during a performance of *Hamlet* and tell the prince sixteen reasons why it's better to be than not to be."

"I am not in the mood for flippancy, Miss Fairchild. I have been humbled, and humility is not a natural state for me. I find it an unsettling, even frightening, experience."

She looked at his austere profile and his white-knuckled hands clutching the steering wheel. She felt a little unsettled herself, as if she were riding an elevator that had just dropped three floors. John Lloyd sounded defeated. Worse, he sounded as if he were feeling sorry for himself. If he were any other man, she'd suspect he was hinting for a little TLC. But John Lloyd Branson resembled other men about as much as a lion resembled a tomcat. Still, she thought as she unfastened her seat belt and scooted closer to him, even a lion needs his ears scratched.

She reached over and patted his arm. "It's all right, John Lloyd. It's natural to feel humiliated when someone beats you. You don't have to pretend to be a good loser just to impress me. I'm not a good loser either, so I understand how you feel."

John Lloyd jerked his head down to stare at her. "What are you blathering about, Miss Fairchild?"

"Losing to Leroy MacPhearson."

She heard him muttering something under his breath that sounded like an obscenity. "I am not humbled because I lost, Miss Fairchild. Even *I* lose occasionally. I am brought low, humbled, if you will, by the realization that I was deceived. I have not been deceived by a case in the past ten years."

"You're only human, John Lloyd . . ."

"Do not recite platitudes, Miss Fairchild, unless you wish to speak of pride going before a fall. I recognized certain deceptions—MacPhearson's stabbing a corpse, the missing beard—but I failed utterly to realize that like a Chinese puzzle, there were deceptions within deceptions. My only consolation is that my adversary is a worthy opponent."

Lydia shook her head. "I don't understand what you're talking about. How were you deceived?"

"Leroy MacPhearson did not shave Charlton Price-Leigh. I did not observe his tremor until I shook his hand just before we left. A trembling hand holding even a safety razor will inevitably leave wounds."

"Maybe he used an electric razor," Lydia suggested.

"Spoken with the authority of a woman who has never worn a full beard."

"I can't help my female hormones."

"Charlton Price-Leigh was shaved by someone with a steady hand using a safety razor, although I would not exclude the possibility of a straight edge. Someone else helped Leroy MacPhearson.''

"The murderer, John Lloyd. The murderer shaved the corpse and Leroy MacPhearson disposed of the body.''

"An altogether calculated plan of action with a logical division of labor in other words?''

"You make it sound like an assembly line, but yes, that's what happened. My God, John Lloyd, just imagine the scene. The murderer stabs what's-his-name, Price-Leigh, then calmly strips him, shaves him like some kind of macabre barber, and calls Farmer MacPhearson, who wraps the body in a sheet and dumps it in a field. Anybody cold-blooded enough to do all that must have to sleep on a rock in the sun to keep his blood from freezing.''

"Your scenario is another deception. Remember the autopsy report, Miss Fairchild. There were no fibers found in the wound. The victim was without his shirt when he was murdered. Also remember the type of weapon used. A knife, unlike a firearm, requires proximity to the victim as well as a degree of personal involvement on the part of the murderer. A knife is not a dispassionate weapon, nor is this crime a dispassionate one. Stabbings seldom are. It requires passion to lift a knife and bury it in a man's chest, and passion leaves a residue of regret, fear, terror, and the inability to act rationally. Yet the final disposition of the body argues a very rational mind. Probability and psychology force me to conclude that the person who shaved the dearly departed was not the murderer.''

She felt as if she were solving some terrifying brainteaser. "And Mr. MacPhearson didn't shave the corpse.''

"Consequently, at least three persons were involved: the murderer; the barber, who is also the master of deceit; and Leroy MacPhearson.''

Lydia began to shiver until she felt her whole body shaking. "I'm cold,'' she whispered, and heard her voice shaking, too.

"Lydia!" John Lloyd's voice wasn't quite calm as usual. "Lydia! Are you ill?"

Scrambling the rest of the way to him, she burrowed her face into his shoulder. She felt him hesitate before he wrapped his arm around her. She'd probably shocked him to the depths of his puritan soul, but she didn't care. He was warm and smelled of bay rum. She heard him calling her name again and smiled. He only called her Lydia when he was concerned.

She squirmed until she was tucked against his side, her head resting comfortably on his shoulder. She looked up at him. He was watching the road just enough to keep from swerving into the bar ditch. "You scared the hell out of me."

He glanced at her, then back at the road. For a moment she thought she saw relief in his eyes. "I do not believe that is possible, Miss Fairchild."

"You came close." She shivered again. "I don't know how you can be so calm. My God, not only were we sitting in the same room with a murderer, but with two people that treated a human being like garbage."

"Possibly."

"Possibly! What do you mean, possibly? You just said at least three"—she stopped and shook her head—"or did you mean there are more? Is that the conspiracy you were talking about? What did they do? Draw straws to see who did what? That's why you said they were all tainted by murder?"

"It is possible. No one expressed shock at the corpse's identity except Elizabeth. No one protested innocence except Elizabeth."

"I don't know why you're leaving out Her Highness. If anyone is tough, it's her. I can see her lathering up the corpse."

She felt his body stiffen. "She does not fit the psychological profile, Miss Fairchild."

"Why not? She certainly didn't hesitate to give orders to

everyone this morning. And she was rational enough to come up with that insanity plea."

"Elizabeth is a very passionate woman."

"Are you speaking from firsthand experience?"

He was now so rigid she thought she was resting her head on a block of wood. "I will tolerate no questions about, nor comments on, my personal relationships, Miss Fairchild."

"Pardon me for living," she snapped back in a voice she hoped was as arctic as his. She slipped out from under his arm and scooted back to the other side of the seat.

"Do not let jealousy cloud your judgment, Miss Fairchild. Elizabeth has so volatile a personality that she was prepared to lay hands on Frances. And her so-called insanity plea bordered on impassioned oratory. She lacks the self-control necessary to plan the disposal of the body."

"And don't let the fact you have the hots for that woman cloud your judgment, *Mr. Branson*!" She folded her arms across her chest and stared straight ahead. "And I'm not jealous."

"I never permit affection for an individual to influence my professional judgment, and I have not done so in this case. Before your vulgar outburst, I was going to say that Elizabeth has more the personality to commit murder than to conceal it."

"E-Elizabeth?"

John Lloyd tightened his hands on the steering wheel. "But to believe Elizabeth guilty of murder is to believe another deception. It would be most unlike her to ask someone for help, and certainly unlike her not to take responsibility for her own actions."

Lydia put her hands over her ears. "I don't want to hear any more about deceptions or possibilities or probabilities. They're all homicidal maniacs." She uncovered her ears. "Withdraw from the case, John Lloyd."

"I have a client, Miss Fairchild."

"Sure, one who fertilizes his wheat with corpses. Give it up. Tell the police what you suspect and let them handle it."

"Leroy is not afraid of the police. However, he is afraid of me. Why, Miss Fairchild? What can I discover that Sergeant Schroder can't?"

"I don't know, and I don't want you looking either. For God's sake, John Loyd, do you want to end up nude in a field pushing up wheat stocks?"

"You exaggerate."

"The hell I do! Ask Charlton Price-Leigh."

He stomped on the brakes and swerved toward an exit ramp. "Miss Fairchild, you just earned a year's salary."

"Good God, John Lloyd!" She rubbed her shoulder where it had slammed into the door. "You just crossed three lanes of traffic and this isn't even our exit. Have you lost your mind?"

"No, Miss Fairchild. I have finally regained it, and you are responsible. We are going to Hereford to do as you suggested. We are going to question Charlton Price-Leigh."

Lydia felt cold again. "In case it slipped your mind, John Lloyd, Price-Leigh is dead."

"Contrary to the popular cliché, dead men do tell tales. Tell me, Miss Fairchild, if you knew you were to die tomorrow, and knew strangers would be looking through your belongings, what would you do?"

"Throw out my torn underwear and burn my love letters," she said without thinking, then felt her face turn red. "What kind of kinky question is that?"

John Lloyd cocked an eyebrow. "I see nothing perverse about my question. Your answer, however, reveals secret aspects of your character . . ."

"You leave my character out of this!"

". . . and by the same token, let us hope Charlton Price-Leigh's undergarments and love letters or whatever, reveal aspects of his. He was not the casual victim of a mugging or a robbery. He was sought out to be murdered for a very specific reason. Why him, Miss Fairchild? What secret did he hold? What threat did he make? Our attention has been distracted by the bizarre aspects of the murder, and we have failed to ask the obvious. Who benefits by his death? Who among those six people at Leroy MacPhearson's farm is richer, safer, happier because Price-Leigh is dead?''

CHAPTER
NINE

"LOCKHART?"

"Yeah, what do you want, Schroder?" asked the Hereford chief as he rolled down the window of his patrol car.

Schroder leaned over and rested both hands on the car. Jenner marveled again that the detective could bend in the middle. "We got a prisoner for you unless maybe you'll accept a material warrant on him."

Lockhart took a sip of coffee and looked at Tinsdale perched in Schroder's backseat. "That's Rory Tinsdale, isn't it?"

Schroder nodded.

"And you want me to arrest him?"

Schroder nodded again.

"You know how often the law enforcement people in this town make the evening news?"

Schroder shook his head.

"Too damn often. You know how many goddamn reporters I catch crawling out of the woodwork every week?"

Schroder shook his head again.

Lockhart leaned his head against the car seat and closed his eyes. "Too damn many, Schroder." His eyes snapped open. "Every time I turn around that Rural Legal Aid bunch is claiming I make all my arrests because I'm prejudiced against Hispanics. Some damn reporter sticks a television camera up my nose and asks what I have to say to the charge. Well, I can't say horseshit on the air, can I? I tell you, Schroder, I got all the mud slung at me I can stand. I don't want no three-piece-suit Washington lawyer threatening to slap a lawsuit on me 'cause I arrested one of the DOE boys. I'll arrest him I have to, but I'd rather you took him back to Potter County on that material witness warrant. Besides, I got high-class prisoners: dopers and thieves and folks like that. DOE would ruin the neighborhood."

Schroder straightened up and ground his minuscule cigarette butt under his heel. "Figured you'd feel that way. I'll call and have Maximum Miller draw up the papers and send them down."

Lockhart had a wistful look on his face. "Maximum Miller. You know, I tried to persuade him to move to Hereford and run for D.A. I figured with a black D.A., the Rural Legal Aid people would give it a rest. Miller wouldn't consider it. He said life was too short to mess with bigots." He sighed again and turned on his ignition. "If you need any of my men to help you question the neighbors, let me know. I'm going back to the office, put my feet up, and count the days until retirement." He waved his hand as he drove off.

Jenner watched Lockhart drive off, then waited for Schroder's next move. The investigator lit a cigarette and stood without moving except for the motion of his lips when he drew on his cigarette. Jenner felt beads of sweat roll down his sides to flatten against the waist of his pants. "Damn it, Schroder, why are we standing out in the sun?"

"I'm thinking."

"Can't we go in the house, or at least sit in the car with Tinsdale? I'm sweating so much my underwear's wet."

"I'm not sitting in the same car with that piss-ant any more than I can help, and we'll be in the way in the house. Now shut up."

Jenner looked resentfully at the investigator. Schroder was overweight, wore a dark brown polyester sport coat, and was standing in the middle of a sidewalk on a hot August day. And the son of a bitch wasn't even sweating. Schroder wasn't human. He was some kind of a damn nicotine-powered android that the chief activated every time there was a murder. But Larry Jenner, traffic cop, wasn't; Larry Jenner was a human being whose tail was dragging. In fact, it was probably leaving a trail in the dirt. Time to haul it back to Amarillo—*if* he could figure out a way to get Schroder to release him. A frontal assault wouldn't work. Better try subtlety.

"Maximum Miller ought to be happy," remarked Jenner, blotting sweat from his forehead with a sodden handkerchief. "He's got his motive. You suppose it'll be enough for an indictment?"

Schroder made an indeterminate sound between a grunt and a growl.

Jenner made another try. "Guess he'll be happy, beating John Lloyd Branson on a murder."

Schroder grunted again. Or maybe growled. It was hard to tell, thought Jenner. Might even be a belch. But it wasn't an answer.

Maybe he was being too subtle, Jenner thought. "Looks like you've got everything under control, Schroder. I guess I'll go back to my regular job tomorrow. No need for me to hang around."

Like a giant humpback whale, Schroder rose to the surface from the depths of a sea of contemplation, spumed out a single word, along with a cloud of cigarette smoke, and sank out of sight again. "No," he said distinctly.

"Why the hell not? We"—he corrected himself when the

humpback rolled one eye in his direction—"*you* found the crime scene, found the motive, and you already had the suspect. You don't need my help. MacPhearson's going to the slammer for ventilating that pervert's hide. Not that I think he should. A man's got a right to defend his property from thieves even if they're government thieves."

Schroder stirred again. "Killing a DOE man ain't going to help MacPhearson protect his property. It's like stepping on dog shit. It just squeezes up around your shoes and you got a bigger mess than you started with."

"It's not fair!" Jenner burst out before he thought. "Those bastards are coming down here to poison us."

The burly investigator shifted his weight like a prize-fighter and Jenner stepped back. "Quit talking like a ten-year-old kid, son. We're cops and we goddamn well know most of what we investigate *ain't* fair, but that's what we got juries for. They decide how to even the score. We just scrape up the dog shit."

Jenner started to wipe his forehead with his dripping handkerchief, and used his sleeve instead. "You can man the pooper-scooper yourself, Schroder. I'm going back to Amarillo. I'd rather resign from the department and set up as a private detective than drive any more nails in MacPhearson's coffin. In fact, that's a good idea. I'll buy myself a fedora and a trench coat, learn to drink straight Scotch out of water glasses, and only work for blondes who look like Lauren Bacall. Hell, I don't know why I didn't think of it before."

"Old man MacPhearson provided his own nails and his own coffin. Hell, he even dug his own grave. All we're doing is serving as pallbearers. So don't give me crap about going back to Amarillo. We're not done until the grave's filled in."

"Jesus, Schroder, want do you want? You've already got enough dirt to fill the Grand Canyon rim to rim."

"We don't even have enough to cover the coffin lid yet. I want MacPhearson's fingerprints in that bedroom. I want a neighbor with insomnia who looked out her window in time to see him walk out of that house with Price-Leigh's body slung over his shoulder. I want the murder weapon.''

"Hell's bells!" exclaimed Jenner. "Why don't you wish for a videotape while you're at it?"

"I want to know why MacPhearson put socks on the victim.''

"So his feet wouldn't get cold, I guess," snapped Jenner, then wished he'd kept his mouth shut. Humpback whales could give dirty looks.

"We've got loose ends, son, enough to unravel the whole case. Maximum Miller doesn't like loose ends. They give him indigestion, and when he's got indigestion, everybody else has gas.''

"Schroder! Where's the car?"

The investigator's head swiveled toward the old Ford, then swiveled back toward Jenner. He expelled a breath of smoke. "Don't do that, son. For a minute there you had me thinking Tinsdale had hot-wired my car and escaped.''

"Not your car. Tinsdale's car. He didn't walk over here carrying a boxful of pornography.''

Schroder scratched a patch of gray stubble underneath his chin, then marched with ponderous steps toward his car. "How come you thought of that?"

"You said gas, and I naturally thought of cars. Then I wondered where his was. It's not parked in the driveway because this house doesn't have one.''

Schroder slapped the younger man on the shoulder. "That's why I keep you around. You're sharp.''

Jenner wished to hell he wasn't so damn smart.

The burly investigator leaned in the window. "Tinsdale, where's your car?"

Still squatting on Schroder's backseat, Tinsdale looked like a scrawny wet buzzard. His face was red and glistening with sweat. Damp patches dotted his clothes. His eyes blinked behind thick lenses. "Parked in the garage, which, in this particular house, opens onto the alley.''

Schroder turned toward the house with the grace of a pivoting buffalo. "Come on, Jenner!"

Jenner looked at Tinsdale's red face. Even the guy's glasses were fogged from the heat. "Schroder, we can't leave him out here. Hell, I wouldn't leave a dog in a car on a day like this."

Schroder didn't miss a step. "I wouldn't either."

Jenner looked at Schroder's retreating shape, and then at Tinsdale's dripping face. He opened the car door. "Get out, and no tricks or I'll lock you up in Schroder's trunk. If you think his backseat is bad, you ain't seen nothin' yet."

Tinsdale wiped his nose on his coat sleeve. "I knew you were the only civilized man in this backward force. My civil rights suit won't mention you."

"Don't do me any favors," said Jenner, leading the way into the house.

The fine fingerprint powder gave a dusty smell to the air and a white coating to every possible surface. Special Crimes investigators were systematically searching the living room. One investigator removed books one by one from the bookcases and meticulously examined each while another stripped pictures from their frames. Cushions from the chairs and couches were lying on the floors. If Price-Leigh weren't already dead, seeing the mess a criminal investigation made of his house would kill him.

The kitchen was even worse, thought Jenner, as he led Tinsdale through the room to the back door. Dishes were stacked on every surface, drawers were pulled out, and silver was piled on the cabinets. The pantry door hung open and canned goods, stripped of their labels, were piled on the floor. There was a faint odor hanging in the air. Jenner closed his eyes and concentrated. Ammonia and rotting potatoes, he decided, as he opened his eyes. Strange combination, he thought as he pushed Tinsdale through the door and into the attached garage. A black Trans-Am was parked on one side, and a conservative tan Dodge sedan on the other.

Schroder was trying different keys on the Dodge's trunk. He glared at Jenner and Tinsdale from under his bushy eyebrows. "What's he doing here?"

Jenner glared back.

"That's not my car," said Tinsdale suddenly.

Schroder froze in the act of trying another key. Jenner thought of a grizzly bear caught in the glare of a park ranger's flashlight. Schroder had that same blank stare and slack jaw. The investigator blinked and ambled over to the Tran-Am like a bear checking out a different garbage can. "Pretty fancy car for a civil servant," he grunted as he lifted the trunk lid.

Tinsdale folded his arms as best he could considering his handcuffs. "Nothing says I have to be boring."

"A Trans-Am doesn't help you," said Jenner as he peered into the trunk.

Schroder looked up at Tinsdale. "You planning on moving?"

Tinsdale pushed his glasses back up his nose. "Is there something wrong with empty boxes?"

"Only if they're in your car," said Schroder. His eyes looked narrow and mean, and seemed to glow with a red light. "I wish I could charge you on one count of tampering with evidence for every empty box in this trunk. You were going to strip this house of every camera, every dirty picture, every one of those disgusting"—he waved his arms—"*things*."

"I think you mean the sex—" began Jenner.

"I know what I mean," interrupted Schroder. "Get the little shit out of here before I lose my temper."

"That's no way to speak to a suspect, Sergeant Schroder," said a voice in a deep, slow drawl.

Jenner looked around the trunk lid to see John Lloyd Branson standing just inside the garage, but it was Lydia Fairchild who drew his eyes like iron filings to a magnet. Just looking at her made his libido speed up. If he ever did chuck the department to become a detective, he wanted her to be his first client. He could visualize rising and walking around his dented and scratched desk, past the rack that held his fedora and trench coat, to pat her shoulder and wipe the tears from those enormous blue eyes. He dropped his gaze below her neck and thought perhaps a warm embrace would be more in character for a macho private eye. Absently he wondered how she got muddy paw prints on her blouse. Maybe he could offer to sponge them off.

"Sergeant Jenner."

Jenner stretched his lips and moved his eyes. Branson's voice had frost an inch thick on it. "Mr. Branson, good to see you again."

"I wasn't aware you saw me." Jenner heard the slight emphasis on the word *me*.

"He saw you and so did I," interrupted Schroder. "Just happen to be in the neighborhood, Branson?"

John Lloyd answered the question with a question, something Jenner had noticed before about the lawyer. "I suppose that your being in this particular domicile means you have identified our anonymous victim as Charlton Price-Leigh? His fingerprints, no doubt?"

Schroder puffed on his cigarette until his head was wreathed with smoke. Jenner hoped the smoke meant the investigator was releasing tension for the same reason an overheated engine released steam. Otherwise there was going to be a hell of an explosion.

"Branson." Schroder's voice sounded hoarser than usual. "You son of a bitch, you knew who the victim was. I ought to charge you for withholding evidence. I ought to haul you up before the Texas Bar for being unethical. I ought to kick your butt."

John Lloyd held up one hand. "Please, Sergeant, watch your language. Miss Fairchild is present, and I do not wish her vocabulary enriched with vulgarities. As for your threats, I suggest you might attempt the third as it only requires strength. The first two require proof and you have none. I had no evidence to withhold. I only had a supposition that Miss Fairchild and I planned to test by attempting to contact Mr. Charlton Price-Leigh. Your presence indicates that test is unnecessary.''

Schroder chewed on the end of his cigarette. "You'd try to argue the devil out of your soul, wouldn't you, Counselor?''

Jenner disagreed. The devil would know better than to mess around with John Lloyd Branson in the first place.

Branson shrugged his shoulders. "Only if it is necessary,'' he said, stepping around Tinsdale to glance in the trunk.

Schroder slammed the lid down. "No free peeks, Branson. You and Miss Fairchild disappear out the front door.''

John Lloyd pointed to the tan Dodge with his cane. "That car is Mr. Price-Leigh's?''

"According to Tinsdale here. Now, get out.''

"Full disclosure, Sergeant Schroder. As attorney for the defense I am entitled to examine the crime scene.''

Schroder chewed on his cigarette again and Jenner sympathized with the other man. Technically Branson was right. However, it was doubtful whether legally the lawyer could examine the crime scene at the same time as the police. Technically, Schroder could kick Branson out. Realistically, Jenner didn't think that was a good idea.

Schroder must have agreed because he capitulated. "All right, but don't touch anything, and stay the hell out of the way.''

John Lloyd inclined his head. "I accept your terms.'' He directed his attention to the DOE project manager. "Mr. Tinsdale, you seem to be involved in this affair.''

Tinsdale shook his handcuffed wrists in John Lloyd's face. "Branson, tell these ignorant yokels to release me.''

"Even a criminal defense lawyer must have some principles, Mr. Tinsdale. I never represent drug dealers, child molesters, or the DOE.''

Tinsdale's face turned red, then white as he grabbed John Lloyd's coat sleeve. ''I'll remember that, Branson,'' he screamed as Jenner pulled him away. ''I'll beat you and the rest of those provincial idiots you represent. The repository will be built, and it will be built in Deaf Smith County. It's the law of the land.'' Tinsdale spat out the words, his eyes seeming to bulge behind his glasses.

John Lloyd brushed his coat sleeve as if something filthy had touched it. ''A half century ago a madman used that refrain as he marched six million human beings into gas chambers.''

''That was Nazi Germany!'' shouted Tinsdale.

''The law of *this* land once declared that I could own a black man. The law of *this* land denied the female sex the right to vote. Both these laws deprived citizens of freedom and happiness. Your infamous law, which I might point out has not been tested constitutionally, threatens to deprive citizens of their very lives, directly as a result of radiation sickness, and indirectly by starvation if the greater portion of our agricultural lands are sterilized. I submit to you, Mr. Tinsdale, that your law is evil. It will not be tolerated.''

Tinsdale twisted out of Jenner's hands to face Schroder. ''You heard him,'' he said, pointing to John Lloyd. ''He's the one who should be arrested. He as much as threatened the DOE. He's the spokesman for STAD. He's guilty of inciting that crazy old man to murder. They're gangsters, terrorists, all of them. They'll be planting bombs and killing innocent women and children next.''

''You pompous ass! You don't give a damn how many women and children you kill with your goddamn dump.'' Lydia Fairchild advanced on Tinsdale like an avenging angel—except Jenner didn't think angels used profanity.

Tinsdale grabbed Schroder's lapels. ''I demand police protection!''

John Lloyd wrapped his arm around Lydia's waist. "Miss Fairchild, please exercise self-control."

"As soon as I exercise my right hook," she retorted, struggling to free herself.

Schroder peeled the clinging limpet that was Tinsdale off his coat. "Jenner, handcuff our friend to the steering wheel of his fancy car."

"I could not help noticing that Mr. Tinsdale is under restraint. Can I assume he is charged with aiding Price-Leigh's departure to the hereafter?" asked John Lloyd, finally subduing his clerk.

"It's all a misunderstanding!" shouted Tinsdale, rattling his handcuffs.

Schroder lit another cigarette and stood clicking his lighter. "Not exactly," he admitted to John Lloyd. "He's a material witness."

John Lloyd cocked an eyebrow. "He witnessed Mr. Price-Leigh's departure?"

Schroder pocketed his lighter. "Not exactly."

"Then exactly what did he witness?"

"He was trying to hide the motive," Jenner blurted out.

"I wasn't aware a motive was a concrete object," remarked John Lloyd, finally loosening his hold on Lydia.

Schroder gave Jenner a look that made him cringe and then proceeded to tell the attorney about the radiation containment area and MacPhearson's threatening Price-Leigh. Jenner watched John Lloyd's face and wondered how a man could show so little emotion.

John Lloyd finally nodded his head. "I see." He glanced over Schroder's head at the tan Dodge and then to the Trans-Am. "Very interesting," he murmured.

"That's one way to put it, Branson," said Schroder. "In any case, you might want to reconsider that examining trial."

John Lloyd smiled. "Perhaps we could see the actual crime scene, Sergeant?"

Schroder led the way back into the house. "I was just

trying to save your face, Branson, 'cause Maximum Miller's gonna leave bruises when he kicks your teeth in.''

"I am fairly agile, Sergeant. Perhaps I can duck his blows.''

"Oh, God,'' gasped Lydia as Schroder led the way into the bedroom. "Oh, God,'' she repeated, then turned her back to the bloodstained mattress. Two Special Crimes investigators watched her as as though they couldn't believe she hadn't fainted. Jenner couldn't either. He'd never seen a face that white.

"Can I get you a drink of water, Miss Fairchild?'' he asked, thinking a belt of whiskey would do more good.

She stumbled backward, bumped into the fountain, shoving it a few inches. She turned to see what she had touched and gasped again. "Oh, God.''

Jenner was glad to see her color had improved. Her face was cherry red, and she stared at the fountain as if she couldn't believe it wasn't a hallucination. "It's just a fountain,'' he said. "It's harmless.''

"It's obscene,'' stated Lydia.

John Lloyd grasped her shoulders and pressed her head against his chest. "It's quite all right, Miss Fairchild. Just take deep breaths. I know how shocking a lady of your sensibilities must find such a display of perverted taste,'' he drawled as he patted her back and stared down at the fountain.

Jenner wasn't sure how sensitive Lydia was. She could really curse when she wanted to. Still, that fountain was strong stuff.

Lydia pushed away from John Lloyd. "I'm all right. It's just that a bloody mattress and that *thing*''—she waved at the gurgling fountain—"are a little much.''

"You should've seen the box of stuff we caught old Tinsdale trying to carry out of here.''

"Sergeant Jenner, if you can't keep that mouth closed . . .'' threatened Schroder.

"Interesting," said John Lloyd, glancing in the closet and touching Price-Leigh's suits. "He was quite conservative in his dress."

"All except his socks," retorted Schroder.

"Ah, yes, those infamous socks. Did you find the mates?"

Schroder had his obstinate look. "You're fishing, Branson."

"Perhaps. Did I tell you that Leroy MacPhearson is not color-blind?"

"Is that so?"

"Yes," said the lawyer as he wandered into the living room. He looked at the pictures stripped of their frames. "Price-Leigh seemed to enjoy our local art. Most of these are Panhandle scenes."

"I'm surprised," said Lydia. "Judging by his bedroom, I expected nudes."

"I guess he needed good taste in something," said Schroder, trailing John Lloyd like a beagle after a rabbit.

The attorney glanced through the stacks of books on the floor. "Mr. Price-Leigh was a man with varied interests. He owned, and judging from the condition of many of these volumes, apparently read, books of poetry, philosophy, Texas history, geology, hydrology, economics, and biography."

"Yeah, Mr. Respectable in the living room and Mr. Name-Your-Perversion in the bedroom. That was the secret life of Charlton Price-Leigh III. And it doesn't help you at all, Branson. The jury might want to vote MacPhearson a good citizenship award for offing the bastard, but won't. You know why? Because that jury's gonna remember that bloodstained mattress. Remember, hell, they'll probably be looking at it. Maximum Miller will enter that mattress into evidence."

"I have no doubt Mr. Miller will attempt it," agreed John Lloyd, flipping though a stack of mail addressed to Price-Leigh. "Given the opportunity, Mr. Miller would attempt to enter the corpse and the wheat field."

Schroder removed the mail from Branson's hands and

slapped it back on the desk. "What I'm getting at, Branson, is that the good folks of Potter County don't like perverts, but they don't like cold-blooded murderers more."

"It wasn't cold-blooded murder," objected Lydia. "It was passion arising from justifiable cause. He was going to lose his land."

Schroder and John Lloyd both turned to look at her. Jenner gave her ten points for not shriveling under the combined stare. But it was a stupid thing for her to say. Sudden passion under Texas law was a kind of shoot-him-while-you're-damn-mad defense mostly used when one spouse caught the other in bed with a third party. MacPhearson didn't fit that definition.

Schroder dismissed Lydia with a final stare that had her shifting uncomfortably. He turned back to find John Lloyd perusing Price-Leigh's bank statements. "You try using that plea and Maximum Miller will make a rug out of your hide," he said, jerking the statements out of the attorney's hands. "This was a planned kill and a planned cover-up . . ."

"An inadequate one," said John Lloyd, unrolling the first of several survey maps. "An intelligently planned cover-up would not involve disposing of the body on your own property."

Jenner noticed a muscle twitching in Schroder's jaw as he caught the lawyer's hand and retrieved the map. "I didn't say it was intelligent, damn it. If murderers were intelligent, we'd never catch them. But MacPhearson did break into the DOE office to leave a phony note saying Price-Leigh'd be out of town for a few days."

"Another deception," said John Lloyd.

Schroder's eyebrows jumped together like two wooly caterpillars. "Of course, and one that didn't work because we discovered the body the next day."

"Wrong, Sergeant Schroder. Leroy MacPhearson *allowed* you to discover it."

"He didn't have time to bury it. He didn't count on Jenner answering a call right across the road."

John Lloyd nodded. "That is a possible explanation, but too obvious. I distrust the obvious."

"The obvious is going to hang your client, Branson. The list of landowners' names which provides motive, the note left in the DOE's office, the threat against Price-Leigh, the disposal of the body—all *obviously* point to MacPhearson. What's missing are the bits and pieces of physical evidence such as fingerprints, fibers, bloodstains, and we'll find those. I got the whole Special Crimes Unit out."

John Lloyd shook his head. "Those bits and pieces can be misinterpreted. Do you recall the six-shot revolver that fired seven times?"

Jenner decided that when it came to making Schroder mad, John Lloyd Branson came in a close second to Tinsdale. The investigator was eating what was left of his cigarette again. "Damn it, Branson, do you have to argue over everything?"

John Lloyd raised one eyebrow, a feat Jenner wished he could duplicate since it always seemed to irritate the hell out of Schroder. "Since the time of Socrates, argument has been the means of ascertaining the truth."

"Bullshit," said Sergeant Ed Schroder.

CHAPTER TEN

"WHERE ARE WE GOING NOW, JOHN LLOYD?" ASKED LYDIA, hurrying down the sidewalk after his tall figure.

"To collect information."

"For God's sake, what kind of information? You wanted to see his underwear and love letters. Well, you saw them, and as far as I'm concerned, Leroy MacPhearson ought to get a medal."

John Lloyd stopped by the curb and looked across the street. "There were inconsistencies, Miss Fairchild, and inconsistencies at a murder scene give me an intellectual itch."

"So scratch it, and let's go back to Canadian. I need a bath and a shampoo, and maybe a general all-around delousing. I feel filthy after being in that house." She opened the car door. "I think I'll burn these clothes. They might be contaminated." Looking up, she saw him still standing on the curb, swinging his cane and looking thoughtful. "If you stand there much longer, the birds will think you're a statue."

"Miss Fairchild, if you wished to know the daily routine

and the dominant personality traits of an individual, whom would you ask?"

"Friends, coworkers, wife, lover, enemies, I guess."

He smiled. "Wrong. Ask an eleven-year-old boy. A boy of that age is old enough to separate fact from fantasy, yet not old enough to be absorbed in the opposite sex. That generally occurs about age twelve. At that point a youngster's curiosity is piqued only by an individual possessing female hormones. They are in effect blind, deaf, and dumb." He pointed his cane toward a group of boys lounging on the sidewalk directly across the street from Price-Leigh's house. "There is our font of information on the victim, Miss Fairchild. An adult does not bother maintaining a social mask in front of children. Those boys are likely to have seen Price-Leigh with his warts exposed."

"I hope that's all they saw. With a pervert like that, you can't be sure."

"Shall we find out?" he asked, leading the way across the street.

He approached the group of boys with the care of an earthling approaching an alien life form. Lydia noticed the boys studying John Lloyd in the same way. John Lloyd stopped ten feet away from the boys and leaned on his cane. Lydia expected him to announce that they'd come in peace.

A skinny youngster with a mouthful of braces and clutching a skateboard under one arm took the initiative. "Hey, mister, what's going on in the hyphen's house?"

John Lloyd looked disconcerted. "The police are there."

The youngster looked at John Lloyd with such disgust that Lydia snickered. "I can *see* that, but why are the cops there? Did the hyphen get kilt?"

John Lloyd hesitated and Lydia felt sorry for him. She suspected that her boss must know children existed, but she was certain that was as far as his knowledge went. She stepped into the breach. "The hyphen got bumped off and the cops are looking for clues. This is Mr. John Lloyd Branson. He's a lawyer and the cops are putting heat on his client.''

The young boy looked up at John Lloyd. ''She your wife?''

''No, she is my clerk?''

''She sure does talk funny, don't she?''

''Umm,'' murmured John Lloyd. ''Why did you wish to know if Mr. Price-Leigh was murdered?''

The boy rubbed one bare foot on top of the other and looked down at the asphalt street. ''Me and my friends''— he pointed a thumb behind him at the other boys, most of them burdened with braces and skateboards—''was just wondering. You know, the cops and all. Who done it?''

''The police think my client did it, but of course he didn't.''

''Cops ain't always right.''

''You are a very astute young man, Mr. . . .'' John Lloyd cocked an eyebrow as he waited.

The boy blushed and gave John Lloyd a quick sideways glance out of one bright blue eye. He must have liked what he saw, thought Lydia, because he straightened his skinny shoulders and puffed out an equally skinny chest. ''Jimmy Jones. Really James Edward Jones, but only my mom calls me that, and then just when she's mad.''

John Lloyd leaned comfortably on his cane. ''I shall call you that because one must always be formal when questioning an important eyewitness.''

The boy rubbed his nose. ''Yeah.''

''I bet Miss Fairchild here that you and your friends knew more about Mr. Price-Leigh than your parents did. I told Miss Fairchild that youngsters were exceedingly difficult to fool. 'Miss Fairchild,' I said. 'If we really want to know what happened at Price-Leigh's house last Friday night, we need to ask those boys over there.' Didn't I, Miss Fairchild?''

''Well, something like that.''

''I said, 'They will know because boys always keep a

watchful eye on people they don't like.' That is true, isn't it, James Edward?'' he asked the boy suddenly. ''You and your friends did not like Price-Leigh?''

Eyes were downcast, and one dirty foot began vigorously polishing the other. Finally, sweat-streaked brown hair flew wildly as the boy shook his head. ''He was a jerk. Me and my friends built a ramp, you know, for skateboards, and he came out and tore it down. Said something about it wasn't safe, and he didn't want any kids getting hurt on his property. It wasn't *his* property. It was on the sidewalk. He don't own the sidewalk. And he was always looking down his nose at us like we was dirty. Besides, he's gonna build the dump and my dad's gonna lose his job. My dad works at the flour mill, and so does my friends' dads. The manager says the company'll close the mill 'cause nobody's gonna buy flour made next to a nuclear dump.''

''It sounds as if Mr. Price-Leigh did not have many friends,'' observed John Lloyd.

''The nerd came to see him a lot,'' said the boy, lifting a knee to scratch a mosquito bite. ''You know, the other dump guy. They went to play golf at the country club. It has a super swimming pool. My folks don't belong to the country club.''

Lydia heard a wistful note in the youngster's voice and felt a sudden spurt of sympathy. Her folks hadn't belonged to a country club either.

''And he had a girlfriend,'' continued James Edward.

John Lloyd glanced quickly at Lydia. ''That's interesting. Can you describe her?''

''Naw. He always brought her at night. He'd hit his garage door opener and zip right in and close the door. Couldn't see nothing but a shape all curling around him like she was afraid he was going to get away. I almost saw her once, though. It was on the weekend—she was mostly there on the weekend—and I heard her talking in his backyard. I started to climb the fence, but a board broke and I landed on my rear end. The hyphen told his girlfriend to get in the house, and then he come over to the fence cussing worse than my dad the time he dropped the car battery on his big toe. Well, I got out of there, and hid in the bushes. I don't think he ever knew who it was, not for sure anyway. But my dad did. The hyphen complained to him 'cause it was Dad's fence. My dad took my skateboard away for a week.''

"Anybody visit him last Friday night?" asked John Lloyd, clipping the end off a cigar and lighting it.

"An old woman."

John Lloyd examined his cigar as if not paying too close attention to what the boy was saying. "What did she look like?"

The boy shifted his skateboard to the other arm and scrunched up his eyes. "She had white hair and big"—he gestured at his chest with one cupped hand—"you know."

"Frances," breathed Lydia. "I knew it!"

"Silence, please, Miss Fairchild," drawled John Lloyd. "Do you know what time the old woman came?"

" 'Fore dark, because I have to go in the house when it gets dark. She left in a hurry, too. Ran over the curb turning around."

"Anyone else?" asked John Lloyd, expelling a cloud of tobacco.

"A van with a guy and a real foxy lady in it. They didn't stay long either. The lady came out and slammed the door. She sat in the van and honked the horn till the guy came out. The hyphen came out on the porch and yelled at them, but the lady shot him a . . ." James Edward's words trailed off and Lydia knew he suddenly remembered he was talking to adults, and adults didn't usually approve of kids using vulgar expressions.

John Lloyd didn't seem fazed. "I see. What did the, um, hyphen say?"

"Trust me."

"Trust the DOE? No wonder she shot him a—" said Lydia. John Lloyd interrupted. "Miss Fairchild, please remember the youth and innocence of our guest. Is that all he said, James Edward?''

"He kinda stood there and watched them drive off, then yelled, 'Remember you alls.' '' James Edward shrugged his shoulders and looked up at John Lloyd. "That's all."

"Did you see or hear anything else?"

The boy swallowed and looked down at his feet. "My mom made me go in the house."

"And where is your house, James Edward?"

The youngster pointed at a beige brick house next door to Price-Leigh's, and John Lloyd studied the two houses. He rolled his cigar between his fingers. "I notice your bedroom is just across from the, um, hyphen's. Did you hear anything later?"

Lydia thought James Edward looked uncomfortable, maybe even frightened. "Uh, I think so."

"What did you hear?"

"I heard a scream, I think."

"Did you see anything, a shadow against the drapes?"

"I was too scared to get out of bed. That scream was . . . it was like in a vampire movie." The youngster put his skateboard on the asphalt and stepped on it, tipping it from end to end. "I gotta go, mister."

John Lloyd removed a business card from his billfold. "If you or your friends remember anything else, James Edward, you may call me collect at either of those numbers."

"You bet," said the boy, clutching the business card in one grubby hand. Making a U-turn on his skateboard, he sped down the sidewalk, his friends scrambling after him.

John Lloyd took Lydia's elbow and led her back across the street. "Interesting, is it not, Miss Fairchild?" he asked, opening the car door.

She slid in and gathering her resources, pounced as soon as he closed his door. "What do you suppose Her Highness and her favored lackey were doing at Price-Leigh's?"

"I do not know, Miss Fairchild," he said, turning on the

ignition. "You are developing the most stressful habit of asking unanswerable questions."

"Then you agree the foxy lady must be Elizabeth," said Lydia, reaching over to poke his arm.

"You are also developing the equally stressful habit of referring to our clients in the most derogatory terms"—he swatted her hand—"as well as manhandling me. First, you patted me as if I were some breed of lapdog, and now you are punching me like a pillow that is not quite fluffy enough."

"I was trying to comfort you," retorted Lydia.

"Comfort me?"

"You don't need to sound so surprised. Everybody needs a little comforting sometimes. Leroy had just made a fool of you, and I was trying to restore your self-esteem."

"Miss Fairchild, if my self-esteem can survive your frequent attacks, it is sufficiently strong enough to fend off damage by a lying client."

"Excuse me! See if I ever scratch your ears again."

"The significance of that statement escapes me, but I lack the time to investigate the perambulations of your cognitive processes," he said as he pulled away from the curb and made a quick U-turn in the street.

Lydia slid into the passenger door. "Damn it, John Lloyd, my ribs can't take much more of your driving."

"Then I suggest you wear your seat belt. If I am fined because of your failure to wear your seat belt, I shall deduct the cost from your wages."

"You just made an illegal U-turn and you're jumping me about a seat belt. I take back what I said about your self-esteem. God himself couldn't dent it."

"Exactly."

"What is our hurry? If you don't mind lowering yourself to explaining your cognitive processes to the hired help."

"We have a financial transaction to undertake," he said, turning into a convenience store parking lot.

"At a 7-Eleven?"

"If the telephone company were not closed on Saturday, I should not find it necessary to enter into such a one-sided arrangement."

"What *are* you talking about?"

"An Amarillo phone book."

"What about it?"

"Go in there and buy one. Please get the type that includes all the surrounding towns," he said, handing her a twenty-dollar bill.

Lydia looked from the money to John Lloyd. "I think you're brain-dead. No one *buys* a phone book at a 7-Eleven store, or anywhere else, for that matter."

"I do. It is either buy one from a merchant, who in these financially strapped times will be eager to sell something that cost him nothing, or commit larceny."

"Larceny?"

"You must consider having your hearing checked, Miss Fairchild. You are still continually repeating whatever I say."

"What about larceny?" Lydia heard an ominous note in her own voice.

"We could take one from the public library and make full restitution later, but I find that alternative distasteful. We are not quite desperate enough to commit a crime against the Deaf Smith County taxpayers."

"*Why* are we buying a phone book?"

"I want you to call all the outlets in Amarillo and elsewhere that process film. Identify yourself as Price-Leigh's secretary, and ask if his latest film is ready."

"That's dishonest."

John Lloyd closed his eyes and Lydia had the feeling he was also counting. She couldn't imagine why. He was the one being obstinate. His eyes snapped open and he took a deep breath. "Miss Fairchild, please don't be picky. We must find that film before Sergeant Schroder begins to wonder where all the pictures are. There were none at the house, which leads me to believe that they were removed. There was no film in any of the cameras. Again for the reason that it was probably removed. However, a man with as many cameras as Price-Leigh must process film every week.''

"He might have sent it off. Did you think of that?"

"I am assuming that he did not dare to send film through the U.S. mail. James Edward said there was a female companion. There is a possibility that Price-Leigh used that female as a model for pornographic snapshots.''

Lydia snorted. "I'd say that was a probability."

"That female companion was sitting in Leroy's living room this morning.''

Lydia felt five years old again, with four of her classmates sent home with head lice. Her own hair was clean, but she felt dirty by association. "How do you know?"

"How many pictures of Price-Leigh did you show this morning?"

"Uh, five, I think. What does that have to do with anything?"

"How many do you have now, Miss Fairchild?"

Lydia grabbed the briefcase and fished out the photos. "One, two, three, four." She looked at him. "Where's the other picture?"

"I would conclude that the female companion wanted a keepsake."

"I bet I know who the girlfriend is."

John Lloyd turned his head to look at her. "And who is that?"

"It's definitely Frances. She's the only one sick enough to want a picture of a dead man. She had a fight with him the day he was murdered. That's why she left like a bat out of hell . . .''

"Miss Fairchild, your language," he murmured.

". . . and the murderer is her husband, what's-his-name . . .''

"Willis."

". . . Willis. He finds out about his wife's affair, and he murders Price-Leigh in a fit of passion."

"I doubt that Frances would arouse sufficient passion in the male breast to serve as a motive for murder."

"Then who's your candidate?"

"I think it probable that the female companion is only part of our missing motive."

"Just part of it? What else could there be? The list of landowners the government is planning to rip off?"

He waved aside that suggestion as though swatting a fly. "The list is another deception. Not even worth mentioning. It is those inconsistencies I mentioned earlier. Why not leave the body in that bedroom? Why dispose of it on his own property so the trail leads directly to him?"

"To protect Frances. You said so yourself."

"Possibly, but that does not explain why Leroy is deliberately acting as a lightning rod, drawing all attention and suspicion. That could have been done by burying it in that field and planting wheat over the grave. He wanted that body found quickly, but not identified. That is an inconsistency."

"Maybe they wanted time to find Price-Leigh's film, too."

"The same reasoning applies. They could have gained time by merely hiding the body, but it is useless to speculate without information." He leaned over and opened her door. "I saw conclusive proof at the murder scene that Leroy is innocent of any wrongdoing except moving the body. That is, by the way, the only thing I am sure of at this point."

"What proof?"

"Get the phone book, Miss Fairchild," he said, tapping his fingers on the steering wheel.

He was still tapping when she returned. "Business must be really bad. Not only did he give me the phone book, he threw in two sandwiches and two Cokes."

"Begin with the Hereford establishments, Miss Fairchild."

"With what, John Lloyd? Two tin cans and a string?"

He heaved one of his long-suffering sighs. "The mobile phone, Miss Fairchild. I do not pay the exorbitant fee demanded each month for the privilege of looking at it."

"Excuse me," she mumbled. "I have basic transportation, and I forgot how the other half lives."

"Sergeant Schroder's automobile is basic transportation. Your car would not qualify to enter a demolition derby, Miss Fairchild. I pay you a generous monthly salary. I fail to understand why you do not invest in a new car."

"I'm frugal."

"You are stingy."

"Mind your own business."

"I am. I have invested a considerable sum in you, Miss Fairchild. I do not wish to waste my investment by having you risk life and limb in that collection of wheels and engine block you call a car."

"The only thing I risk are my ribs, and they're only at risk when I'm riding with you. Would you like to see my bruises?"

"You should have negotiated with the convenience store clerk for a bottle of liniment. If you will begin calling now, please."

"What are you going to do, oh, master, while your downtrodden employee is slaving over a hot receiver?" She bowed her head.

"I am going to see a man about drilling a well."

She looked up. "What about a well? An oil well?"

"Miss Fairchild, if I knew that, I would not need to see him, would I?"

She picked up the mobile phone. "That's all right. Don't tell me anything. I'm just a lowly employee, a lowly *female* employee, fit only for secretarial duties. I wouldn't dream of stepping out of my place."

"Miss Fairchild?"

"Yes, John Lloyd."

"Shut up."

CHAPTER
ELEVEN

"DO YOU THINK THERE WAS ANYTHING BRANSON MISSED?"
asked Jenner.

Schroder's left eyelid was jumping. Short-circuited nerve
was Jenner's best guess. "That son of a bitch has the stickiest
fingers I ever saw. One of these days I'm gonna chop them
off at the knuckles. I'm just surprised he didn't try out some
of them sex apparatuses in there."

"Branson? He wouldn't know what to do with them. He
acts like he's neutered."

Schroder's eyelid twitched even more. "Lot of women
around here wouldn't agree with you. He kept company with
some relation of Leroy MacPhearson's for about three years.
Good-looking woman, too. She's on the board of directors
for STAD. Elizabeth Thornton's her name."

"Kept company? You mean old Branson was sleeping with
her?"

"I don't figure there was much sleeping done. But don't
you go saying anything to him about it. He'll knock you on

your behind with that cane of his. He never tells tales about his women.''

''Do you suppose he's got something going with that clerk of his?''

''I'd wipe that thought out of my mind if I was you. I figure he'd take after you with his cane for even thinking it. He keeps his business life and his personal so far apart you can't find the two in the same town, much less the same office. He's got respect for women even if he don't respect much else.''

''You do like him, don't you, Schroder?''

Schroder's twitch became a full-scale blink. ''I can't stand the bastard, and I'd sure like to know why he ain't worried. John Lloyd Branson's dangerous when he ain't worried. Flores!'' he suddenly roared at a Special Crimes investigator.

The slim young Hispanic dropped a book he was examining. ''Yeah, Schroder.''

''Take over here. Jenner and me are going to take a walk around the neighborhood, see if anybody noticed anybody sticking Price-Leigh.''

''What about that whining office boy in the garage? He's threatened to sue us for about sixteen civil rights violations.''

''Call Cleetus Miller and tell him we need a material witness warrant for the son of a bitch. The Hereford police aren't real anxious to offer Mr. Tinsdale their hospitality.''

''Maximum Miller? You want me to call Maximum Miller on a Saturday?'' Flores wiped his forehead. ''You're the sergeant in charge here. Why don't you call him?''

Schroder grinned and Flores flinched. Schroder's grins always affected people like that, thought Jenner. The burly investigator poked Flores in the chest. ''Because I'm pulling rank.'' He sauntered out the door, leaving a sweating Flores behind.

''Will he call Miller?'' asked Jenner when he and Schroder were outside.

''Hell, no. The investigator with the least seniority'll do

it. That's 'cause the one with the least seniority won't have anybody to pass the buck to.''

He turned down the sidewalk and stopped in front of an elaborate wooden ramp. Nudging it with his toe, he glowered at its engineers. "You kids do this?" he asked.

A young boy, indistinguishable from a crowd of other boys, stepped up. "Yeah," he said, scratching a mosquito bite.

"It's blocking the sidewalk. You need to tear it down," said Schroder.

Jenner stepped behind a convenient bush. He had a ten-year-old boy at home, and he didn't intend to be the butt of any ten-year-old type pranks. Not over anything as foolish as a skateboard ramp.

"You the cops?"

"Yeah."

The boy rubbed his nose. "That figures."

"What are you doing with my son?" A young woman dressed in shorts and a man's shirt and carrying a baby on her hip came running down the sidewalk. "I've been reading about men like you. Trying to sell drugs to young kids. Did he hurt you, James Edward?" she asked, turning to the young spokesman. James Edward whimpered.

She whirled back to Schroder. "I knew you were trying something nasty the minute I saw you. You just get away from here, or I'll call the police."

"I am the police," began Schroder, reaching in his pocket for his identification.

"He's got a gun!" screamed the woman. "Run, James Edward!"

Jenner stepped from behind the bush. "Is there any trouble, ma'am?"

"Officer, arrest that man. He's got a gun, and he's accosting my son."

Jenner smoothed his hair back as he wondered how long he could drag out the act. He caught sight of Schroder's eyes, and sighed. He'd seen friendlier eyes on a crocodile in the zoo just before he bit the zookeeper. Since he was the zoo-keeper, in a manner of speaking, he'd better get Schroder off the hook.

"Well, you see, ma'am, this is a policeman, too. This is Sergeant Schroder with the Special Crimes Unit out of Amarillo. We're investigating the suspicious death of your neighbor, Charlton Price-Leigh."

The woman forgot about Schroder as a drug pusher. "What do you mean, suspicious death?"

"We have cause to suspect that Mr. Price-Leigh was a victim of homicide," said Schroder.

"Homicide? You mean, murder?"

"He sure didn't die from a nosebleed," said Jenner, then wished he hadn't been so flippant.

"Yes, ma'am," said Schroder. "We'd surely appreciate it if you'd tell us about anything you saw last Friday night."

The young woman jiggled the baby on her hip. "Heavens, it's been too hot to sit outside lately. My husband and I usually stay in the house and watch TV in the evening. The kids always play out until dark, though. James Edward, did you and your friends see anything at Mr. Price-Leigh's last Friday?"

Schroder had a ludicrous expression on his face as if he'd bitten into a chocolate and found a rock instead of a cherry. Jenner snickered. Served the old fart right. Maybe he'd learn to stop giving orders so damn fast.

James Edward looked up at Schroder with wide, innocent eyes. "Gosh, mister, us kids were just playing with our skateboards, and kind of hanging out. You know."

Schroder swallowed, and Jenner gave him credit for trying to talk his way out. "You boys know how serious murder is, and how god"—he skidded and changed course—"how *very* important citizens are in helping to apprehend a murderer. I know you'll tell your mother if you remember anything at all." He handed James Edward's mother his card, and retreated back down the sidewalk.

"Little shit knows something," said Schroder as soon as they were out of earshot. "I arrested a con man once for selling lots in heaven. He had eyes just as innocent-looking as that kid's."

"Lots in heaven. You're shitting me."

"Deeds of trust had gold lettering. Last I heard he escaped from Huntsville. Forged his own parole papers." He tucked his shirt back in his pants and straightened his tie. "Back to work, Jenner. You take that side of the street, and I'll take this one. Somebody knows something. The whole damn block wasn't watching TV."

Jenner pulled the front of his shirt away from his sweaty chest. His deodorant had failed hours ago, and he smelled like a locker room. His feet had swollen at least two sizes, and he'd probably have to cut his boots off. And what had he learned? Not much. He dropped down on Price-Leigh's porch and watched Schroder walking up the sidewalk. Schroder didn't look hot and sweaty, probably didn't even stink unless you counted nicotine. That was it. His pores oozed nicotine instead of perspiration. Son of a bitch saved on deodorant.

"What'd you get?" asked Schroder, easing his bulk down on the porch.

Jenner looked at him resentfully. Bastard wasn't even breathing hard. "Suspicious looks, and a lot of gasps. Nobody much liked him. One woman said he walked around with his nose so far in the air, that if it ever rained, he'd drown. Another said he started trying to be friendly about six months ago, but he didn't know how. Started wearing cowboy boots and western shirts about the same time. I did get one bit of information, but I don't think it helps. The lady that lives across the street saw a white-haired woman about seven, seven-thirty, the night of the murder. The only reason she remembers is because the woman drove over her flower bed making a U-turn. The description sounded like Mac-Phearson's daughter, the one with the big tits."

"Frances Whitley," said Schroder with a disapproving look at the younger man.

Jenner shrugged his shoulders. So what if the fat investigator didn't approve of his language. He was too damn hot and tired to care. Besides, it was an accurate description. She did have big tits.

"This place was as busy as a whorehouse on a Saturday night," remarked Schroder. "But all the visitors were too early. The lady two houses down saw a van with a man and woman in it about eight o'clock. But everybody is deaf, dumb, and blind after that."

Schroder heaved himself up, a stupendous feat given his size, thought Jenner, as he eased his shirt away from his chest again. "Where you going, Schroder?"

"If you were carrying a dead body out of a house, would you bring it out the front door?"

"Hell, no. The neighbors might talk."

"I wouldn't either. I'd pull my car into the garage. The garage opens on the alley, so let's go talk to the folks that live across the alley from Price-Leigh."

"Jesus, what I wouldn't give for a beer," groaned Jenner as he grabbed a bush growing beside the porch and pulled himself up.

"You youngsters have got no stamina," said Schroder, setting a fast pace around the house and toward the next block.

"Shit," said Jenner, following the older man. "Slow down, Schroder. This isn't the damn Boston marathon."

"Move it. We ain't got MacPhearson tied down yet."

Jenner passed Schroder and made it to the doorbell first. He wiped the sweat off his forehead, and pressed his arms against his sides, hoping to trap the sour smell inside his shirt. The door opened, and he plastered a smile on his face. "Good afternoon, ma'am. I'm Sergeant Jenner and this is Sergeant Schroder of the Special Crimes Unit of Potter and Randall counties." He stopped with his mouth open. Had he really included himself as part of Special Crimes? The heat must be cooking his brain.

Schroder's gravelly voice took over. "Ma'am, there's been a homicide across the alley from you, and we'd like to ask you some questions."

She shook her head, multiple chins quivered, a bosom like the prow of the *Queen Mary* wobbled, and waist-length blonde-by-request hair flew in all directions. "I didn't do it. Heavens, I don't have time to go around murdering people. Don't believe in it anyway. Messy business, and I'm a poet. A rhyming poet, I might add. I like form and structure. None of this loose free verse for me. If rhyme was good enough for Shakespeare, it's good enough for me."

Jenner wasn't sure, but he thought maybe Shakespeare's plays were written in some kind of poetry, and it didn't rhyme. But he couldn't be sure. He'd spent most of his English lit courses writing dirty notes to Twilla Lynn Mac-Cormick, who had the biggest boobs in the junior class.

Schroder nudged Jenner in the ribs. "A poet. Ain't that great, Jenner? Poets are observant. I bet Mrs . . ." he raised his eyebrows.

"*Ms.* Aurora Silliphant." She twittered. Like a bird in mating season, thought Jenner. "It's not the name I was born with, but I had it changed. I told the judge that a poet named Bertha Myrick just wouldn't look good in a college text-book." She opened her door. "Do come in, gentlemen. May I offer you some tea?"

"That'd be fine," said Jenner, visions of amber-colored tea seeping down his throat and percolating a needed burst of caffeine into his bloodstream, making his mouth water. He followed the poet's caftan-clad body into the house.

Aurora Silliphant floated into her kitchen and piled cups and saucers on a tray. "I always serve hot herbal infusions to my guests. They're so good for you. I never put additives in my body. It's so unhealthy, don't you think?"

Jenner felt additional sweat break out on his body. "Yes, ma'am."

"Do come into my study, gentlemen," said Aurora, carrying the tray and preceding them into a room lined, piled, and overflowing with books. It was also inhabited by a Pekingese with a sinus condition. The dog jumped off a chair, growled at Schroder, then proceeded to sniff Jenner's legs.

"Just move the books, gentlemen, and sit down. Sweetie Poo, now leave the nice man alone."

Jenner shifted a pile of books and sat down on a couch upholstered in bright yellow. Sweetie Poo promptly jumped in his lap and licked his face. "Hey, fellow, get down now," he said, trying to disengage the dog from his sleeve. Sweetie Poo's teeth hooked through the material, and he hung on with the tenacity of a piranha.

"Isn't he the cutest thing?" cooed Aurora, handing Jenner a cup of steaming liquid that smelled faintly of alfalfa.

"Yeah," agreed Jenner, shaking his arm with the dog suspended in midair from his sleeve. There was an ominous ripping sound and Sweetie Poo landed on his furry rump and gave a yip. He then nipped Jenner's ankle and scampered onto his mistress's lap.

"Quit playing with the dog, Jenner, and get your notebook out," said Schroder. He twisted around in a chair scarcely large enough to support his ample hindquarters, and smiled at Aurora. The poet seemed dazzled. She ought to be, thought Jenner sourly. Schroder's smile made him look just like the Pekingese, except without the bulging eyes.

"Now, Ms. Silliphant, your neighbor Charlton Price-Leigh was murdered last Friday night. We have reason to believe that the murderers parked in the garage in order to transport the body into a car."

"Pickup," said Aurora, taking a small sip of her tea.

"Beg pardon," said Schroder.

"I said, it was a pickup, not a car. That is, if we're speaking of late Friday night. I'm often up quite late. Inspiration, you know. The moonlight is a source of inspiration to me. The way it silvers the shrubs, and dulls the sharp edges of this weary, cruel world just inspires me to the heights of poetical expression.''

If that was a sample of Aurora Silliphant's poetical expression, Jenner thought he'd forgo purchasing the finished product—when, or if, published. ''You saw a pickup parked in Price-Leigh's garage?''

''I didn't see it parked there. I saw it back in, then saw it leave an hour or so later. I assume it was parked during the intervening time.''

Schroder smiled again, and Aurora's hand fluttered up to rest against her bosom. ''Now let me get this straight, Ms. Silliphant. You were in the backyard looking at the moon . . .''

''Experiencing the moonlight.''

''. . . and you saw this pickup back into Price-Leigh's garage?''

She nodded. ''It was very strange, you know. I mean, it was a little late to be moving, and I couldn't imagine why anyone other than Charlton would back into the garage.''

''They were moving something, all right,'' agreed Schroder.

''I only saw one.''

''Ma'am?'' asked Schroder.

''You said *they*. I only saw one person.''

Schroder moved to the edge of his chair. ''Can you tell me what he looked like?''

''It was dark, but . . .''

''Yes?'' said Schroder, leaning forward.

''. . . the moonlight was very bright. It was a full moon last Friday, and it was just so inspiring.''

''Can you describe him?'' repeated Schroder. Jenner saw perspiration beading the older man's forehead. Nice to know what it took to make Schroder sweat.

''It was a man, not as tall as Sergeant Jenner. I could tell that by how tall he was sitting in the pickup cab, and he was wearing one of those gimme hats. I could tell by the silhouette of his head.''

''Ma'am,'' asked Schroder with the desperation of a cop who sees his case sinking into quicksand. ''Did you see his face at all?''

''I told you it was dark. But I saw the pickup quite clearly.''

Schroder clutched her comment like a lifeline. ''What did it look like?''

''It was a Ford, and a lovely aqua blue color like the softest, purest ocean water.''

In Jenner's opinion, any water that was home to millions of fish was not pure. And he wished to hell Leroy Mac-Phearson's pickup was some other color than aqua.

''But it was dirty and dented. It had mud guards on the rear wheels, was a 1983 model. I'd recognize that pickup out of thousands.'' She pursed her lips. ''And it had a gun rack across the back window. I don't approve of guns killing little animals, do you, Sergeant Schroder?''

''Well, ma'am, generally it's the people holding the guns that do the killing. Now is there anything else you can tell us about Friday night?''

''Sweetie Poo got out.'' She cuddled the Pekingese. ''Him was a bad boy, running away from Mama like that.''

''I don't think Sweetie Poo''—Schroder had trouble saying the dog's name—''can testify.''

''He ran into Charlton's backyard. He loved Charlton.''

Schroder reached out to pet Sweetie Poo, but the dog bared sharp teeth the size of needles, and the investigator jerked his hand back. ''What time was this?''

''About ten-thirty. Charlton came to the back door with his visitor.''

''Visitor,'' interrupted Schroder. ''What did the vistor look like? Who was he? Did you know him?''

''I didn't see him at all. I heard Charlton speaking to him. He said, 'You can stay around here all night arguing with me, but it won't change a thing. You've lost. Can't you understand that?' Then he yelled at Sweetie Poo. Called him a very bad name.''

"What did he call him?" asked Jenner.

Ms. Silliphant's chins wobbled and her lips quivered. "He called Sweetie Poo a mangy mutt. Charlton didn't like Sweetie Poo.''

Jenner thought that was the only good thing he'd heard anybody say about Charlton Price-Leigh.

CHAPTER
TWELVE

LYDIA CRUNCHED A MOUTHFUL OF ICE. "THAT DOES IT, JOHN Lloyd. Charlton Price-Leigh didn't leave any film in Hereford, Canyon, Vega, or Panhandle."

"And Amarillo?"

"Give me a break. I'm getting laryngitis. Do you know how many places I've called?"

"Exactly ten. And if you would not insist on assuming different regional accents with each phone call, your throat would not hurt. For future reference, your Bostonian accent was a trifle overdone, but your Georgia peach was almost perfect. One would swear that 'Dixie' was playing in the background."

"It's boring to say the same thing ten times in a row," said Lydia through another mouthful of ice. She looked around. "Where are we?"

"Near the Tri-State fairgrounds."

"What for?"

"It is incorrect to end a sentence with a preposition, Miss

129

Fairchild. Members of a jury, however ungrammatical their own English, expect yours to be perfect."

Lydia nodded. "I'd better rephrase that. What for, pompous ass? Is that grammatically correct?"

John Lloyd tightened his hands around the steering wheel, made an illegal left turn, and pulled into a parking lot noteworthy for the number of ruts per square foot. "To quote a familiar homily, you are skating on thin ice, Miss Fairchild. We are near the fairgrounds because the drilling company, *this* drilling company"—he waved his hand at a corrugated tin building—"hired by Charlton Price-Leigh, is near the fairgrounds."

"I just wanted an explanation. I don't like being kept in the dark. That's another homily." She wondered if the sound she heard was John Lloyd grinding his teeth, or the ice cracking under her feet.

He slowly loosened his hands from the steering wheel, turned off the ignition, and turned to face her. "Miss Fairchild, you have a tongue like a rapier. Do you suppose you could sheathe it for the duration of this investigation? We cannot afford to waste our time fencing with each other."

"Then stop baiting me. You criticize my car . . ."

"That is not a car. It is a death trap."

". . . and my grammar," she finished, then horrified herself by bursting into tears.

John Lloyd whipped a white handerkerchief out of his pocket and blotted her tears. Cupping her chin in his palm, he tilted her face up and examined it closely. Sighing, he released her. "Lydia, it's all right to be frightened."

She grabbed the handerkerchief and blew her nose. "I'm not frightened. I'm upset because of . . ." Some feminine instinct she wasn't aware she possessed stopped her before she finished her sentence with "that damn bitch, Elizabeth." She looked up at him, drew a sobbing breath, and held it. His eyes, those ebony eyes, held an expression of regret.

"You're sorry," she said, exhaling her pent-up breath. "And you called me Lydia. That's twice in the same day."

He turned his head away. "So I have. No doubt a sign of creeping senility. But I am sorry I pushed you, Miss Fairchild."

She sniffed, enjoying herself immensely. A contrite John Lloyd was worth squeezing out a few more tears, particularly since she'd been acting like a jealous adolescent, and he was feeling guilty. God, but being an emotional female was sometimes wonderful. "You ought to be," she said, dabbing her eyes again. "Criticizing me like you were my father."

He looked at her, an expression of incredulity on his face. "I am hardly that ancient. And under ordinary circumstances, you would verbally or physically assault me for any remarks, however trivial, that angered you. By the way, the ribs you broke during your last attack have healed nicely. In conclusion, Miss Fairchild, bursting into tears is out of character for you. Therefore, I am apologizing."

"What for?" She corrected herself. "For what?"

"For frightening you," he said impatiently.

She sniffed again. An apologetic John Lloyd was nearly as fun as a contrite one. With any luck she could stretch out his apology for at least another five minutes. He deserved it for slobbering over some bad-mouthed, brassy, *middle-aged* woman, while he treated Lydia Fairchild like a kindergartner. But she did wish she could figure out why he thought he scared her.

"You don't frighten me," she said, carefully letting her lip quiver.

He looked incredulous again. "Me? Miss Fairchild, the likelihood of my personally frightening you is remote indeed. Whenever you are being particularly infuriating, I wish I *could* frighten you."

"Then why are you apologizing?"

"I am apologizing for subjecting you to a crime scene.

My technique of throwing you into water over your head in order to teach you to swim is reprehensible.''

Lydia twisted the handerkerchief into a knot. ''Oh, that.''

''Objectivity is a learned skill and I''—he blinked—''what do you mean, oh, that?''

Lydia slapped the knotted handkerchief against her eyes and bent over, shaking her head violently so that her blonde hair veiled her face. ''It was awful, John Lloyd''—she surreptitiously pinched an earlobe until tears came—''and I was afraid you'd think I was a coward if I said anything. I didn't want you to send me back to Dallas. If Elizabeth can look at pictures of a dead man and not faint, I should be able to look at a crime scene without crying.'' She cautiously glanced at him out of one eye. He had a speculative look on his face. Maybe she'd gone too far.

He rubbed his fingers over his chin. ''Miss Fairchild, I think this case is having a detrimental effect on you.''

Oh, God, he really is going to send me back to Dallas, she thought wildly. She sat up and smoothed her hair back. ''I'm fine, John Lloyd. See!'' She held out her hands. ''No shaking hands. Steady as a rock.''

''And how is your nose?''

''My nose?''

''Is it growing like Pinocchio's? Because I suspect this case has taught you more about deception than I care for you to know.'' He still had that speculative look on his face.

She rubbed the handkerchief over her cheeks. Maybe he'd mistaken the guilty blush for simple friction. ''Now you're insulting me.''

''Am I?''

''Yes, and I refuse to sit here and be insulted.''

''Excellent! You may come with me to visit with the owner or manager or janitor if need be, of M. M. Myers Drilling Company.''

''Why? If you don't mind explaining, that is.''

''Sergeant Schroder prevented a lengthy examination of

Price-Leigh's bank statements, but even a quick perusal showed several checks written to M. M. Myers for rather large sums. Don't you find that curious, Miss Fairchild?''

She folded his handkerchief and laid it on the seat. ''The DOE is supposed to be drilling boreholes for site characterization, John Lloyd.''

''Those drilling operations will be paid for with checks drawn on our pocketbooks, otherwise known as the U.S. Treasury. This is something Price-Leigh didn't want known. Otherwise, he would've used a Hereford drilling firm. Our victim had secrets, and when we know those secrets, we shall know the rest of the missing motive.''

''But what does drilling an oil well have to do with the female companion and pornographic pictures?'' she asked as she climbed out of the car.

''Not an oil well. This company specializes in water wells. As for the connection between Price-Leigh's perverse sexual tastes and his secret drilling operation, both parts of his life were hidden and that makes both equally interesting.'' He opened the dented, mud-splotched door of the steel building and waved her in. ''Shall we find out how interesting?''

The building was like nothing Lydia had ever seen before. Of course, she'd never been inside the headquarters of a drilling company, but she expected more than a warehouse of racks loaded with steel pipe of varying lengths and diameters, drill bits numbering in the dozens, miles of cables like braided steel coiled around huge pulleys, more miles of rope and chains, derricks that vaguely resembled oil derricks except much smaller, and tools whose function she could not even begin to guess. Through an overhead door at the far end of the building she glimpsed trucks with drilling rigs mounted on the rear, and more stacks of pipe. An aroma compounded of oil, mud, hemp, and dust assaulted her nostrils and made her eyes water.

A glassed-off cubicle to the right of the door divided what were obviously the corporate offices from the warehouse.

That is, if battered filing cabinets, equally battered desks, a two-way radio, and a shiny new computer could be said to constitute a corporate office.

A tall man with a battered face and a harried look abruptly opened the cubicle door. "Can I help you? Need a water well maybe. Running a special this month, two for the price of one. Cash in advance."

John Lloyd introduced himself and Lydia. "I came for information concerning some work you did for an acquaintance of mine."

The man shook hands. "M. M. Myers, call me Mike. Come on in the office; find yourselves a chair that ain't stacked to the ceiling with files. We had a break-in the other night, and the damn bastard, excuse me, ma'am, made a mess of the files. Damn fool of a thief. I don't leave money laying around. That is, if I had any money. Between the natural gas companies charging an arm and a leg for gas to run irrigation pumps, and the farmers going broke, nobody wants any wells drilled." He sat down in the oldest swivel chair Lydia had ever seen. "Now what did you want to know?"

John Lloyd sat down and folded his hands to his cane. "You did some drilling for Charlton Price-Leigh, is that correct?"

Myers propped his feet on the desk top. "Sure did. What do you want to know for?"

John Lloyd hesitated, and Lydia knew he was debating how much to tell. "Price-Leigh was murdered," he said finally. "I am the attorney for the man accused of murdering him."

Myers's shrewd blue eyes studied John Lloyd. "What made you decide to tell me the truth? You were debating about it."

John Lloyd smiled. "You are an astute man, Mr. Myers."

"I can recognize bullshit, if that's what you mean. Now, you gonna answer my question?"

John Lloyd leaned back in his chair and crossed his legs.

"I have been knee-deep in deception all day, Mr. Myers. It goes against the grain to add to that deception. Besides, I also am an astute man. Had I lied, you would have suffered a sudden memory lapse."

Myers nodded. "Is your client guilty?"

"No, he is not."

Myers's feet hit the floor and he hitched his chair closer to his desk. "Ask your questions. I ain't a priest, and besides, I don't promise to keep my jobs confidential. No reason to."

"What kind of wells did you drill for Price-Leigh?" asked John Lloyd, motioning to Lydia to take notes.

"Didn't drill any wells. It was a kind of funny deal, Mr. Branson. He came in here about six months ago. It was still winter, no work to speak of, and I was getting desperate. I was carrying men on the payroll for sitting on their behinds. Anyway, this guy comes walking in here like his feet hurt, and I knew right away he was a Yankee trying to dress like a Texan. His boots were so new, the soles weren't scuffed, and he had his shirt unbuttoned one button too many. When he opened his mouth, I knew I was right. Had a flat-sounding accent of some kind. To tell the truth, I felt sorry for him. He was trying hard to fit in, and he just wasn't making the grade. But to make a long story short, he hired me to drill a bunch of boreholes all over hell and half of Georgia. Didn't care how much it cost, he said. That comment marked him as a fool in anybody's books. Nobody around here, even if they're rolling in money, ever says cost doesn't matter. Hell, I thought, his money is as good as anybody else's, and like I said, I was desperate, so I told him I'd take the job."

Myers picked up a pencil and tapped it against the palm of one hand like a man who wasn't used to sitting still. "He unrolled a survey may and started marking sites, said he'd already gotten releases from the landowners. That was something else funny. I found out those farmers and ranchers thought the drilling was all part of a geological survey sponsored by a university I never heard of. Price-Leigh didn't tell me that, but I figured it wasn't any of my business. I mean, I saw the releases, and they looked legitimate. So I drilled, mostly on the weekends, because he said he wanted to be there. I'd hardly get the pipes jerked out of the hole before he was checking the core samples. Sometimes we'd drill all week and he'd come by every afternoon and he'd check the samples.''

''What were his instructions?'' asked John Lloyd, his eyes intent.

''That's just it. He didn't give any. He just said drill, so I drilled. Sometimes he'd tell me to stop at four hundred feet, and sometimes I'd drill deeper.''

''How deep?''

Myers tapped his pencil faster. ''He wanted me to go to three thousand a couple of times. Well, I could do it, but it was a strain on my equipment. I told him he needed oil drilling equipment, but he said his budget wouldn't stretch that far. I could understand that. Oil drilling equipment don't come cheap.'' He grinned. ''I don't either, but he managed to pay on time, or almost on time.''

''Did you know, or can you guess what he was looking for?'' asked John Lloyd. Lydia wanted to tell him that he just ended a sentence with a preposition, but decided this wasn't the time.

''I figure it was brine.''

''Brine?'' echoed John Lloyd.

''Yeah, saltwater. It didn't take me long to figure out that whenever we hit saltwater, he stopped that drilling operation and sent us to the next site.''

''Could you point out the drilling sites on a map?''

''Sure,'' said Myers, pushing his chair back and getting up to point out locations on a huge survey map pinned on the wall behind his desk. Using his pencil he drew circles on the map, counting as he marked. ''. . . twelve, thirteen, fourteen, all in a huge circle right in the middle of the Panhandle.''

John Lloyd studied the map, and tapped the middle of the circle. "Here is the site of the nuclear waste dump. Price-Leigh's sites are all around it at varying distances. Was there anything peculiar, or anything in common, about the sites you drilled?"

"Sure as hell was," replied Myers. "All the sites were playa lakes."

"And you found brine water under all the sites?"

"All but one, but I wasn't surprised about that site. It was an old playa, several thousand years old, probably been around since the high plains rose up out of the ocean. All the others were younger, geologically speaking, and I wasn't surprised to find brine. Did I mention I was a geologist by training? My family's owned this drilling company since the 1890s. My daddy was a geologist, and so am I. It made sense to us. If you're gonna fuck around with the earth, especially in the Panhandle, you ought to have a little schoolin'. Excuse the language, ma'am," he said to Lydia.

"Why especially in the Panhandle?" asked John Lloyd before Lydia could acknowledge Myers's apology.

"You don't always know what you're going to find. The Ogallala Aquifer sort of confuses the issue. Then we got the Permian Basin around three thousand or so feet down. Now that's bad shit down there. We don't want any of that stuff mixing with the aquifer. Then we got the salt beds, which are all mixed with clay. Terrible stuff to drill. Your damn borehole is always collapsing."

"But it's the salt beds where the DOE is planning to drill those huge shafts," said Lydia, breaking into the conversation.

"They're gonna kill a lot of men, too," said Myers flatly. "They're talking about drilling two shafts between twelve and twenty-six feet in diameter twenty-six-hundred feet in the ground like it was a piece of cake. My family's been drilling in this area for damn near a hundred years, and I'm telling you that cake is gonna crumble. Those boys in DOE don't know much and they don't want to know much. We're talking science and they're talking magic. They're gonna wave their policy act over the ground, and by magic, that salt won't shift, the aquifer won't leak, the shafts won't collapse. They're wrong on all counts. Salt is the only rock known to man that moves like plastic under stress. You can't punch two big holes through aquifer without it springing a leak. As for those shafts, hell, you couldn't pay me enough to get close to one of them.''

Lydia heard the wheeze of the air-conditioner as it fought the late August heat. She could also make out the faint sounds of traffic on the street outside. Other than that the only sound was Mike Myers restlessly tapping his pencil on the map. ''Why did Price-Leigh want to drill just in the playa lakes?'' she asked Myers.

''Damn if I know, young lady,'' he answered. ''He never confided his reasons, but I'll tell you one thing. He got more and more antsy every time I struck brine. The last hole I drilled, he finally asked if I had any ideas about how playas were formed. I do, of course, so I told him.''

''What did you tell him?'' asked John Lloyd.

''Salt dissolution. This whole area used to be an inland sea. There are underground salt beds all over the place. With a very few exceptions, everywhere you got a playa lake, you got a dissolving salt bed underneath. You see, those playas don't just evaporate; they also infiltrate the ground. In other words, the ground soaks up water, too. That water percolates down through the strata, hits the salt beds, and dissolves them, so you got brine. The earth just kind of hollows out into a shallow depression as that happens. Most of the year those playas are dry as a bone, can't even see where they're supposed to be. Come a rain, they fill up.''

He scratched his head and looked back at the map. ''If I was taking a wild guess, I'd say Price-Leigh was trying to prove that we got active salt dissolution going on in the Panhandle.''

"But if the salt beds are dissolving, how can the DOE store the casings full of nuclear waste in them?" asked Lydia.

Myers grinned. "Now that's a damn good question, ain't it?"

"Do you have a drilling record on each hole?" asked John Lloyd.

"Sure. I think my secretary got the files straightened up through the S's. Let me check." He pulled out a filing cabinet and sorted through the manila folders. Frowning, he sorted them again. He slammed the drawer shut, and pulled out another. "Secretary must have filed those records in the B's," he said by way of explanation.

After another five minutes of searching, he closed the drawer and turned to John Lloyd. "Guess those files are misplaced."

"Or stolen," said John Lloyd.

"Why would anybody want to steal my files? They were just work orders and invoices. I got all the straight skinny on a floppy disk. I was kinda interested in what we were finding because of the dump. I'd always wanted to do some straight research like that, but, hell, who's got the money even if you do own a drilling company? This job was manna from heaven. I was proving a theory of my own and somebody else was paying for it."

"Did you know Charlton Price-Leigh worked for the DOE?" asked Lydia.

Myers sat back down. Lydia had the feeling his legs had collapsed under him. "That explains some of the questions he asked. He asked how corrosive brine was, and I said just as damn good as acid, just not as fast. He walked off mumbling to himself."

Myers slammed his fist on the desk top. "Goddamn it! That bastard knows for a fact now that storing nuclear waste in the salt beds is dangerous as hell. He's got all the raw data he needs to prove it. Put what he's got together with what the University of Texas has, and what that professor down at

Texas Tech has been doing, and we got the DOE stopped cold. They can't weasel their way out of salt dissolution. No way can they claim it's safe to store hot waste in brine."

"How come?" asked Lydia. "Other than the brine will corrode the casings the garbage is stored in."

"Plain salt will do that, young lady. Brine will do it faster, but that's not the problem."

"What is the problem?" demanded Lydia.

"Brine is salt in solution, in this case, ground water infiltrating from the playas, but any kind of ground water will do. Now you put water next to a used fuel rod that the DOE admits will be around eight hundred degrees, and what do you get?"

"Steam," answered Lydia, hearing her voice beginning to shake.

"That's right. Now you don't have to be a geologist or hydrologist, or even a college graduate, to know that steam keeps building up until it's vented or blows up. Now we got boreholes around that site that folks have forgotten about. Hell, Texas didn't even have a water commission until the 1950s, and there's been drilling around here for sixty years before that. The landowners on that site say they know of thirty-eight boreholes. Natural vents, little lady, which radioactive steam can use as chimneys. But that still ain't the biggest problem."

"For God's sake, what *is* the problem?" demanded Lydia.

"The small boreholes won't adequately relieve the pressure buildup, Miss Fairchild," said John Lloyd, his skin looking bloodless.

"You got it, Mr. Branson. The DOE's gonna blow the fucking Panhandle right off the map."

CHAPTER
THIRTEEN

"WE GOT HIM, WE GOT HIM," SANG MAXIMUM MILLER AS he did the Texas two-step around the U-shaped table in the old grand jury room, now a work room at Special Crimes. "Schroder, you old coon dog. I knew you'd come up with something, but an eyeball witness, that is supreme!"

"She's one brick shy of a load, Cleetus, but she can identify that pickup."

"She's flaky as hell," muttered Jenner, eyeing the three-corner tear in his shirt.

"Hell, I don't care if she puts on a tall black hat and flies around the moon on a broomstick. She's still a witness."

"Must be a million blue pickups in Texas," said Jenner, rolling up his pants leg to check the tiny red Pekingese puncture marks on his calf.

Miller stopped in mid–two-step. "Aqua, not blue. Didn't you read the statement?"

"Read it? I took the damn thing," said Jenner. "Had to drink two cups of her godawful herbal tea just to keep her talking. I tell you, the woman's a candidate for the loony bin.''

"Schroder, tell this kid to stop raining on my parade. Jesus, I've seen happier faces at a funeral.'' Miller started dancing again. "Who's afraid of the big, bad Branson?" he sang.

Jenner sat at one end of the table, watching the black prosecutor and trying to ease his boots off his feet. He gave up and just watched Cleetus Miller instead. He was glad somebody was happy because he sure as hell wasn't. His feet hurt, his stomach was doing a rolling boil that threatened to erupt into the granddaddy of all bellyaches, and his armpits stank. It was probably just as well he couldn't get his boots off. His feet undoubtedly stank, too. He wanted a shower, a dose of Pepto-Bismol, and one of his wife's special back rubs. What he was going to get was a quick face-wipe in the Special Crimes bathroom, a cold hamburger, and the privilege of looking at, and listening to, Schroder and Cleetus Miller congratulate each other. Suddenly he was sick of them, sick of the job, and doubly sick of having to help send Leroy MacPhearson to prison. Piss on it, he thought. Let the old man walk. He didn't do anything that didn't need doing, because if ever somebody needed killing, it was Charlton Price-Leigh. For the first time in his career, he was on the side of the defense.

He locked his fingers behind his head, propped his feet on the table, and belched. He felt better, certainly good enough to let Schroder and Miller have it. Who's afraid of the big, bad Miller? he sang to himself. If he got fired, he could open up his private detective agency, and the first person he'd hire himself out to would be John Lloyd Branson. By God, he'd investigate this case for the right side.

"You two bastards make me sick," he announced, and grinned at the two astonished faces. He guessed their expressions were astonishment. It was either that, or they both were trapping flies with their open mouths.

"What did the younger Hardy boy say?" Cleetus asked Schroder.

"He said we were bastards."

Miller's eyes seemed to swell until the whites were twice their normal size. "He did, huh?"

Jenner crossed one foot over the other, and slid down until he was resting his weight on the end of his spine. "I damn sure did. You're dancing around on MacPhearson's grave like two ghouls."

"Jesus, the boy's literate, Schroder. Ghouls, no less. Next he's going to be quoting Shakespeare." Miller advanced down the length of the room like a Sherman tank, and Jenner wondered if the police department's health policy covered being run down by a mad assistant district attorney.

"Listen," Jenner said quickly, driven by the fear of having to explain to his wife why he was fired when he still owed the orthodontist for Melissa's braces and the credit union for his new, used car. "I might have come on a little strong . . ."

"He came on a little strong," said Miller to Schroder as they surrounded Jenner's position.

". . . but damn it, Charlton Price-Leigh was a horse's ass, and Leroy MacPhearson was just trying to defend his land."

"Listen, boy," roared Maximum Miller. "To a cop and to a prosecutor, a man might be a low-life son of a bitch while he's alive, but when he's murdered, he becomes a *goddamn saint*. Is that clear?"

Jenner's feet hit the floor and he leaned his elbows on the table and supported his head on his hands. "I'm no good at this, Schroder." He looked up at the investigator. "I've told you that before. I don't like murder, but sticking a desperate old man in jail is worse. How can you two act so fucking happy about it?"

Miller pulled out a chair and sat down on Jenner's left. He looked at Jenner for several seconds until the young man felt like a virus under the microscope. "Son," said the prosecutor, "there's not much that the bleeding hearts haven't persuaded John Q. Public is okay. Every damn statute in the criminal code can be explained away. But do you know the one crime that no wild-eyed do-your-own-thing fanatic hasn't managed to persuade your average man on the street isn't wrong? *Murder!*"

Miller picked up a crime scene photo. "Look at that mattress, son. Look at the blood. No one person's got the right to decide that another person ought to bleed their life away like that." He shoved it in Jenner's face. "Look at it!"

Jenner shoved it away and swallowed the bile burning in his throat. "I've seen it! I've seen the real thing, and believe me, the pictures don't do it justice. But damn it, there were mitigating circumstances. Doesn't what the DOE planned to do to MacPhearson count for anything?"

Schroder sat down across from Miller. "It's still murder, son." His voice sounded as kind as Jenner had ever heard it.

Jenner clasped his shaking hands together. "I know it. I guess I was just trying to make excuses because there's so much at stake. MacPhearson's chairman of STAD. What's going to happen to the anti-dump movement? If Tinsdale uses this against the movement, we all might as well hand the DOE the title to the Panhandle, and go look for jobs in Nicaragua. It would be a lot safer than here."

"I was thinking of signing on at a weather station in Antarctica myself," mused Miller. "I don't think Nicaragua's far enough away." He slapped the table. "Damn it, son, I don't need a kid to teach me how to suck eggs. I don't need you to tell me there's a lot more involved here than MacPhearson sticking a thieving carpetbagger. I just wish to hell he'd been satisfied with burning a cross on his front lawn." He grinned. "Maybe I can suggest that to STAD. Might even volunteer to dress up in a white sheet myself. Sort of role reversal."

"It's not funny, damn it!" shouted Jenner, knocking over his chair as he stood up.

Schroder moved, his square body coming off his chair like a piece of rubber. Jenner felt the bones in his elbow grind together as the investigator grabbed him. "That's enough, Jenner!" said Schroder, his cigarette bobbing with each word. "You ain't got a corner on the market in being sorry. Miller and me ain't exactly happy about the situation."

Jenner pulled away and rubbed his elbow. "You were sure as hell acting like it."

"That's right," agreed Miller. "I'm always happy to catch a murderer. I'm not ever gonna let one walk if I can help it. Murder demands retribution, son, and I'm the man society hired to win it. But I'm not totally a bastard. God said an eye for an eye, a tooth for a tooth, but he put some conditions on that edict. I can't do any less. So what can I do about Leroy MacPhearson? He committed murder, no question about that, but there are those mitigating circumstances you're so concerned about. So maybe we ought to be talking expiation instead of retribution. Leroy MacPhearson's got to atone for his crime, and that gives me some room to maneuver. He can plead to voluntary manslaughter, and I'll recommend ten years probation, a fine, and five thousand hours public service. That way we won't have that damn examining trial *and* the publicity that goes with it. With any luck, we'll file this case away with minimal damage to STAD. It's the best I can do because I'm not going to let him off. God knows I'd like to wring his damn neck for killing a DOE employee in the first place. Or maybe I'm just pissed because he didn't do it in front of forty witnesses who would swear he was provoked beyond what a reasonable man could stand."

Miller got to his feet and stretched, every bone in his large body cracking. "Call John Branson, Schroder, and tell him to hightail it down here and look at the evidence. When he sees his goddamn mutilation of a corpse ain't gonna fly, he'll play ball. Ordinarily, I wouldn't let the bastard see anything that I wasn't going to introduce into evidence, but this is an exception. We've got to keep Branson quiet, or all hell's gonna break loose in the press."

"Who's going to keep Tinsdale quiet?" demanded Jenner. "He'll invite so damn many reporters, he'll have to hold his press conference in the Civic Center."

"He won't open his mouth, or I'll mention his tampering with evidence," said Schroder. "He ain't gonna throw any stones, or I'll kick his glass house in."

"Speaking of that penny-loafered toad," said Miller. "He bonded out of jail this evening. Didn't like his accommodations in Potter County. He hopped back to Hereford in company with his lawyer who is as big a slimeball as he is. And while I'm on the subject of lawyers, get in gear and call Branson. I want this settled so I can watch the Cowboys' exhibition game tomorrow without worrying about getting my ass kicked on Monday morning."

Jenner looked at his watch. "It's one-thirty in the morning. Branson isn't going to drive down here at one-thirty in the morning for God himself."

Miller slapped Jenner on the back. "Maybe not for God, but he'll come for a client. Go call him."

"Me? Why me? I'm not in charge of this case."

Miller looked at Schroder and they both grinned. "Shit, boy," said Miller. "You think the sergeant and I are stupid enough to call John Lloyd Branson and get him out of bed?"

CHAPTER
FOURTEEN

LYDIA HEARD THE EARTH RUMBLE BENEATH HER FEET AND ran faster. Sweat stung her eyes and pain twisted her calves. She gasped for breath, and each breath she took seared her lungs. Radiation, she thought. The radioactive steam is burning my lungs into cinders. She'd be coughing up ash and phlegm until the earth exploded and rained nuclear waste onto her exhausted body until she was buried forty feet deep. Ten thousand years from now some archaeology student would dig up her petrified remains and exhibit it in some damn museum. Her toes stiffened as her foot cramped into one fleshy arch of pain and she went down to lie groveling in the dirt. A heavy pounding echoed in her head and she buried her face in her arms. Heated steam was punching its way through the earth's crust like some giant fist to incinerate the land and extinguish its caretakers.

"Miss Fairchild."

Lydia awoke clutching her pillow in her fists and shivering. God, what a nightmare was her first thought, quickly followed by the second. Her foot was cramping, and a real fist was pounding on her apartment door. Stumbling out of bed, she hopped around the floor on one foot, her other foot a stiff, arched, toe-twisted appendage. "Oh," she groaned, and collapsed on the floor.

"Miss Fairchild, are you all right?" He pounded again. "Lydia, open this door or I'll break the damn thing down." The voice was deep, commanding, and loud enough to be heard a block away.

"John Lloyd," she shouted. "Is that you?" It couldn't be, she thought. John Lloyd Branson never allowed a contraction nor a profane expression to pass his lips.

"And who else might be knocking on your door in the middle of the night?" The voice was still deep, still loud, still commanding, but another note had been added. John Lloyd sounded suspicious as hell.

"I'm coming," she called, crawling to the dresser and pulling herself to her feet. Limping grotesquely into the living room, she unlocked the door.

It slammed open, bounced against the wall, imprinting the shape of the doorknob into the plaster, and swung back to be stopped by John Lloyd Branson's outstretched hand. He stepped over the threshold and kicked the door shut. "What took you so long?"

Lydia hobbled backward with John Lloyd stalking after her like an angry father whose daughter stayed out past curfew, and finally fell into a wingback chair, cradling her foot in her hands. "Quit yelling."

"I never yell," he replied.

"Tell that to the neighbors down the block. What are you doing anyway? Making a bed check?" Her cramped foot jerked and contracted and she bit her lip, decided to hell with being brave, and screamed. "Ouch! Damn, damn, damn!"

"Miss Fairchild! What is it?" He dropped his cane and hunkered down by her chair.

"Foot," she moaned.

"What?"

"Foot. Cramp. Hurts like hell."

"Let me," he said, pushing her fingers aside and pressing his own deep into her arch.

"Oh, God," she screamed, and grabbed for his hands and encountered his cotton-clad shoulder instead as he turned sideways and pulled her foot and leg across his thighs.

"Relax, Miss Fairchild," he murmured, pressing, releasing, pressing again.

"But it hurts!" she protested, digging her own fingers into the muscles of his shoulder.

He winced. "Please, Miss Fairchild, I would rather not have to explain to my housekeeper why a brand-new shirt has ten crescent-shaped holes in the shoulder."

"Sorry," she gasped as his lean fingers massaged another tight muscle. She clasped his upper arm and leaned her head against his shoulder, rubbing her forehead against the stiff cloth. She jerked her head up and stared at him. "You're wearing a cotton shirt. And jeans."

"I do own other clothes besides three-piece suits," he said dryly.

Lydia leaned against his shoulder again as her protesting muscles eased into an aching soreness. "You look like the Marlboro man."

"A compliment, Miss Fairchild?" he asked, moving his hand up her leg to massage the tense muscles in her calf.

"Um, yes," she said, closing her eyes. "You have magic fingers. You'd make a fortune as a masseur."

He immediately let go of her calf, loosened her grip on his arm, and pushed himself up. "I have occasion to practice," he said with the first note of bitterness she'd ever heard in his voice.

She glanced at his left leg, then up at his face. She imagined him awaking in his lonely four-poster bed and rubbing his own cramped muscles in tight-lipped silence. She didn't know if he limped as a result of a birth injury, an illness, or an accident, and she'd learned never to ask. He never referred to his handicap, and she sensed he regretted doing so now.

She smiled, felt her lips quiver, and stretched them wider. "Well," she said in what she privately referred to as her jolly good sport voice. "Let me know if I can return the favor." She stood up and tested her foot. "I may not be as good as you, but I'll put on soft music, use scented oil, and wear something silky and slinky."

"Miss Fairchild, what are you wearing?" His voice would have made a Sunday School teacher feel guilty.

She looked down at herself, felt her face heat up several degrees, and crossed her arms over her breasts. "A-a Mickey Mouse T-shirt."

"And apparently nothing else. Are you in the habit of answering your door in the middle of the night wearing that?"

"Oh, for God's sake, John Lloyd, I knew it was you."

"Miss Fairchild, I am not a eunuch."

Lydia's mouth felt dry, and she swallowed nervously. "Does that mean you're going to make a pass at me?"

"It means nothing of the sort. Please get dressed."

"Does it mean you're *thinking* about it?"

"My thoughts are none of your business," he drawled.

"Then you are thinking about it," she said, moistening her lips and attempting a seductive look she'd practiced in front of her bathroom mirror.

"If memory serves me, Miss Fairchild, I told you at the beginning of our association that I was not a suitable candidate for your romantic fantasies," he said as he turned her around and gave her a gentle push toward the bedroom door. "Now get dressed. Sergeant Schroder is waiting."

She waited until she reached her bedroom door before turning her head to look at him over her shoulder. "But we're not talking about my fantasies. We're talking about yours. Am I a suitable candidate for your romantic fantasies?" She heard him curse as she closed the door behind her.

* * *

"I don't understand what is so urgent that Sergeant Schroder had to see you tonight?" Lydia complained as she stood on the sidewalk in front of the Special Crimes building across the square from the Potter County courthouse.

"Sergeant Jenner," said John Lloyd, taking her arm and guiding her up to the glass door.

"Well, the sphinx talks," she quipped, and felt his hand tighten around her arm. "I thought you said Schroder. As I recall, it was the last thing you said to me, and that was two hours ago."

"Jenner called. Sergeant Schroder is aware that I dislike being awakened at night," he said as he pulled open the glass door and ushered her into a tiny entry hall containing a chair, a telephone, and another set of glass doors.

"Apparently that's not all you dislike at night," she snapped.

He pulled open the second set of doors. "You misinterpreted my earlier remarks. I was only pointing out that I am not blind to your physical charms, and your continued assumption that I am is putting an unnecessary strain on our professional relationship. Equality of the sexes does not imply impotence of either gender."

"Are you saying I'm not safe?"

His eyes glittered in the dim light. "On the contrary, your virtue is unassailable."

She walked into a foyer with a reception desk, a few chairs, and many filing cabinets, and whirled to face him. "Then you're saying I can't be seduced?"

He smiled. "No. I am saying I can't be." He touched her shoulder and pointed. "To your right, Miss Fairchild, through that door."

"Arrogant bastard," she muttered as she stalked into a large room with a huge U-shaped table stacked with what looked like the entire contents of Price-Leigh's house. She was glad to see the mattress wasn't in sight.

"Took you long enough, Branson. What happened? Did

you finally get stopped for speeding and decide your driving record couldn't stand more than one ticket a night?'' asked a tall black man with the massive shoulders of a linebacker. An overweight, overage linebacker, thought Lydia, but still an impressive physical specimen.

"Lydia Fairchild, may I introduce Assistant District Attorney Cleetus Miller, better known as Maximum Miller for his formidable record in obtaining the maximum sentence allowed by law. Felons, even innocent ones, quail at the mention of his name. In some sections of this fair city mothers evoke his name to insure their children's good behavior. He has replaced the bogeyman in the hearts and minds of an entire generation. Mr. Miller, my assistant and soon-to-be law partner, Miss Fairchild.''

Lydia felt her mouth drop open, and looked up to meet John Lloyd's totally unexpressive eyes. "I-I . . .'' she stuttered.

"Miss Fairchild, shake hands with Mr. Miller. He does not eat innocent young women. Only guilty ones.''

Lydia held out her hand and felt it engulfed by Maximum Miller's. He had hands more like a running back, she thought; large and graceful. "How do you do,'' she said, and inwardly winced. God, what an original greeting.

Miller pumped her hand vigorously. "Miss Fairchild, what is a beautiful young woman with her whole life ahead of her doing burying herself in a backwater town like Canadian partnered up with this nineteenth-century throwback? Come to Amarillo; do some important work.'' He released her hand and took a step closer to John Lloyd. "Put those guilty bastards in jail instead of defending them.''

John Lloyd applauded. "Excellent, Cleetus. Spoken like a true prosecutor. Off with their heads.''

Lydia thought of two fighting pit bulls circling around and around, each searching for that one opportunity to disembowel the other. It was dangerous to stop a dogfight, she thought as she nervously stepped between the two men, but she'd be damned if she'd watch the blood flow. They could postpone the match until Monday morning when a judge could referee.

"I'm flattered by your offer, Mr. Miller, but my mother always taught me to leave the party with the man I came with. Speaking of parties, where is it? I mean, why did Sergeant Jenner call us?" Her voice trailed off when Cleetus Miller started laughing.

"I think we scared your new partner, John Lloyd," he said. "Don't worry, Miss Fairchild. Branson and I always insult each other. Sort of marking our territory."

"Like dogs wetting down fireplugs?" asked Lydia.

Miller's laughter rumbled up from deep in his chest. "That's it exactly. I like her, John Lloyd. When I first heard you'd hired yourself a woman attorney, I figured you'd have her too intimidated within a week to open her mouth. Hell, the legal community in Amarillo had a bet going on how long she'd last. I think I'll throw my bet in the pot at the next bar meeting."

"Don't risk your financial future," said Lydia, flouncing over to sit in a chair by Jenner. "I may decide I want to be a prosecutor after all." She smiled at Jenner. "How about it, Sergeant? Should I join the D.A.'s office? Fight for truth, justice, and a maximum sentence?"

"Be a private investigator, Miss Fairchild. Then you can choose your own side." He grinned, and she thought again how terribly attractive he was. She'd always been a sucker for blue eyes and black hair. Too bad his personal hygiene was lacking.

"A private eye," she said, propping her chin on one hand. "I guess I could exchange my three-piece suit for a trench coat."

"A trench coat always reminds me of smog-shrouded street corners and refuse-filled alleys, both unsuitable places for you," drawled John Lloyd as he slid into the chair next to her.

"Unsuitable seems to be your favorite word," she retorted, turning her head to look at him. "And you always define it as behavior that doesn't suit you."

He regarded her with a bland expression on his face. "I am only trying to look out for your best interests"—he inclined his head in Miller's direction—"without intimidating you."

Maximum Miller gave another roar of laughter. "Yes, sir, I'm gonna win that bet."

"You will not, however, win the MacPhearson case," said John Lloyd, his drawl conspicuous by its absence. Gone, too, was any trace of humor. His face was hard-looking, as though it were carved from marble, his eyes two chips of coal. They glittered in the light without reflecting any emotion. They expressed only cold, merciless logic.

"The hell you say," said Miller, his own black eyes a reflection of John Lloyd's. "You ain't seen the latest evidence, Branson. Evidence that's snapped your client in a mousetrap. Schroder!" he said without taking his eyes from John Lloyd's. "Show the defense attorney here Ms. Silliphant's statement. Give him Tinsdale's while you're at it. And that list of names we caught the little bastard with. Hell, I'll be generous. Give him the neighbors' statements."

Schroder pushed himself away from the far wall and walked to the table. Leafing through a stack of papers, he extracted several and handed them to John Lloyd, then went back to lean against the wall.

Lydia sat quietly watching the four men in the room. They all sat or stood without moving. Like statues, she thought, but statues carved from different materials. Miller was granite, hard, unyielding, almost impervious to anything but the strongest force. Schroder was quartzite, massive, hard, resistant to change. Jenner was carved of a softer material, sandstone perhaps. Yes, definitely sandstone. Someday he would metamorphose into the quartzite hardness of Schroder, but not yet. John Lloyd was not carved of stone at all. He was a diamond, polished, faceted, without flaws. No one could shatter John Lloyd Branson except his equal. And he had no equals.

Silently he passed the statements to Lydia. "Your inference is a non sequitur, Cleetus. Your conclusion does not follow the evidence."

Miller's neck expanded one collar size as complacency changed to fury. "Goddamn it, Branson, don't pull that fancy talk on me. That Silliphant woman is an eyeball witness." He slammed his fist on the table. "Let's reconstruct the crime so you can see your client has had it. Schroder! Front and center and tell Mr. Defense Attorney how it was done."

Schroder walked to the table again and picked up a pointer. His face was expressionless, too, Lydia noticed. His and John Lloyd's. Miller looked mad, and Jenner looked, well, reluctant.

Schroder placed a large sheet of poster board on an easel. "According to the forensic pathologist, Charlton Price-Leigh was murdered between twelve-thirty and one o'clock on the morning of Saturday, August 26 of this year."

"Closer to twelve-thirty, I believe, Sergeant Schroder," said John Lloyd in that hard, sharp voice.

"Could be, Branson, but the pathologist won't be pinned down any closer. Now earlier, on Friday afternoon about four o'clock, MacPhearson was overheard threatening Price-Leigh in the DOE field office in Hereford, Texas . . ."

"By Mr. Tinsdale, is that correct?" asked John Lloyd.

Schroder was beginning to frown, "Yeah, that's right, Counselor. Now, as I was saying . . ."

"Surely a very foolish thing to do, threatening a man in front of witnesses, then going to his home to kill him."

Schroder's frown was making interesting designs on his forehead. "Murderers ain't so damn smart sometimes. Otherwise, they wouldn't be murderers. If I can get on with what I was saying. MacPhearson threatened Price-Leigh over a letter informing MacPhearson his land was in the so-called containment area and would be bought—"

"Confiscated," interrupted John Lloyd. "The doctrine of eminent domain is a legally sanctioned form of land confiscation by the federal government."

"All right! Confiscated! Anyway, after delivering the threat MacPhearson left. Price-Leigh also left the office, arriving at his home somewhere around five o'clock. At eight he received a visit from a woman believed to be Frances Whitley, the daughter of Leroy MacPhearson—"

"You know she's got to give us a statement," interrupted Miller. "I'm just telling you so you'll know."

Schroder's eyebrows were meeting and his eyes seemed to be protruding. "I don't want that airhead fainting every time I ask a question, Branson, because this time I'm gonna have some answers if I have to stick a bottle of smelling salts up her nose and hold it there."

"I trust you will remember my client's civil rights, Sergeant Schroder," John Lloyd said. "Shall we meet tomorrow at two on neutral ground. I will have Mrs. Whitley in my office for her interview."

"That's neutral ground?" demanded Schroder. "Like hell it is. You're trying to pull something, Branson. I can feel it in my bones just like I can feel a thunderstorm coming. The back of my neck hurts in the same place in both cases."

"Mrs. Whitley is of a nervous disposition. To subject her to brutal questioning in the sterile environment of Special Crimes is an unnecessary hardship."

"Nervous disposition, my ass. That woman has ground round for brains," said Schroder. Lydia agreed wholeheartedly.

"You were saying, Sergeant Schroder?" asked John Lloyd. Schroder stood blinking. "About Frances Whitley visiting Price-Leigh."

Schroder twisted the pointer in his hands. "After she left, a man and woman driving a van were seen at Price-Leigh's house. After checking the list of people who received letters, and investigating their circumstances, we believe the woman to be Elizabeth Thornton and her boarder, a man named—''

''The letter,'' exclaimed John Lloyd. ''Of course.''

It was too much! Schroder broke the pointer in two. His eyebrows were so close together, they overlapped like two mating caterpillars. ''Goddamn it, Branson! Will you let me finish a sentence?''

John Lloyd looked down the table at Schroder, his eyes absolutely blank. Lydia wondered if he'd even heard the sergeant. ''Certainly. I would not dream of interrupting.''

Lydia thought the investigator might have a stroke or at least go into convulsions. He was all but foaming at the mouth. Jenner, on the other hand, spent a lot of his time bending over with his shoulders shaking. She'd suspect he was laughing except that was impossible. He was on Schroder's side.

''Get on with it, Schroder. It's four o'clock in the morning and I'm in low gear. I want Branson to hear the rest of this; then he and I are going to do a little plea bargaining.''

John Lloyd must have heard Miller, thought Lydia, because his eyes sharpened into focus. ''There will be no plea bargaining. Leroy Macphearson is innocent.''

''And I'm Peter Rabbit,'' shouted Miller. He held up one finger. ''We got MacPhearson with the body.'' He held up another finger. ''Two. We got motive.'' He held up a third finger. ''We got a witness who saw him back his fucking pickup into the garage at the time of the murder. And thanks to Sweetie Pie . . .''

''Poo,'' said Jenner.

''What?'' demanded Miller, distracted by the interruption.

''The dog's name is Sweetie Poo, not Pie,'' said Jenner. ''And Charlton Price-Leigh didn't like him.''

''Thanks to Sweetie Poo, we got that same witness hearing Price-Leigh telling somebody that it was no use fighting it, that it was all over. Or words to that effect. Now who might that be, Branson, but your client. The government's going to take his land, and there's no way he can win even if he goes to the Supreme Court. And you sit there and tell me your client's *innocent*?''

John Lloyd's eyes were hard obsidian again. ''Yes, Clee-tus, he is.''

''Just suppose you tell me who murdered Charlton Price-Leigh?''

''I do not know at the present time . . .''

Miller looked at Schroder. ''The great white hope doesn't know. Mark that down, Sergeant. It's the first time I ever heard him admit he didn't know something.''

''. . . and neither do you. I will bargain with you, Cleetus. I will ask that the examining trial be continued a week if you will delay presenting your case against Leroy MacPhearson to the grand jury.''

Miller folded his arms and jerked his head from side to side. ''No deal, John Lloyd. I've got your man.''

''Your motive is invalid, and your eyewitness mistaken. I will win, Cleetus, and the judge will dismiss the charges against Leroy MacPhearson. Your investigation will escalate and so will the danger.'' John Lloyd's foreboding voice seemed to drop the room temperature at least ten degrees, and Lydia felt a chill shiver down her back.

Maximum Miller felt it, too, because an expression of uncertainty flashed across his face like a bolt of lightning only to be eclipsed by the rumble of thunder in his voice. ''Danger? What the hell are you talking about, Branson? The only danger will be a murderer on the loose.''

''Exactly,'' said John Lloyd. ''The period of greatest danger will be after Leroy MacPhearson is released, and the murderer realizes that the hunt is once again on. Then he will kill again if necessary to protect himself. If, on the other hand, we use delaying tactics in the legal procedure to reassure the murderer that all is well, while at the same time intensifying the criminal investigatory process, it may be possible to apprehend him before he kills again."

Miller tapped his fingers on the wooden table. "And just who do you think this mythical beast is going to kill?"

"If I knew that, I would know the identity of the murderer."

"We could let everybody be killed off, and then arrest whoever is left," suggested Jenner. Lydia hoped he was being sarcastic.

"Shut up, Jenner," snapped Miller without looking at him. "You're scared, aren't you, John Lloyd? You wouldn't be suggesting letting your client hang in limbo between being charged and being indicted if you weren't. You know something, don't you? You've got some evidence that you haven't turned over to Special Crimes. I'll get your ass disbarred for withholding evidence in a murder case. You defense attorneys are officers of the court. You can keep quiet if your client confesses to you, but you goddamn well can't keep quiet about physical evidence."

"I have found nothing!" shouted John Lloyd, and Lydia flinched. John Lloyd never shouted.

Miller knew it, too. He scratched his face and considered. "What about the evidence you *say* is going to clear your client?"

"I do now have solitary physical possession of one piece of that evidence, and you possess the other."

Maximum Miller's mouth opened, then closed. Finally he spoke. "You're shitting me."

"No, I am not."

"What the hell is it, Branson?" demanded Schroder from the other end of the table.

John Lloyd shook his head. "Sergeant, what you are asking me to do is unethical. If I voluntarily revealed my defense to the prosecution, then my client could have me disbarred. We are at an impasse, gentlemen," he said, rising and standing behind Lydia's chair. "Miss Fairchild, shall we go?"

Maximum Miller's comments on John Lloyd's character, legitimacy, and possible physical relationship to female members of his family as well as to animals of the field echoed in Lydia's ears long after she and John Lloyd left Special Crimes. She'd expected to be pelted by rotten cabbages and eggs as they walked out of the workroom. She had heard something crack as they reached the foyer, but she thought it was Sergeant Schroder breaking his pointer again.

"Was that a lesson on professional relationships, John Lloyd?"

"Stories of lawyers having lunch or a golf game together after battling in court do not apply to prosecutors and defense attorneys, Miss Fairchild. We deal in black and white. The suspect is guilty beyond a reasonable doubt, or he is innocent. There are no split decisions allowed to a Texas criminal jury as there are to a civil jury. It is all or none, and that does not make for close personal friendships between defense and prosecution."

"Does anybody like a defense attorney?"

John Lloyd chuckled. "Your client. While he's in jail, at least. Once he's acquitted, he will argue over your bill."

"That's pretty ungrateful."

"Better than the alternative. If your client is convicted, he doesn't pay you at all. Another lesson for you, Miss Fairchild. Always ask for payment in advance. Mrs. Dinwittie insists on it, and I do not wish to upset Mrs. Dinwittie."

"Afraid she might take after you with an ax?"

"No. I am afraid she might take after the clients," he replied, turning right on Amarillo Boulevard.

CHAPTER
FIFTEEN

THE FIRST THING JENNER NOTICED WAS HOW MUCH LEG Lydia Fairchild's narrow denim skirt exposed. The second thing he noticed was the cold look John Lloyd Branson was giving him. Jesus, that guy could freeze the balls off a buffalo, he thought as he hastily searched the lawyer's reception area for something else to look at. Not Branson's secretary, that was for damn sure. Except for the pink glasses, she looked like an ugly doll his sister had won at a carnival one year. And didn't Schroder say she was an acquitted ax murderess? Some collection of women Branson kept around: a blonde built like a Barbie doll and Canadian's own version of Lizzie Borden. No wonder the guy was weird.

"Where are your clients, Branson?" demanded Schroder, opening a new pack of cigarettes.

"In my office," replied John Lloyd. "Mrs. Dinwittie, if I could trouble you for some coffee."

She bobbed her head and smiled. "I'd be just as pleased as punch, Mr. Branson. You and Miss Fairchild will just be as busy as two little bees, so just don't worry your heads about refreshment. I'll just slip in quiet as a mouse with a tray.''

Jenner had never heard so many clichés in so few sentences in his life.

Schroder nudged him. ''Quit staring at the help and get your notebook out. We're here to take statements,'' the investigator muttered.

''I wasn't staring.''

''The hell you weren't. Your eyes were on stalks when you were looking at Miss Fairchild.'' Schroder's voice was a low rumble in Jenner's ears as the burly sergeant urged him through the door into John Lloyd's office.

''Quit shoving,'' whispered Jenner as he tripped over the doorsill and staggered into the sitting area. The Victorian couch was full of MacPhearsons, he noticed, as he grabbed the back of a chair to keep from sprawling on the floor.

''I see the fuzz have arrived.'' The beautiful dark-haired woman tilted her head back to look at Jenner.

''Yes, ma'am,'' he said, straightening up and stepping around the chair to face her, hoping he didn't look as much like an idiot as he felt. He noticed the woman was also wearing a denim skirt, but in his opinion she didn't do as much for it as Lydia Fairchild did for hers.

''You're Elizabeth Thornton?'' asked Schroder, shouldering Jenner aside.

''That's right, and as usual, you cops are never there when you're needed.''

''I do not believe Deaf Smith County is in Sergeant Schroder's jurisdiction, Elizabeth,'' said John Lloyd, standing by her chair and smiling down at her.

''Did you need a policeman?'' asked Jenner, deciding he didn't like her skirt because it was gathered instead of long and narrow with a slit in the back like Lydia Fairchild's.

''Not as much as I need to fix the sight on my rifle. I had a damn prowler, if you can imagine that. My place is so far back in the sticks I have to keep my own tomcat, and some fool tries to break in. I keep a couple of dogs around the place so he didn't get as far as the house. By the time I got to the door with my rifle, he was jumping the fence and heading for the road. I got off a couple of shots, but my sight was low and all I did was kick up some dust behind him. First time I ever saw a man outrun my shepherd. He jumped in a car parked behind a windbreak of trees and took off.''

"What kind of car was it?" asked Schroder.

Elizabeth's upper lip curled in disgust. "That's just the kind of question a city cop would ask. That's a dirt road out there and it hasn't rained for two months. I didn't see anything but a cloud of dust. I didn't hear the engine either. I've got a beagle that's just big enough to chew off a man's knees, but he's got a howl like the hound of the Baskervilles. You couldn't hear a jet plane over that dog."

"The danger has begun, Sergeant Schroder," said John Lloyd.

"Real convenient timing, isn't it, Branson?" asked Schroder.

"What are you talking about, John Lloyd? What danger? I wasn't in danger. Probably just some damn kid looking for a house to wreck, and figured an isolated farmhouse was a good bet. He won't try it again."

"I don't think so, Elizabeth," said a tall redheaded man sitting in the chair on the other side of her.

That must be the one Schroder called Hap, thought Jenner. Good-looking bastard, but there was something about the eyes that raised the hair on the back of his neck.

"You got some reason for saying so?" asked Schroder, his attention focused on the other man like an exterminator studying a rat in order to determine the proper dose of poison.

Hap shrugged his shoulders and smiled, laugh lines crinkling around his eyes. "John Lloyd Branson isn't known for making idle conversation. If he says danger, it's time to duck behind a barricade.''

"Is that so?" asked Schroder, still studying Hap.

Jenner studied him, too. He was a cool bastard, wasn't even squirming. Most men, even innocent ones, couldn't sit still under one of Schroder's famous visual examinations. And there was still something about Hap's eyes that bothered Jenner. Somewhere he'd seen eyes like those before. Not the same color or shape, but that same quiet, waiting expression. Hap was smiling, but those damn eyes weren't.

"Oh, God, we're all going to be killed in our beds!" shrieked Frances Whitley.

"Now, Frances, you calm yourself down," said her father, patting her knee.

Elizabeth wasn't as patient. "Shut up, Frances. I can't hear over your yelping like a scalded cat, and I want an explanation." She looked up at the attorney. "What are you hinting at, John Lloyd?"

"You are all involved in Charlton Price-Leigh's murder . . ."

"I didn't kill him!" screeched Frances, twitching and jerking in her denim dress. Denim must be in this year, thought Jenner. Too bad for Frances, because she looked like the backside of a fat cowboy in it.

"Willis, if you don't keep her quiet, I'll gag her," said Elizabeth.

"Quiet!" John Lloyd's voice caught Frances in mid-squeal. "Thank you," he continued. "As I was saying, you were all involved with Charlton Price-Leigh in some fashion. He is dead and his murderer is unknown." Schroder frowned at that remark. "And each of you were at his house on the day of the murder just prior to his forced departure for eternity. *On a bloodstained mattress in his own bedroom.*"

Frances covered her mouth with her hands and closed her eyes. Elizabeth glanced at the floor and restlessly crossed her legs, but Hap didn't react at all. It was unnatural how calm the man was, thought Jenner.

"All of you but Willis were seen there by witnesses. Thus all of you have some knowledge, perhaps more than you think."

"For God's sake, John Lloyd, none of us saw anyone kill him. Do you think Frances could keep her mouth shut for one minute if she had? She would have screamed the house down."

"Unless it was her daddy," said Schroder in his low, hoarse voice. That brought another long silence.

"You may not be aware that you saw something, or heard something, Elizabeth," said John Lloyd. "And perhaps you did not. *But* the murderer might not know that, and a murderer by the nature of his crime becomes paranoid. He has a secret to keep and will not hesitate to kill again to protect that secret."

The atmosphere in the room reminded Jenner of the heavy, ominous feeling before a thunderstorm. He held his breath in anticipation. MacPhearson's voice was anticlimatic. "There ain't no danger," he stated flatly.

"Because you're not planning to kill your family and friends?" asked Schroder.

"Mr. MacPhearson is not obliged to talk to you, Sergeant Schroder," interrupted John Lloyd before the farmer could answer. "You may take statements from everyone else in the room. I cannot stop you, but you will not speak with Mr. MacPhearson." John Lloyd smiled, a particularly nasty smile in Jenner's opinion. "Rather you may speak *at* him, but I will not allow him to answer."

Schroder sucked in a breath and Jenner braced for an explosion. It never came. The investigator smiled back at John Lloyd, two alligators grinning at each other. "I guess I'll just have to be satisfied talking to these other folks, won't I, Branson? Mrs. Whitley, we'll start with you. We'll just go in Mr. Branson's library over here. It looks real comfy . . ."

Frances Whitley rolled her eyes back in her head and fainted.

"Shit!" exclaimed Schroder.

"Oh, God," said Elizabeth in disgust.

"Frances always does get in a state," said her father, patting her hand. "Gotta handle her real careful."

"Miss Fairchild, get the brandy."

John Lloyd's voice was urgent, and Jenner watched Lydia dash to the attorney's desk and retrieve a squat bottle. John Lloyd unscrewed the cap and dribbled some of the liquor into Frances's open mouth. She sputtered, and her nose twitched. Bulging eyes opened and she smacked her lips.

Jenner had seen winos make the same smacking motion, like babies seeking the breast. The woman was a secret alcoholic, and all her twitching and squirming meant she probably hadn't had a drink in several hours. He glanced at John Lloyd and decided the attorney knew it, too. No wonder Branson insisted she be questioned in his office. The woman might have gone into convulsions at Special Crimes.

"Frances," said John Lloyd gently. "I will be with you, Miss Fairchild and I. Sergeant Schroder will ask questions, and I will tell you whether to answer or not. No one will browbeat you. I will not allow it."

"Ma'am," said Schroder, extending his hand. "You just don't get yourself so upset. Miss Fairchild, do you suppose you could check on that coffee. I could use a cup, and I bet Mrs. Whitley could, too."

Frances patted her hair back. "I might be able to drink a little. Caffeine makes me so nervous, I try not to drink too much."

"I understand, ma'am," said Schroder, leading her into the library with Jenner trailing along behind. All the faces in the room were slack with astonishment at Schroder's about-face. All but John Lloyd's. But then Jenner would bet only he and John Lloyd Branson knew Schroder's wife had been a helpless alcoholic before her death. So far as Jenner knew, sympathy for a sick alcoholic woman was the only chink in Schroder's armor.

"Now, ma'am, can you tell me why you went to see Charlton Price-Leigh?" Schroder asked as soon as they were seated in the library and had watched Frances down two cups of coffee.

John Lloyd held up his hand. "Factual questions only, Sergeant. Nothing to do with motive. I cannot allow Frances to incriminate herself."

Schroder's mouth tightened around his cigarette, but Jenner guessed he didn't want to start a fight with John Lloyd in front of Frances. "Did you go to Charlton Price-Leigh's house at about seven-thirty or eight the night of the murder?"

Frances glanced at John Lloyd and he nodded. "Yes," she said. "But I didn't kill him."

"Yes, ma'am," said Schroder. "Did Charlton Price-Leigh say anything to you?"

Frances's lips started to quiver. "He said he couldn't talk to me, that I was a . . ."—she hesitated—"he called me a name."

"What did you want to talk about?" Schroder may have been sympathetic, but he was still a cop.

"To leave—"

"No!" said John Lloyd, interrupting.

"What time did you leave his house?" asked Schroder.

"I don't know. I was upset. I'm terribly nervous, you know." Substitute drunk for nervous, thought Jenner. No wonder she ran over somebody's flower bed.

"Did you go home?" asked Schroder.

"Is this where you ask me for an alibi?" twittered Frances. Jenner wondered if someone had slipped some brandy into her coffee. She was acting like it. Or maybe she wasn't worried about questions dealing with after she left the house.

"Yes, ma'am," said Schroder.

"I went straight home, picked up my daughter, Rachel, and took her to her Aunt Elizabeth's for a visit. I stayed for a while—Elizabeth insisted on feeding me coffee—and then I started home. Willis and I went straight to bed. It was, oh, I don't know, eleven o'clock.''

Schroder looked hurt. "Mrs. Whitley, in your first statement you told me you had called your father about eleven-thirty? We checked with the phone company. You didn't call him.''

Frances's eyes began to roam the room, and she licked her lips. Probably needs another drink, Jenner thought. "I thought I called him that night, Sergeant. Maybe it was the night before. I'm getting forgetful." She laughed.

"Yes, ma'am," said Schroder. "I believe that'll be all. Sergeant Jenner, take her back, and bring in Willis Whitley.''

"Did you get a letter from Price-Leigh?" John Lloyd asked her suddenly.

Her face looked blank and slack, like melting leather. "Willis picks up the mail and he didn't say anything about it. What kind of a letter?''

"About the containment area for the dump?" replied John Lloyd.

Her face suddenly looked animated, as if the lawyer had touched the right chord. "The dump! I hate the dump! It's ruined everything. And I hated Charlton Price-Leigh! And . . ." Her face slackened as if a battery had run down, or if she realized what she was saying. "I didn't kill him." She twisted her fingers together until Jenner wondered why they didn't break. "I didn't kill him. I *didn't*!"

"Of course, you didn't, Frances," said John Lloyd in a quick, jovial voice. "Everyone knows that. Sergeant Jenner, pour Mrs. Whitley a cup of brandy when you escort her back. Strictly for medicinal purposes.''

Jenner noticed Schroder frowning at John Lloyd as Frances nearly ran out of the library toward the brandy bottle. Probably didn't think the lawyer should give Frances a drink. The investigator ought to know better. The woman was too far-gone to be denied without risking delirium tremens. She was so pickled with alcohol it would almost kill her to take it away.

He watched her fill a coffee cup with brandy until it sloshed over the rim. Elizabeth made a sound of disgust, but it was Hap who surprised Jenner. The man looked sad, as if he felt as sorry for Frances as Schroder had. "Mr. Whitley, Sergeant Schroder wants to talk to you now."

Willis Whitley rubbed a large hand through his hair and nodded. He patted his wife's shoulder, but Jenner doubted if she noticed. "I'll be back, hon," he said, and he followed Jenner into the library.

"Did you know your wife went to see Charlton Price-Leigh?" asked Schroder.

The big farmer rubbed together his rough, cracked hands. "Yeah. Told her not to do it, that it wouldn't do no good, but she was bound and determined to go. She came home about eight-thirty or nine." He stopped.

"Go on," urged Schroder.

"Did you get a letter from Price-Leigh, Willis?" asked John Lloyd.

"Letter? You mean like Leroy's? No, we didn't. Guess he slipped up and missed us."

"If you don't mind, Counselor, I'll take the statement," Schroder told John Lloyd. He swung his head back to the farmer, a cloud of smoke trailing behind him. "What did your wife do then?"

Whitley filled a pipe, tamping the tobacco down with a finger. "She went to my sister's, visited awhile, and came home. We went to bed about eleven-thirty."

"What did Price-Leigh say to your wife, Mr. Whitley?" asked Schroder.

Whitley lit his pipe with a lighter Jenner swore was almost as old and battered as Schroder's, and puffed for a minute, studying the investigator through a wreath of smoke. He finally tucked the pipe in one corner of his mouth. "He called her a lush," he said matter-of-factly.

"Didn't that make you mad?"

Whitley took his pipe and tapped it on the ashtray. "I've been married to Frances for twenty years. She's been drinking for most of that time. I didn't catch on for a long time, thought she had states as her dad calls them, and broke a lot of faces before I learned better. I try to take care of her, keep her away from the public when she's having a bad time, but I just can't fight everybody who says something about her. I'm too tired, Sergeant. So if you're thinking I went over to Price-Leigh's and killed him because he threw my wife out of his house, you're thinking wrong."

He stood up. "If that's all, Sergeant, I'd better go see how Frances is doing, maybe keep her from drinking all Lawyer Branson's brandy."

Jenner followed him out and beckoned to Elizabeth. "Your turn, Mrs. Thornton."

With a swish of her flounced denim skirt, Elizabeth preceded him into the library. "Don't bother to get up, gentlemen," she said as she sat next to John Lloyd. Jenner hadn't noticed anyone making any effort to rise.

Jenner sat down next to Schroder on one side of the long library table. Seated on the opposite side were Lydia Fairchild, John Lloyd Branson, and Elizabeth Thornton. He felt his heart start pounding and knew the first two interviews had been scrimmages. This was it, the big one, the championship game. Talent scouts were in the stands watching the magic moves of the witnesses, the strong arm of Sergeant Ed Schroder, winner take all. And Branson. He was the umpire.

The game started, and Schroder pitched. "Did you recognize the prowler at all, Mrs. Thornton?"

"If I had, I'd already have his ass in jail," she answered tartly. Ball one.

Schroder wound up for another pitch. "Are you sure you saw a prowler at all?"

"If that's your way of calling me a liar, we're going to

finish this interview real fast, Sergeant. You'll get my name, address, and the fifth amendment.'' Ball two.

"You can't take the fifth during an interview,'' said Schroder. An argument at home plate.

"You may ask your questions, Sergeant, but I will not permit you to cast aspersions on Mrs. Thornton,'' said John Lloyd. A ruling by the umpire in the batter's favor.

Schroder studied the batter, then let loose his famous fastball. "Did you receive a letter from Charlton Price-Leigh concerning the so-called containment area?''

"That sneaky little bastard, that mealymouthed son of a bitch. Never a word during the public hearing about a containment area, then he sends that letter. Between the land I own on the site itself, and the land in the containment area, I'll be wiped out. And for what? Because the DOE boasted they could take care of the nuclear waste by 1998. A bunch of bureaucrats taking on the most serious scientific challenge of the twentieth century. They can't handle a wet dream, much less nuclear waste. And you know what that pseudo-cowboy prancing around in his designer jeans had the nerve to say? That I should come by to discuss my options, like this was some kind of penny-ante business deal. You know what I've discovered, Sergeant Schroder? That the more important the deal, the fewer the options. This is the most important deal of my life and I have exactly two options: fight or flight. I'm damn sure not going to flee.''

Strike one, thought Jenner, drawing a baseball diamond in his notebook.

"Just answer the question, Elizabeth,'' cautioned John Lloyd. "Do not give Sergeant Schroder any options.''

Two balls, one strike. Schroder wound up and let go. "What did you say to Price-Leigh when you and Hap went to his house?''

"I told him where to stick his dump, and that I figured there'd be enough room for the containment area there, too,'' said Elizabeth. Ball three.

Schroder on the pitcher's mound. Would he throw a fast-ball, or a curve. "What did Price-Leigh say to you?"

"He opened the door and pulled us in like he didn't want the neighbors to see. He even peeked through his front window drapes. God, he was acting paranoid. Then he whispered. He did, so help me God," she repeated when Schroder looked disbelieving. "He walked around his living room looking like his feet hurt in those boots he insisted on wearing, and talked about his enlightenment, his awakening. Damn it, I didn't care about the state of his psyche. I was mad as hell about that containment area. Four generations of my husband's family farmed that land. They outlasted drought, the depression, inflation, deflation. And now, by the stroke of somebody's pen who's not worth the cowshit on his boots, *poof*, it's gone. I wasn't in the mood to listen to him blather about a spiritual experience. I told him to call Oral Roberts, and I walked out. If I were going to kill him, I would've done it then."

Strike two.

Three balls, two strikes. Crucial pitch. Schroder wound up again and let fly. "Where were you between midnight and one o'clock the night of the murder?"

"Listening to my niece, Rachel, cry her heart out after her lush of a mother dumped her at my front door, and I was still listening at two o'clock and three o'clock. God, being a teenager is hell. Between acne and young love, life just isn't worth living." Ball four. Elizabeth took her base.

"Get Hap," said Schroder, his voice between a snarl and a growl.

Jenner stuck his head out of the library door. "Batter up."

Schroder took his time studying Hap as the redheaded man sat down by John Lloyd. Hap met the investigator's eyes with a bland expression in his own. Bland? Or experienced? Jenner mentally weighed the two descriptions and picked experienced. That was what had bothered him about Hap's eyes. He'd seen that same expression in a hundred pairs of eyes in his career. Hap had been interviewed by cops before, probably several times, because it took more than once to learn to hide your thoughts. In spite of that, Jenner couldn't sense any violence about the man, nor any smell of his being an ex-con.

Jenner glanced at John Lloyd. The attorney's eyes held a watching, waiting expression like a man expecting nothing, but prepared in case he was wrong. Jenner had a gut instinct that the lawyer was protecting Hap, and thought if anybody could take care of himself, it was Hap. Then he wondered what Hap needed protection from. A murder charge? Or something else?

He heard the burly investigator light another cigarette and knew Schroder was ready to pitch.

"What is your name besides Hap?" asked Schroder.

Hap smiled. "John Smith," he said, handing over a driver's license. Ball one, thought Jenner, even though he didn't believe Hap any more than he knew Schroder did. But Hap wasn't a suspect, so there was no legal way to take his fingerprints, a mug shot, or to make him hand over any more identification.

Schroder evidently agreed because he didn't pursue it. Instead he pitched a fastball. "What did Charlton Price-Leigh say to you and Elizabeth Thornton?"

Hap ran his fingers through his hair and smiled. Jenner studied the lines around his eyes and decided Hap was older than he'd first thought. Maybe mid-thirties. "The man was incoherent, Sergeant," said Hap in his best frank and honest voice.

"He must have said something you could understand," insisted Schroder.

"He was speaking English, if that's what you mean, but none of his sentences made any sense." Ball two, decided Jenner.

"Quote me a sentence," demanded Schroder.

Hap shrugged his shoulders. "I really can't remember."
Ball three.

"Where did you go after you left Price-Leigh?" asked
Schroder.

"We returned to Elizabeth's home. Part of my salary as
an employee of STAD is room and board. I have a room at
her home." His eyes turned from bland to cold. "And don't
read anything into that statement. Elizabeth and I are interested only in the dump. Not in each other." Close call, maybe
a strike, thought Jenner.

"What time did you get to Mrs. Thornton's?"

"I wasn't watching the clock. Perhaps nine, nine-thirty.
It was almost dark, anyway."

"Anything else happen that night?" Schroder snapped off
another fastball.

"Mrs. Whitley came by with her daughter, Rachel, shortly
after we arrived. Mrs. Whitley was . . ."—he hesitated—
"drunk. I insisted on making coffee." He spread his hands
in a helpless gesture Jenner swore was sincere. "It wasn't
what she wanted, but it was all I could do. Everybody wres-
tles with demons in his own way, and she doesn't want any
help. I wish . . ." His voice trailed off, and his eyes revealed
the first emotion Jenner had observed. Hap felt as sorry for
Frances Whitley as Schroder did.

He ran his hands through his hair and continued. "I went
to my room about eleven, and Elizabeth stayed up with Rachel, I think most of the night. I checked a little before twelve
to see if I could help. I couldn't, so I left. I know it was after
five before things settled down and I was able to sleep. So
you see, Sergeant, I can't help you with your murder."

Ball four and Hap takes his base.

CHAPTER
SIXTEEN

"YOU KNOW WHAT THIS MEANS, DON'T YOU, BRANSON?" asked Schroder.

John Lloyd looked up from his legal pad, where he'd been doodling what looked like mathematical formulas to Lydia. "It's the first time Mrs. Dinwittie has typed statements for the police? Don't be concerned. During her incarceration in the county jail while awaiting trial for the demise of the late Mr. Dinwittie, she had ample opportunity to read and sign several statements of her own. She is familiar with the form."

"That's not what I'm talking about," said Schroder, lighting a cigarette.

Lydia made a mark on her notebook page. That was the investigator's twenty-fifth cigarette since the four of them had sat down in the law library. She'd never seen anyone go through a pack of cigarettes in less than two hours. Clean air would probably kill him.

John Lloyd doodled another formula on his legal pad and circled it. He capped his pen and slipped it back in his pocket before looking at Schroder. "I have never known you to be less than straightforward, Sergeant Schroder. May I ask why you are talking around the subject now?"

Schroder took a deep drag on his cigarette and let the smoke trickle out his nose. "Because I can't figure you out. You sat here this afternoon and listened to four people put the noose around your client's neck, and you never said a damn thing to shut them up. Except for cautioning Mrs. Whitley not to tell me why she went to see Price-Leigh, and warning Elizabeth Thornton against elaborating too much, you never said anything period. Why is that, Branson?"

"I believe I asked about the letter."

Schroder snapped his fingers. "That's right, you did. I appreciate that, Branson. Saved me from asking them. So how come you were so damn helpful?"

John Lloyd poured himself a cup of coffee. "I want to know who murdered Charlton Price-Leigh as badly as you do, Sergeant. When the judge dismisses charges against Leroy MacPhearson tomorrow, I do not want you to waste time investigating the innocent."

"Meaning those four people I interviewed?"

"Of course."

Schroder ground out his cigarette in the ashtray. "Real cozy group sitting out there. They alibied each other six ways from Sunday. Except your client. Leroy MacPhearson is the only one who has no alibi. None whatsoever."

John Lloyd took a sip of coffee and set the cup down. "He is not the only one."

"Now you're calling your own clients liars?"

"There is one person involved in this case who does not have an alibi."

Lydia dropped her pencil and turned her head to stare at John Lloyd. He simply couldn't be planning to turn over one of his clients to the police. It was unheard of, impossible.

Schroder evidently thought so, too, because his mouth

gaped open, leaving his cigarette clinging precariously to his lower lip. "Who the hell are you talking about?"

John Lloyd pushed his coffee cup away and rested his elbows on the table. "Tinsdale."

"What!" Schroder's cigarette peeled away from his lip and dropped on the table. Lydia saw Jenner grab it and grind it out in the ashtray.

John Lloyd raised one eyebrow as if puzzled by Schroder's reaction. Which was a lie, thought Lydia, because John Lloyd had probably planned the whole day's revelations. "I read his statement, and he said he was working late. As any wife can tell you, that particular alibi is most suspicious."

"He doesn't have a motive."

"Ah, yes, the motive. That elusive motive. One might even say deceptive motive."

Schroder half rose from his chair and leaned over the table until his face was close to John Lloyd's. The bear and the fox, thought Lydia. And folklore says the fox is slier. "What the hell are you getting at, Branson? Come on, spit it out. You've been sitting here with a shit-eating grin on your face most of the afternoon, and I want to know why."

John Lloyd sat up straight, and Lydia noticed his eyes held that same cold, merciless expression they had held last night. "Deception, Sergeant Schroder, is the game we have been playing. Leroy MacPhearson, the alleged guilty party, has an apparent motive and no alibi. I shall prove he has *no* motive and *does* have an alibi. Tinsdale has an apparent alibi and no motive. Logic tells me he has *no* alibi and *does* have a motive."

Schroder sat down again, and lit another cigarette. Lydia made another mark on her pad. "What motive, Branson? That he didn't like Price-Leigh's bedroom games?"

John Lloyd dismissed Schroder's comment with a wave of his hand. "If you had checked Price-Leigh's bank statements, as I did, you also would've noticed checks written to a drilling company. Being curious, I checked with the driller and discovered that Price-Leigh had the data necessary to prove that the Panhandle salt beds were dissolving, and thus were unsafe as a burial for nuclear waste.''

"Hot damn!" exclaimed Jenner.

John Lloyd ignored him. "I thought at first that our departed friend was planning to hide the evidence, but upon reflection I have decided that is a deception. I believe now he was planning to use it to stop the dump. This would leave Mr. Tinsdale with no project to manage, thus reducing him to just another bureaucrat. In other words, Price-Leigh was a threat to Tinsdale's power, and that makes a superlative motive for murder."

"Where's this data?" asked Schroder, beginning to look uncertain.

"I do not know."

"Shit!" the investigator said. "I might've known you're up to your old tricks. Throw suspicion on everybody but your client. It ain't gonna work, Branson."

"I can, however, prove the data exists. Please call the Amarillo Police Department, and ask for the incident report on the break-in of the M. M. Myers Drilling Company. Then call the owner and ask him what was stolen." John Lloyd pushed a telephone closer to Schroder. "Go on, call."

Schroder looked at the phone as if he thought it might explode. He tapped his thick fingers on the table, and puffed furiously on his cigarette. Lydia decided there must be a correlation between the investigator's rate of smoking and his brain activity.

"You'd better be giving me the straight skinny, Branson," he warned as he picked up the phone. "Otherwise . . ." He didn't finish the sentence, but then Lydia didn't think he needed to. It was dangerous to bait a bear even if you were John Lloyd Branson.

It took several calls before Schroder finally hung up the phone and looked at John Lloyd through the haze of smoke that layered the air. "Interesting conversations, Counselor. You got any more wild geese you want me to chase?"

John Lloyd froze until Lydia wondered if he had turned into the diamond she'd compared him to. "Perhaps you would like to share your information, Sergeant," he said, his voice holding only the slightest drawl.

Schroder leaned back in his chair and folded his hands over his square torso. "There was a break-in, and some invoices on a drilling job done for Price-Leigh were gone. But, and it's a very big but, Branson, it was a professional job. The burglar alarm was wired around, the door was jimmied without any scratches, and there were no fingerprints anywhere. Not a single one. And no fibers or smudges from gloves either. The thief wore disposable rubber gloves, and that with everything else, means a pro. Do you think Tinsdale can break in like a pro? I don't. The little pip-squeak does well to zip his pants in the morning. It was a good try, Counselor, but you're going nowhere."

John Lloyd frowned. "Don't you think it's odd that only the proof of salt dissolution was stolen?" Two contractions in one sentence, thought Lydia. He must be more upset than he acts.

"You keep talking about data, but according to Mr. Myers, there was just raw figures on those invoices. He put it together on his computer and came up with some hairy figures, but that's no sign Price-Leigh did. Besides, seems to me *if* that data exists, Leroy MacPhearson had a better motive for stealing it than Tinsdale. MacPhearson is losing land that's been in his family for all of this century. He's got to stop that dump. Tinsdale's just gonna lose a title—maybe. And maybe he'll just get shuffled off to give somebody else a pain in the butt."

John Lloyd rose and paced the length of the library, finally stopping behind Lydia's chair. "Then why hasn't MacPhearson called a press conference or released the information?"

Schroder got up and tucked his shirt in. "Now that's a problem, isn't it? If he admits he's got it, then we know he took it from Price-Leigh, probably over the dead body, and he's got an even stronger motive for murder than before. If he don't release the data, then he can't stop the dump and he killed for nothing. He's kind of between a rock and a hard place. That's assuming there's any data or report or whatever to start with."

"Are you insinuating that I am lying?" asked John Lloyd.

"You've never done it before, and I don't think you're doing it now. I just think you're desperate, and you're seeing things that aren't there—like the data. You know what I think? I think that data's gonna be like the lost dutchman's mine. Everybody's heard about it, but nobody's ever found it." He nudged Jenner. "Up, Sergeant, and let's get those statements signed."

He followed the younger sergeant to the library door, then turned back to John Lloyd. "I wish there was some data, and I wish MacPhearson stole it, because I think any jury would let him walk as soon as they heard the DOE's dump was gonna blow a good chunk of Texas sky-high. That's a good motive, a hell of a lot better than MacPhearson's killing him to save his own piece of ground. He was trying to save all our hides. Jury might even vote him a reward. Too bad you can't use any of the story. It's all hearsay, and Maximum Miller ain't gonna let you get it within smelling distance of the judge tomorrow, or a jury when this case finally comes to trial. You know, I just thought of it, but you're between a rock and a hard place, too. If you do find the data, your client's bought the farm. If you don't find the data, the Pan-handle's gonna get the shaft." He lifted his hand. "See you in court, Branson."

"Who was the prowler, Sergeant Schroder?" asked John Lloyd.

Lydia saw Schroder's back stiffen. When he turned, his eyes were wary like those of a man who suddenly realizes he's walking down an unfamiliar street. "What's that got to do with anything?"

John Lloyd frowned impatiently. "Come now, Sergeant. First you tell me the break-in has nothing to do with the murder, and if it does, MacPhearson is the guilty person. Are you telling me that Elizabeth's prowler is another coincidence?"

Schroder's eyes still looked like those of a man walking down an unfamiliar street, but now he noticed the streetlights were out. "I didn't say the break-in was a coincidence."

"But you implied it. What explanation do you have for Elizabeth's prowler?"

Schroder's eyes were beyond wary and close to desperate. Not only were the streetlights out, but three rough strangers were approaching. "Maybe MacPhearson thinks she knows something."

"Now you are the one who is desperate, Sergeant. She would have recognized Leroy MacPhearson."

"It was dark. She probably couldn't see him."

John Lloyd shook his head. "Leroy MacPhearson has a handicapped left foot. He limps badly. Do you really believe he could outrun a three-year-old child, much less a German shepherd?"

Schroder had been mugged.

Lydia watched the investigator stumble out of the library, and close the door behind him. "What do you think he'll do, John Lloyd?"

John Lloyd dropped into a chair. "He will investigate Tinsdale's alibi."

"Then he believed you?"

John Lloyd rubbed his forehead. "Miss Fairchild, I don't believe me. Why should he?"

Somewhere the sun shone and flowers blossomed. Somewhere a boy and girl made love, a father played catch with his sons, a mother hemmed her daughter's dress. Somewhere men fought and died, women gave birth and worried, children ate moldy bread and hungered. Somewhere life continued, fueled by laughter, suffering, pain, longing, love, generosity, greed, selflessness, and hope. Somewhere, thought Lydia. But not in Canadian, Texas. Here normalcy had failed. John Lloyd Branson had struck out.

Impossible.

She stepped behind his chair and massaged his temples. "What are you doing, Miss Fairchild?" he asked without moving.

"You gave me a massage when I had a muscle cramp. I'm returning the favor."

"My head does not have a cramp."

"No, but your brain does."

He caught her hands and held them against his chest so that her arms circled his shoulders. "I am sure you have a very logical explanation for that statement."

"Certainly. Don't I always? I concluded your brain was cramping because you're talking crap."

He twisted his head to look at her. "Miss Fairchild, your language is deplorable and your logic worse."

"How so? My logic, that is. My language's fine. You're just a Victorian prude."

John Lloyd sighed and rested his head against her breasts. She braced her knees to keep from collapsing from shock. "I am not infallible, Miss Fairchild, and this afternoon proved it. I built a house of cards, and Sergeant Schroder knocked it down."

"I thought you mugged him."

He looked up at her again, one eyebrow raised. "Mugged?"

"Never mind. Go on with what you were saying."

"My explanation had several weak spots and Sergeant Schroder very kindly stepped in each one, leaving gaping holes from his size twelve shoes."

"I think you're exaggerating because I didn't see any holes. You pointed out that since all our people have alibis, Tinsdale must have done the dirty deed. Schroder certainly left looking as if his whole case had fallen in on his head.''

"I showed him the selling points of my house of cards, Miss Fairchild, and hoped he would not notice the flooded basement or leaking roof. In other words, I practiced deception in order to gain an objective. I will not deceive him for long.''

"I don't understand," complained Lydia. "How did you deceive him?''

"The burglar and the prowler logically must be the same person. The burglar could not be Tinsdale because our DOE lackey would have set off the alarm, fallen into a rack of pipes, or tripped over a coil of rope and broken a leg. I am assuming, of course, that he is not Superman in disguise . . .''

"I haven't seen him changing clothes in any phone booths.''

". . . however, our prowler was stupid enough to be Tinsdale. He did not know that every farm has dogs, that those dogs would bark at any stranger, and that Elizabeth would not hesitate to shoot whatever portion of his anatomy happened to be in range. Schroder will also realize the illogic of Tinsdale committing both crimes. But it must be Tinsdale.''

"What if he has an alibi?''

"Miss Fairchild, you are making my headache worse. But it is a valid question. I wish I had an answer. To put it simply, if Tinsdale has an alibi, then I don't know who murdered Price-Leigh.''

"Mr. Branson?" Mrs. Dinwittie opened the door. "Oh, I'm sorry. Did I interrupt something.''

John Lloyd released Lydia's hands and sat up. "Certainly not, Mrs. Dinwittie.''

"Certainly not, Mrs. Dinwittie," echoed Lydia. And winked at the secretary.

"Miss Fairchild was massaging my temples. Sergeant Schroder often gives me a headache.''

"I was massaging his temples," echoed Lydia.

"It is not necessary to repeat everything I say, Miss Fairchild," snapped John Lloyd, slipping out of his chair and straightening his vest. "What did you require, Mrs. Dinwittie?"

"Everyone's gone, and I'll be leaving, too, if you don't need anything else. I like to be home snug as a bug in a rug on Sunday night so I can watch my TV programs."

John Lloyd walked around the table and leaning over, kissed her cherry-red rouged cheek. "Mrs. Dinwittie, you are a jewel. Run along home, and I thank you very much."

Mrs. Dinwittie blushed and twittered. "Oh, Mr. Branson, you're just a prince among men."

"He has his moments," agreed Lydia. "Not many, but some."

"You're such a card, Miss Fairchild," said the secretary as she walked through the door. She stopped and clapped her hand to her head. "Oh, I forgot. I picked up the mail at the post office and sorted it. I guess you didn't have a chance to get it yesterday what with all the excitement. Do you want to look at it? There are some packages and a letter marked personal that's smells to high heaven of some kind of cheap perfume. And it's purple."

John Lloyd picked up his cane and grasped Lydia's arm. "No, I do not."

"I do," said Lydia. "Put it in my briefcase. We can't have a letter from one of John Lloyd's admirers lying around the office losing its scent."

"I wouldn't worry about that, Miss Fairchild," said the secretary. "I believe that letter will still smell when we're all in our graves." She waved her hand and went out.

"Come along, Miss Fairchild," said John Lloyd, urging her out of the library. "We have work to do."

"Like what?" Lydia asked, her mind still on the purple letter. What kind of a woman would use purple stationery?

"We must find Price-Leigh's film. I must know if that is the motive."

"And if it isn't?" she asked, watching him walk toward the other end of his office. His limp was more noticeable. She wished he'd go home and rest.

He sat down in one of the easy chairs and propped his feet on a hassock. "Then I have been deceived again, Miss Fairchild."

Nine calls and two hours later, she reverently opened the first envelope of photographs. The phone calls hadn't taken long, but the drive into Amarillo from Canadian had. She'd twitched worse than Frances at her twitchiest on the ride down until John Lloyd had finally threatened to tie her to her seat and bind her hands.

"What do you think, John Lloyd?" she asked as she held the pictures against her chest. "Doubles, triples, a foursome?"

John Lloyd snapped his fingers and held out his hand. "I despair of the future of our country if a well-brought-up young woman is even aware of the possibility of multiple participation in a sexual encounter."

"For God's sake, John Lloyd, sexual experimentation is the subject of talk shows and magazine articles," she said, reluctantly handing over the pictures.

"So is serial murder, but I trust you will not indulge in that either," he said fanning the photos like a hand of cards.

She crooked her neck to look. "But there's nothing there. Just a bunch of ponds." She quickly opened the other two envelopes, and spilled out the photographs on the seat of the car. "All ponds and"—she grabbed one picture and pointed to a figure—"look, it's Rachel!"

John Lloyd examined the photo. "I believe you are correct. That young woman in the foreground holding the placard is Rachel Whitley. Fully clothed, if you will notice. And the rest of these photographs are of playa lakes, several of them of the same lake at different times. The plot both clears and thickens, Miss Fairchild.''

"What do you mean?"

"I now theorize why Frances Whitley visited Price-Leigh. She was warning him away from her daughter. To insure that her daughter was safe, she took the girl to Elizabeth, knowing that an isolated farmhouse owned by someone who hated Price-Leigh was nearly as secure as a prison. Willis Whitley carefully avoided mentioning his daughter in his statement at all, perhaps in an effort to protect her. I suspected Rachel's feelings, but it is gratifying to have it proved.''

"Wait a minute! You didn't say anything about Rachel.''

"Miss Fairchild, I do not air my theories until I have more than mere psychological supposition. When a photo of our deceased friend turned up missing after yesterday's meeting, I immediately suspected Rachel. It is teenagers who collect posters and photos of their idols. Also recall our young witness who said Price-Leigh had a girlfriend, but was careful never to allow anyone to see her. That argues either a married woman, or a very young girl whose parents would disapprove of the affair.

"Deception, deception, Miss Fairchild. Where does it end?'' He slipped the photographs back in the envelopes. "Now the central question becomes why did Leroy move the body at all? We know now it was not to protect a member of his family from a murder charge because they all have alibis. Yet he is protecting someone. Damn it, Miss Fairchild, I am missing something.''

Lydia swallowed. John Lloyd was cursing, and that meant he was frustrated beyond his control and that was saying a lot. "At least you know now it wasn't a conspiracy.''

He turned on the ignition and backed out of the parking place in front of the photography shop. "On the contrary, now I know that it was.''

"But who?''

"You are asking unanswerable questions again, Miss Fairchild. Buckle your safety belt, please. We are going to the dumpsite."

"The dump?"

"It may inspire me."

"The *dump*?" she asked.

"It is the one constant in this whole confusing case."

"Are you saying it's the motive?"

"It must be. Yet a stabbing is not consistent with that motive. A stabbing is"—he drew a breath—"a passionate means of murder. A passionate murder and a cerebral motive? Or another deception? If I might have silence until we reach the dumpsite, Miss Fairchild, I must sort the pieces again."

"Really, Miss Fairchild, you should wear appropriate clothes for an outing such as this," said John Lloyd, stepping on one strand of barbed wire and holding another up.

Lydia hiked her denim skirt up to her thighs, and gingerly crawled through the fence. She stood up, wiped the sweat off her forehead, and gave a look that should have put him six feet under, but didn't. John Lloyd Branson was impervious to killing looks. "I didn't know we were going to be walking across somebody's north forty, for God's sake." She dusted her skirt. "Don't you people believe in roads?"

"Not if it means chopping up a perfectly good field." He pointed his cane into the distance. "Just another hundred yards or so, and we will be there."

"Why walk another hundred yards?" she asked, standing on one leg and emptying the dirt out of her shoe. "One yard of plowed ground looks just like another."

"But it is not, Miss Fairchild. A hundred yards away will be the center of one of the shafts. Provided the efforts of STAD are unsuccessful. Do not dawdle. Come along."

He walked off, swinging his cane, and she stared at him. How could anyone walk around wearing a black three-piece suit in ninety-plus temperature, and not even sweat. And he wasn't dusty, either, while she felt as if she'd been rolling in the dirt. Of course, she had at one point. No one had warned her that plowed ground and high heels were mutually exclusive. She'd stepped in a plowed furrow, sunk in up to her ankle, and landed on her face. She hadn't appreciated John Lloyd's grin one damn bit.

She trudged after him, heels sinking into the ground with every step. She wondered what kind of crop was planted in this particular field. It could be elephant grass for all she knew. She was a city girl, by God, used to walking on concrete, and admiring small plots of grass. She stopped and looked around. But this, this was incredible. A huge field of green shoots as far as she could see with an occasional fence-row or aerial irrigation system with its pivot arms to break the monotony. She appreciated how vast the world must seem to an ant. She felt as small as an ant standing in the middle of this land, and much more impermanent. She shook her head and walked on. The Panhandle always made her feel dwarfed. It must have something to do with being able to see the horizon on all sides.

It was late, and the western sky was beginning to streak into the bloodred and bright orange colors of another spectacular sunset as she walked toward John Lloyd's black silhouette. She stepped up beside him and settled her heels comfortably into the ground. "Are you inspired?"

He continued looking into the setting sun, the softening light mellowing his blond coloring into a pale gold. His profile might have been chiseled on an ancient coin. "Man dams up rivers to create lakes, he builds bridges and tunnels, defies gravity to fly. He has been to the moon, and photographed the galaxies, but he cannot replace one gram of this land once it is destroyed."

He scooped up a handful of soil and placed it in Lydia's palm, closing her fingers around it. "Feel its texture, Miss Fairchild. Feel its warmth, like a living being, and forget the slogans and speeches of both sides. This is what it is all about. The fertility of the earth, and whether man has the right to sterilize the womb that nourishes him.''

Lydia squeezed her fist and felt the warm, slightly damp earth. It smelled of sun, and water, and growing things. Yet incongruously, it smelled of age. As well it should, she guessed. She was holding molecules five billion years old. "How can the bastards do it, John Lloyd?" she whispered as she opened her hand and watched the dirt trickle back to the ground.

"Man has an infinite capacity for destruction, Miss Fairchild. More correctly, the question is: how can we stop them?"

"Leroy MacPhearson tried."

He shook his head. "No, but someone else did."

"Then you've definitely decided the dump is the motive?"

He poked his cane into the earth. "If it is not, then my only other solution is impossible."

Lydia opened her mouth to ask how, but a loud, threatening voice interrupted. "Stop right where you are, you sons of bitches!" A black pickup roared across the field, bouncing over the furrows like a ship over waves. A long, narrow object jutted out of the driver's window.

Lydia screamed and jumped for John Lloyd, leaving both shoes securely stuck in the ground. She landed against his chest and wrapped her arms around him. "Oh, God, don't let him shoot me." She'd been shot earlier in the summer during one of John Lloyd's cases, and the very thought of it happening again made the fresh scars on her arm and side burn.

John Lloyd hesitated, then put an arm around her. He raised the other one and hailed the pickup. "Elizabeth, don't shoot. It's John Lloyd."

Lydia jerked her head out from John Lloyd's shoulder. "Elizabeth?"

The black pickup swerved at the last minute, spinning its wheels in the loose soil and showering the back of Lydia's skirt. Elizabeth Thornton climbed out of the cab, a rifle cradled in the crook of her arm. "You don't know how close you came to getting your butt shot off, John Lloyd. Don't you know better than to wear a suit on the dumpsite? Some other farmer might have figured you were DOE, shot first, and worried about it later. The only reason I didn't was because you had her with you." Elizabeth gestured at Lydia with the gun barrel. "Nobody in the local office looks like her."

Lydia let go of John Lloyd and turned around. "My name is Lydia, not *her*, and you may call me Miss Fairchild. What right do you have running around with a gun anyway?"

Elizabeth Thornton studied Lydia for a moment. "The best right, Miss Fairchild. This is my land, and I don't like trespassers." There was a slight emphasis on that word, and a pointed look at Lydia. "Particularly ones in suits."

Lydia had the oddest feeling that she was a trespasser, but not on the land. Tough, she thought. John Lloyd wasn't posted. "Why?" she demanded.

"Because anybody in a suit walking across this field is probably a DOE man, and I hate those vultures. You know what a vulture is, don't you?"

"A scavenger."

"That's right. They feed on dying and dead animals. You see them a lot on the highways eating roadkill. Well, the DOE is a lot like those vultures. They think that the announcement that we're a first-round dumpsite killed opposition like a truck running over a skunk; so they've been perching in their offices in Hereford and Vega waiting to feed on us. But we're not dead yet, and I don't intend to let them run over me. DOE will have to carry me off my land, and I'll go kicking and screaming the whole way."

"You're going to fight for your land, then?" asked Lydia.

"It's my land and my son's land now, but in two hundred years, I'll just be a name on a tombstone or on some dusty record book in the courthouse, and somebody else may own it.''

She grabbed a fistful of earth. ''I want to save it so two hundred years from now it'll be growing wheat and corn and barley and sugar beets to feed some bastard who grew up on concrete and skyscrapers and couldn't raise an acre of food if he had to.'' She looked at Lydia again.

Lydia swallowed and looked down at the tiny green stalks at her feet. She was one of those who had been raised on the sight and feel of concrete and skyscrapers. She'd never produced an ounce of food for her own consumption or anybody else's. Food came wrapped in cellophane or packaged in cardboard. Maybe that was why Elizabeth Thornton always intimidated her so badly. Elizabeth produced and Lydia Fairchild merely consumed.

She looked up, caught John Lloyd and Elizabeth exchanging glances, and looked down again, feeling as if she were not only trespassing, but also eavesdropping. She tried to step away, but John Lloyd's fingers dug into her shoulders, holding her motionless. ''Some people fit into both worlds, Elizabeth, but like Miss Fairchild, they need time to acclimate.''

''You're transplanting her?''

''She is taking root nicely.''

''Just a damn minute,'' shouted Lydia. ''I'm not a hothouse rose, and I don't like being talked about in the third person.''

Elizabeth tilted her head back and laughed, her chestnut hair swinging freely down her back. She sobered and faced John Lloyd. ''All right, I'm not dense. I can see the lay of the land. I just hope you don't get your finger stuck on her thorns.''

She finally pointed her rifle toward the ground, and Lydia let out a trembling breath. ''So what are you doing out here?'' asked the dark-haired woman.

"Showing Miss Fairchild the dumpsite and waiting for you."

"Waiting for me?" asked Elizabeth.

"Waiting for her?" echoed Lydia with a startled look at John Lloyd. "That's not what you told me."

Elizabeth laughed again, and Lydia wished she knew what the woman thought was so damn funny. "He'll never tell you everything, Lydia, and if there are two ways of doing something, he'll find a third just to be obstinate." She turned to the attorney. "So how did you know I'd come, and what do you want?"

"The road passes your house and dead-ends in this field. I knew you would investigate. As for what I want, it should be obvious. I wish to discuss your rather ridiculous statement outside the presence of your boarder." His voice had sharpened from its usual drawl to a hard, precise tone that sliced. "Your feelings for Frances do not include giving her coffee to sober her up, nor do I for a minute believe she would drink it. Your statements were very clever, just different enough to be believable to someone like Sergeant Schroder who does not know you. I, however, do know you. I want the truth, Elizabeth."

Elizabeth's mouth twisted in a wry gesture. "I told Hap you wouldn't fall for the coffee story, but we didn't have much time to concoct a different one, just since your little meeting yesterday morning when you said the police would question us. And Hap did make coffee, but Frances didn't stay long enough to drink it."

"You are trying to protect Rachel?"

"If the victim had been anybody but a DOE man, I'd have let Rachel, Frances, and even Leroy sink or swim. But we couldn't have STAD involved in a messy scandal over some silly teenager."

"But DOE would've come out on the worse end having an employee who was involved with a young girl," objected

Lydia, watching John Lloyd watch Elizabeth and trying to decide if he still had the hots for her.

Elizabeth cocked her head. "Would they? I doubt it. They get immediate media attention. By the time Rory Tinsdale finished with STAD, we'd all look like a bunch of hillbillies grabbing for a gun the first time some outsider looked at one of our womenfolk. Frances's alcoholism would have come out. Just imagine what kind of an image she would give us. We'd all look like the dumb hicks the DOE would like the rest of the country to think we are." She shook her head. "It's better for everyone to believe Leroy killed Price-Leigh over the dump. Everybody with a grudge against the government will understand that motive. It's not the best option, but it's the only one we have."

"Then you don't believe the dump was the motive?" asked Lydia.

Elizabeth gave her a disgusted look. "Of course not. Leroy's smart. He knows killing off DOE employees is not the solution."

"He is also too smart to kill over an eighteen-year-old girl," said John Lloyd. "She is of legal age. He would be seen as an interfering grandparent, not as a protector of family honor, and he is smart enough to know that, too. Obviously you believe Frances is the guilty one, so tell me your story again."

Elizabeth gave him an incredulous look. "Frances! Are you out of your mind? I know for a fact she's innocent. She's got an unbeatable alibi."

"A husband's testimony is dubious at best, Elizabeth," said John Lloyd.

"Yeah, but a cop's is great, isn't it?"

"A cop?" said Lydia.

Elizabeth nodded. "Hap didn't want to use that alibi because again it would call attention to Rachel and to Frances's alcoholism." She sighed. "I guess I'd better tell you the whole story. Frances dropped off Rachel about nine-thirty.

Kicked her out would be more accurate, I guess. She wasn't here any longer than to blurt out some drunken story about Rachel and Price-Leigh, and to call Leroy. She did call him that night, but she used my phone so it showed up on my phone bill, not hers. Then she went roaring back to town. Willis called about a quarter to eleven looking for her. She wasn't here, of course, so I told him to sit tight. When the bars closed, she would be home. As it turns out, he didn't have to wait that long. Frances rammed into Tinsdale's car about eleven-thirty. A county deputy got the call, ticketed Frances for drunken driving, called Willis, and got a wrecker for Tinsdale's fancy car. Willis hushed the whole thing as best he could, and Tinsdale helped him. I still can't understand that.''

John Lloyd's face was white and still. "And Schroder does not know about it because the county sheriff's office handled it, and our sergeant has been dealing with the city police.''

"But that means Tinsdale is innocent, John Lloyd,'' said Lydia.

John Lloyd's face stiffened even more. "Only of murder, Miss Fairchild.''

CHAPTER
SEVENTEEN

JENNER YAWNED, RUBBED HIS HAND OVER HIS FACE, NOTICing several patches of whiskers he missed shaving, and gingerly felt the pouches under his eyes. Damn it all, he was only thirty-two. He was too young to have bags under his eyes. That was for men Schroder's age. He glanced across the table at Schroder and blinked at the unfairness of life. The overweight investigator didn't have bags under his eyes, and the son of a bitch didn't look tired either. How in the hell could anyone stay up until four o'clock in the morning, get up four hours later, work, then drive to Canadian and back to Amarillo and the Special Crimes building and not look tired? A robot, that's who. Schroder was a fucking robot.

The sergeant looked mad, though, and his forehead was creased into a landscape of hills and gullies. Did robots look mad, or just mean? Jenner glanced at Maximum Miller, who sat next to Schroder. Miller definitely looked pissed, but then that was to be expected. Schroder had called him out in the middle of the Cowboys' exhibition game.

"So what the hell's this missing data got to do with the price of peas, Schroder?" demanded Miller, popping open a can of Coca-Cola. "Are you telling me it's the motive? If it exists, that is. You don't even seem too sure of that."

Schroder wiped his face with a grimy handkerchief. It wasn't dirty, thought Jenner. It was just gray like everything else the investigator owned. Probably smoke damage from his cigarettes.

"A correlation turned up that might prove the data exists."

"Might prove? What are you talking about, Schroder? I don't want to hear any *might prove*s. They don't go over worth a shit with the judge. Cases get reversed on *might prove*s. We don't *might prove*. We fucking well prove, period. No ifs, ands, or buts."

Miller crushed his Coke can, which was a mistake since it was still full of liquid. The soft drink spewed over the black assistant, Schroder, and the stack of Mrs. Dinwittie's carefully typed statements. "Shit!" he yelled as he and Schroder dived for the statements and began blotting them on whatever was handy, primarily Miller's white T-shirt. Jenner crossed his legs and enjoyed the sight, or what he could see of it since his eyes were so puffy from lack of sleep, they were nearly swollen shut.

Miller slapped a sheet of paper against his chest, letting his shirt absorb the droplets of soft drink. He slammed it down on a dry spot and picked up another. All the while he was breathing harder. "Would you like to tell me what the hell your *might prove* is, Schroder, before I really lose my temper."

Schroder mopped a statement dry with his handkerchief, now damp with brown splotches of Coke. "Remember I told you the break-in at the drilling company looked like a professional job, no fingerprints, and so on?"

"You only told me about it five minutes ago, Schroder. You think I'm losing my hearing, or maybe my memory?"

"No, I just wanted to make a point of the fingerprints because it ties in to the murder."

"How, since there weren't any fingerprints at the break-in?"

Schroder laid the last statement down, and tucked his handkerchief back in his pocket. He lit a cigarette and flipped the top on his Zippo lighter several times. Finally, he took a deep breath. "There ain't any at the murder scene either."

Miller opened and closed his mouth several times before he found his voice. "What?" he yelled.

Jenner scooted down further in his chair to make himself a smaller target. The way the assistant D.A. looked, he was going to turn on his deep fat fryer and start cooking Schroder's balls. Jenner wanted to keep his intact.

Schroder whipped out his handkerchief and wiped his face again. Jenner was amused to see he was sweating. "I said that there weren't any fingerprints at the crime scene. Oh, there were, but they don't count. We found Tinsdale's in the shower and the back door. And Jenner's on the toilet seat . . ."

"Don't you know not to take a crap at a murder scene, Sergeant?" asked Miller.

"I wasn't," protested Jenner.

". . . and a bunch of Price-Leigh's on his books, on the backs of pictures, and on the inside of one shoe. Nothing else. Not one goddamn thing. The cabinets in the kitchen had been completely cleaned out and the dishes, pots and pans, utensils, even the canned goods had been put through the dishwasher. I've never seen anything like it. No crippled-up old man could've wiped that house down like that, not in the length of time he had. Remember we had him in jail from Saturday until Branson bailed him out late Thursday, and we were working the scene two days later. He would've missed some places anyway. I tell you, Cleetus, that house was wiped by a pro. Just like the break-in.''

''So what are you saying, Schroder?'' asked Miller, leaning back in his chair and looking as worried as the investigator.

''The same person who wiped the house broke into the drilling company.''

''Coincidence?'' suggested Miller, then waved his own comment away. ''Don't bother answering that. I don't believe it either. So what's your conclusion, Sergeant?''

''Maybe that data exists, and maybe our pro was looking for it in both places.''

''Either you're saying that MacPhearson's our pro, and we agreed he isn't, or you're saying we've got two different people in that murder house, one croaking the victim and hauling off the body, and the other looking for data and cleaning up afterward.''

''I think we got two different people, and maybe the data's the motive.''

''You're talking out of the other side of your mouth, Schroder,'' said Jenner, sitting up now that it appeared he was out of danger. ''You were telling John Lloyd he was full of shit when he suggested the same thing.''

Miller turned his bloodshot eyes on Jenner. ''You mean Branson suggested his client had help?''

Schroder glared at Jenner and the younger man scooted down in his chair again. ''Branson had some kind of theory that the data was the motive, and that Tinsdale had more to gain by killing Price-Leigh than MacPhearson did.''

Miller started chuckling until the chuckles turned into guffaws of laughter. Finally, he stopped and wiped his tearing eyes on his sleeve. ''Now I know Branson's desperate. Suggesting Tinsdale as a murderer? Jesus Christ, Tinsdale is a total dipshit. He'd never figure out how to clean up fingerprints.''

''With ammonia,'' said Jenner suddenly. He looked at the

two other men. "I smelled ammonia in the kitchen. It had to be a pro, Schroder. He knew enough to wipe down walls and woodwork with ammonia to cut the oils that make fingerprints. If I told the ordinary person to clean off fingerprints, he'd grab a cloth and start polishing. You've got to take it slow and easy to get all the prints that way. You'll smear them, sure, but not absolutely erase all trace of body oil. Whoever cleaned Price-Leigh's house was really clever."

"So who is it, Jenner?" asked the assistant D.A. "Come on," he cajoled when Jenner hesitated. "You've convinced me we really are dealing with somebody besides Farmer MacPhearson, so give me your best guess."

"Everybody's got alibis," began Jenner.

"Including Tinsdale," interrupted Schroder. "A real dilly of one. He and Mrs. Frances Whitley had a fender bender between eleven and eleven-thirty that kept them both tied up until after one."

"Why'd Tinsdale lie?" asked Jenner.

"He didn't want us to know where he was," replied Schroder.

"Where was he?" asked Miller.

"At Price-Leigh's, but according to the autopsy, the victim was still alive until about twelve-thirty, maybe a little later. Anyway, twelve-thirty's the earliest he could have died. So Tinsdale and the Whitleys have alibis independent of one another. Mrs. Thornton, Hap, and the Whitley girl alibi one another."

"You're leading up to something, Schroder," said Miller. "Out with it. My afternoon's already been spoiled. A little more bad news isn't going to make it any worse."

Schroder cleared his throat. "The way I see it, Cleetus, if Branson proves MacPhearson didn't do it, then nobody did it."

"Would you like to run that by again," said Maximum Miller ominously.

"I said, if MacPhearson didn't stab Price-Leigh, then nobody did. We got nothing. We got no fingerprints, no fibers, no eyewitnesses.''

"We got Ms. Silliphant," said Jenner, rubbing his leg.

"Sure, and she says she saw MacPhearson's pickup. If Branson comes up with something better, then we've got an unsolved case on the books.''

"We're not having an unsolved case on the books because *MacPhearson did it*! I don't care if he hired Al Capone to wash down the walls in that house, he's still the one who hauled off the body. Maybe we can't get a murder conviction on him because we can't prove what went on while the two of them were in that bedroom, but we'll damn sure get him on voluntary manslaughter. Charlton Price-Leigh was alive at about eleven o'clock or thereabouts because Ms. Silliphant talked to him. At twelve-thirty or a little after, Leroy MacPhearson's pickup backs into the garage and hauls off the body. How would MacPhearson know he had a body to carry off if he hadn't already been inside that house at the time the pathologist believes is the most likely time for Price-Leigh to have died?'' He looked at each one of them. "Either one of you sad sacks got an answer to that one?''

"Sir?"

Miller grimaced. "I might have known it would be the younger Hardy boy. What do you have to say?''

"Maybe it was the pro who killed him, and MacPhearson just happened on the scene.''

"Then how come MacPhearson's still alive?'' asked Miller, pointing his finger at Jenner. He changed directions and pointed at Schroder. "You thought of that, Sergeant? If MacPhearson saw the pro off Price-Leigh, then Mac-Phearson ought to be dead. A pro, a real honest-to-God professional killer, doesn't leave witnesses. And if MacPhearson killed him, why is the pro covering up? You ever think of that?''

"The pro came later looking for the data, and saw there'd been a murder, so he wiped the house down.'' Jenner's voice trailed off as he realized how ridiculous he sounded. ''Never mind. The pro wouldn't have any reason to do that. He wouldn't leave any prints, so why worry about somebody else.''

Miller drank the rest of his Coke out of the crushed can. ''You got it, boy. So if we eliminate all your *might proves*, Schroder, what we end up with is what we started with. Leroy MacPhearson murdered Charlton Price-Leigh and dumped his body in a wheat field. Everything else is bullshit.''

CHAPTER
EIGHTEEN

LYDIA LAID HER BRIEFCASE ON THE COUNSEL TABLE, IF THE laminated walnut-colored creation could be called a table. Actually, it was more a modified desk. But in a courtroom they were called counsel tables even when they looked like desks.

She smoothed her hair, eased her feet out of her shoes under the cover of the table/desk, and looked around the courtroom. Evidently the interior decorator of the new County Courts Building decided wood was out of style. The only wood in the entire courtroom was the railing, or bar, that separated the officers of the court from the spectators, and the one that separated the jury from the rest of the world. If the interior decorator disliked wood, the architect disliked straight lines with an equal vengeance. There was one ordinary wall at the back of the courtroom. Every other wall was series of fabric-covered curved panels. As far as she could tell, the only lines that met in a ninety-degree angle were the doorways. She wasn't sure if she was in a courtroom or on a set for some science-fiction movie.

She looked across at the prosecutor's table to see Maximum Miller drinking coffee and visiting with the bailiff, a slim brunette with a .38 unobtrusively strapped around her waist. Straight ahead and to the right of the witness stand, the court reporter was setting up her equipment, which these days included a tape recorder in addition to a steno machine. Behind her were the seats for the spectators, and she noticed that they were playing to a full gallery. She recognized the reporter from the newspaper, as well as all the regional TV anchormen and their cameramen or -women. The witnesses were waiting to be sworn in by wholesale lot and sent to the witness room. Only in the movies did witnesses sit in the courtroom listening to one another's testimony. In reality, no prosecutor or defense attorney would allow that.

"What are you going to ask the MacPhearson bunch and Hap?" she asked, nudging John Lloyd.

He cocked an eyebrow. "Nothing."

"Nothing? Then why did you subpoena them as witnesses?"

"To prevent Mr. Miller from doing so."

"Why?"

"My dear Miss Fairchild, if I ask them nothing, then Miller will be unable to cross-examine them. While I do not believe they will damage our case, I do not want them confusing the issue. I shall explain the extraneous details of the murder at another time."

"When?" she asked.

He sighed. "When I have the answer to two questions. Now please be quiet so I may think."

She glanced at John Lloyd. He was looking more like a gambler than an undertaker today. Must be the turquoise bolero he wore in place of his usual string tie. Or the off-white silk vest embroidered with tiny rosebuds.

On the other side of John Lloyd sat Leroy MacPhearson,

obviously uncomfortable in a suit and without his gimme hat. His hair was parted on the side and slicked down with hair oil.

She opened her briefcase to take out her yellow legal pad. Maybe John Lloyd could remember every word of testimony without taking notes, but she couldn't. A strong odor that immediately evoked images of brothels and unwashed bodies rose from the briefcase. She could hear conversation die behind her as a sniffing sound from forty noses took its place. Maximum Miller stopped in midsentence and turned his head toward Lydia. He raised his head and wrinkled his nose in one large inhalation. He coughed and waved a hand in the air.

"Miss Fairchild," hissed John Lloyd, his long aristocratic nose quivering. "Have you changed perfumes, or do you have a spoiled cheese sandwich in there?"

Lydia peered in the briefcase and wondered if it was even hers until she saw the corner of a purple envelope sticking out from under a brown mailing bag. "It's the mail," she hissed back at John Lloyd. "I forgot about it. And the stink, for your information, is coming from your private correspondence, the infamous purple letter. Would you like to read it now? I can't promise it won't ferment if not read immediately."

Spectators and witnesses were beginning to crane their necks to see inside the briefcase, and John Lloyd glared at her, "No, I will not read it, and please close that briefcase. You will get us cited for contempt of court for that ungodly smell. The judge will suspect us of some nefarious scheme, like asphyxiation."

She grabbed her legal pad and slammed the briefcase lid. "Don't get on my case, Mr. Branson. I don't know anybody sleazy enough to wear something that smells like sweaty socks doused in Evening in Paris."

Before he had a chance to answer, the bailiff announced the judge's arrival and everyone stood. Judge Abraham Delaney, the son of a Jewish mother and an Irish father and with the humor of neither, waved them to their seats. "Be seated. Officers of the court may smoke. Witnesses come forward to be sworn."

The witnesses filed between the two counsel tables to form a line in front of the judge's bench. Schroder gave an experimental sniff as he walked by. Frances Whitley was green and twitchy, but Lydia put it down to lack of a bottle rather than the perfumed letter. Frances's sense of smell had probably been pickled years ago. Tinsdale walked by, a handkerchief against his nose. Lydia opened the briefcase and grinned as he stared at it and gagged, and joined the other witnesses.

"Do you swear the testimony you are about to give is the truth, the whole truth, and nothing but the truth, so help you God!" intoned Judge Delaney, glaring at each of the witnesses. Lydia watched as each nodded solemnly. She imagined a witness would rather be caught in a lie by God than by Judge Delaney.

"Off to the witness room, or wherever you want to wait so long as we can find you. My temper wears thin when I have to wait on a witness."

Lighting a cigarette, he leaned over the bench to peer at John Lloyd and Cleetus Miller over the top of his Ben Franklin glasses. "Gentlemen, approach the bench, please. Lillian, this goes on the record." His court reporter pushed the record button on her tape recorder, then sat with fingers poised over her steno machine, an expectant look on her face.

John Lloyd sighed. "Come along, Miss Fairchild," he said, pulling out her chair.

Lydia rose and smoothed her skirt. "What's he want?" she whispered.

"To warn us not to hit below the belt."

"Who is this young lady?" demanded the judge, giving Lydia a quick once-over that left her feeling as if she'd been sorted, labeled, and stored.

"My legal clerk and partner, Miss Lydia Fairchild," replied John Lloyd, lightly touching her arm.

Another quick look from the judge. "Is this true, young lady?"

"Yes, Your Honor," said Lydia. Actually it wasn't. John Lloyd had left the impression that she'd already been admitted to the bar without actually saying so.

Judge Delaney gave a brusque nod of his head. "I hope you are a woman of strong character." He concentrated his pale blue eyes on the two attorneys. "Gentleman, we meet again, and I wish to set the ground rules. We will not have a rematch of the last encounter between you two. My bailiff took early retirement as a result of that trial. Mr. Miller, we have a brand-new jury railing to replace the one in which you buried the murder weapon. Maintenance was able to get the ax out without splitting the wood. We shall not have a repeat of any such action. Mr. Branson, you will not verbally incite Mr. Miller to violence, nor will you indulge in any graphic descriptions of the murder scene. The female juror who fainted during your last trial, fell out of her chair, and suffered a broken leg as a result of your dramatic gifts has been persuaded not to sue the judicial district. She may, however, sue you."

He frowned at each of them, and shook his finger. "There is no jury to impress today. This is an examining trial, and I am the only one you must convince. I am immune to histrionics. In fact, they irritate my ulcer, so don't bother with your usual antics. Do I make myself clear, gentlemen?"

"Perfectly clear, Your Honor, and I am sure my opposite number, Mr. Miller, will present his case in as clear and straightforward a manner as I myself intend to do," said John Lloyd.

"Speak for yourself, Branson," said Miller out of the side of his mouth.

"What did you say, Mr. Miller?" asked the judge, tilting his head toward the prosecutor.

"I said, yes, Your Honor," answered Miller, an innocent expression on his face.

The judge's eyes swiveled between the two lawyers until Lydia thought they would drop out of his head like marbles. Apparently satisfied, Delaney waved them back to their seats. "Mr. Miller, do you have an opening statement?"

"Yes, Your Honor, I do." Miller took up a stance between the bench and the defense table. "The State intends to prove that at about twelve-thirty on the morning of August 26, this year, Leroy MacPhearson did stab to death Charlton Price-Leigh and dispose of the body in a wheat field on his property."

"On the victim's property?" asked the judge.

"No, Your Honor, the defendant's property." Maximum Miller pinched the bridge of his nose. To avoid pinching the judge, guessed Lydia.

The judge made a note, then looked over his glasses at Miller. "Go on," he said testily.

"That's all of my statement."

"At least it's short," said the judge. "That's a change for the better. Mr. Branson, your statement?"

John Lloyd stood up. "We intend to prove Leroy Mac-Phearson did nothing of the kind." He sat down and folded his hands.

Judge Delaney blinked. "Anything else?"

John Lloyd shook his head.

The judge leaned over the bench. "Mr. Branson, while I appreciate your unusual brevity, a headshake can't be recorded on tape."

"Defense has nothing further to say because anything else would be superfluous."

"Yes, well, all right." Judge Delaney sniffed, looked startled, and sniffed again. He motioned his bailiff. "Call maintenance. Tell them something died in the air duct, or between one of these cockeyed walls, and to find it and get rid of it." Lydia surreptitiously set her briefcase on the floor, while several of the spectators snickered. The judge glared at them. "If the gallery finds it too difficult to control themselves, I shall find a means to do it for them." He sniffed again, coughed, and spoke. "Call your first witness, Mr. Miller."

"Dr. Patrick T. MacElvoy."

The bailiff repeated the name, and a small, square red-headed man slipped through the side door. The pathologist sat down and pushed his bifocals back up his nose. Maximum Miller rose, opened his mouth, and was interrupted.

"Defense will stipulate that Dr. MacElvoy is qualified as an expert witness." John Lloyd spoke without rising, his long legs stretched out as far as possible under the desk.

Maximum Miller slapped his legal pad down on the desk, then picked it up again, and flipped to another page. A custodian entered from a side door carrying a long ladder. "Dr. MacElvoy, did you perform an autopsy on August 26 of this year?"

The pathologist crossed his legs and shifted closer to the microphone. "I did three that day. Which one did you want to talk about? I've got two more subpoenas for court appearances today, both on murders. It was a hot summer, you know. Lots of folks forget to check their guns at the door when they stopped to have a beer."

Maximum Miller gripped his legal pad. "Specifically, the autopsy on a white male of between thirty-five and forty years of age. The stabbing victim," he added hopefully.

MacElvoy rubbed his head. "That one, a John Doe later identified as a Charlton Price-Leigh. Interesting case."

"Yes, it is," said Maximum Miller quickly.

Lydia felt sorry for the prosecutor. There was no way around the medical evidence of the two stab wounds several hours apart. It was just a matter of Miller biting the bullet and letting it come out. She doodled on her legal pad while the prosecutor asked every conceivable question except about the stab wounds. The custodian in the meantime had set his ladder up in the middle of the courtroom and was sniffing the air duct. He took a break to peer down at the autopsy photographs as Miller introduced them, gagged, and went back to sniffing the air duct.

Finally Miller asked the question. "Dr. MacElvoy, what did you determine was the manner and mechanism of death?"

"The victim died of hypovolemic shock and cardiac arrest from a stab wound to the heart."

"Did you determine the cause of death to be homicide, Dr. MacElvoy?"

"Objection," said John Lloyd. "Calls for a conclusion on the part of the witness."

"Oh, for Christ's sake, Branson. The victim was found nude in the field. What else could it be?" demanded Miller before the judge could get his cigarette out of his mouth.

"He could have been a nudist performing a ritual and fell on a knife. You have not proved homicide. You have proved nothing except the doctor performed an autopsy."

"Gentlemen! That's enough! Objection is sustained."

Miller slapped his legal pad against his leg like a riding crop. "Your witness, Mr. Branson."

John Lloyd rose to feet. "How many wounds to the heart did you find, Dr. MacElvoy?"

"Two." MacElvoy glanced apologetically at Miller. The question was going to come and there was nothing the pathologist could do to stop it.

"Were both fatal?"

"He might have lived a few minutes from the first wound, perhaps three or four. There are many cases on the books of that happening. The second wound would have killed him except he'd already been dead several hours before the second wound was administered." There was a buzz from the spectators and the custodian stopped sniffing to stare at the pathologist.

"Somebody stabbed a dead body?" asked Judge Delaney.

The pathologist rubbed his head again. "Yes, Your Honor."

"Was the knife found in the body the weapon that killed him?" asked John Lloyd.

"No. It was much larger, and had a slightly different angle of entry, actually bisecting the path of the original weapon. The larger knife was pushed straight in while the first wound took a downward angle."

"Were there any other wounds on the body?" asked John Lloyd.

"The victim had a dislocated toe."

"That will be all, Dr, MacElvoy," said John Lloyd as he sat down.

Miller signaled he had no more questions, and the judge dismissed the pathologist, who left the courtroom at a run. Judge Delaney folded his hands and glared at the custodian. "You have been smelling that air duct for a good thirty minutes. My conclusion is that there is nothing dead in that vent, or you would have toppled off that ladder in a faint twenty-nine minutes ago. Do you suppose you could move on to the walls?"

"I guess so," said the man, and folded his ladder. He then climbed into the jury box and began a systematic sniff test of its back wall.

Judge Delaney rolled his eyes toward the ceiling as if asking for divine guidance. There was a sound of almost inaudible muttering coming from the bench for a few moments. Finally he drew a deep breath. "Next witness, Mr. Miller."

"I call Sergeant Larry Jenner."

Lydia smiled at Jenner as he passed, then settled back to listen. Jenner recounted his finding the body, calling Special Crimes, and arresting Leroy MacPhearson. It was not much different from his incident report, and Lydia drew pictures of the custodian on her yellow pad. She did the same during Schroder's testimony, lifting her head only at Judge Delaney's various outbursts at the custodian. John Lloyd made a few halfhearted objections, but seemed more intent on the mathematical formulas he was writing on a small memo pad.

She jabbed him when the list of landowners was introduced into evidence. "Aren't you going to object?" she whispered.

He cocked an eyebrow. "Certainly not. Even if Cleetus had improperly introduced it, which he did not, I still would not object. That list and their eyewitness will free my client."

"Your witness, Mr. Branson," said Miller, a falsely casual note in his voice.

John Lloyd's eyes had a speculative expression as he gazed at the prosecutor. Finally, he rose. "Did you find any fingerprints at the murder scene, Sergeant Schroder?"

Miller was on his feet. "Objection. Not proper cross-examination. Fingerprints were not discussed during direct."

John Lloyd smiled. "You did discuss Special Crimes' investigation of the crime scene. Ordinarily"—he stressed the word—"that includes the taking of latent fingerprints. Your Honor, defense contends that since the State introduced the investigatory procedure, the subject of fingerprints is proper cross-examination."

The judge glanced at Miller, who was sitting at his table, his face buried in his hands. "Since I hear no cases cited from the State, I will overrule that objection."

Schroder cleared his throat and looked John Lloyd in the face. "There were no prints in that house except on a few books, the backs of pictures, and the inside of a shoe."

John Lloyd tilted his head. "Interesting, don't you think, Sergeant? No further questions."

"I have a few, Sergeant," said the judge, his brows drawn so far down they threatened to cover his eyes. He took a deep breath, coughed, and rounded on the custodian who was lounging in the jury box taking a gentle inhalation occasionally and listening to the testimony. "If you want to continue working for Potter County, you'd better find where that odor is coming from."

He glared at the spectators, several of whom Lydia noticed were red-faced and snickering. "If I discover anyone in this courtroom is the source of that odor, I shall see to it that they have the opportunity to do a close-up study of whether the Potter County facility meets state jail standards!"

"Get rid of that briefcase, Miss Fairchild," said John Lloyd. "Lock it in the car"—he corrected himself—"the trunk, preferably, throw it away, or otherwise dispose of it. You would not enjoy the Potter County jail. The decor is very depressing."

"What about your letter?"

"I will read it later," he said, his voice coming between clenched teeth. "Get it out of here."

"All right, don't get nasty about it," she said, opening the case and transferring all the mail except the purple letter and a spare legal pad to her large shoulder bag.

"When one carries a purse the size of a carpetbag, I fail to see the necessity for a briefcase," he said, leaning over to pat her shoulder, then making arm signals in the air.

Judge Delaney stopped in mid-tirade. "What is it, Mr. Branson? Do you have a cramp in your arm?"

John Lloyd inclined his head. "No, Your Honor. I was merely giving Miss Fairchild directions to the . . ."—he hesitated, a perfect picture of embarrassed masculinity— "ladies' room."

"It's down the hall and to your right, Miss Fairchild," said the judge, smiling at her while Lydia felt herself blush all the way down to her toes.

"Thank you," she mumbled, picked up the briefcase, gave John Lloyd her best killing look—which he ignored—and stumbled out of the double doors at the back of the courtroom.

"That absolute bastard," she muttered as she walked down the hall, took a right through a curving hall, and turned left to the elevator. "When I get back, I'm going to spill coffee on his trousers right where it will do the most good. Or maybe I'll do something more direct, like hitting him over his thick skull.''

The elevator opened and she stepped forward. When she felt the blow, she had a split second to hope that she, too, had a thick skull.

CHAPTER
NINETEEN

"HOW COME BRANSON'S NOT ASKING QUESTIONS?" JENNER asked Schroder as the investigator sat down.

Schroder looked across the spectators' heads at the defense table. "Bastard's got something up his sleeve besides an arm."

"Like what?"

"How the hell do I know?"

John Lloyd stood up. "Objection, Your Honor," he said, and Jenner couldn't figure out why. There wasn't any witness in the box, and none had been called.

The judge evidently couldn't figure it out either because he kept looking from the witness box to Branson and back again. "What are you objecting to, Mr. Branson?"

"I do not wish to excuse Sergeant Schroder, Your Honor. I will recall him when defense presents its case."

Delaney peered over his glasses at the spectators. "Sergeant Schroder, you heard Mr. Branson. Find another seat outside the courtroom."

Schroder stood up and began tucking his shirt back in. "Yes, Your Honor."

Jenner got up, too, and stretched elaborately. "I'd like to stay and listen, maybe find out what Branson's going to do before I head back to the police station. But if I don't get back to work, the Chief'll assign my patrol car to somebody else. Be seeing you, Schroder." He started to edge past the investigator, and ran into a thick arm barring his way. "Excuse me," he said politely.

Schroder looked at him, and pointed to the seat Jenner had just vacated. "Sit down. You ain't going anywhere."

"The judge excused me."

"I haven't," said Schroder. "This case isn't over until the fat lady sings. Or in this case, until the skinny lawyer sings. We might be out looking for another suspect before the sun goes down, so you just plant your butt back in that seat until *I* tell you you're excused."

"Just a goddamn minute, Schroder," said Jenner. "You're not my boss."

Schroder pushed him down. "You want to bet? Ask the Chief."

The investigator looked so smug, like a bear who had his own private honeybee hive, that Jenner knew instinctively that the Chief had sold him, Sergeant Larry Jenner, traffic cop extraordinaire, to Schroder for the duration. He broke out in a sweat. If Branson got the charges against Leroy MacPhearson dismissed, the duration might be one hell of a long time.

"That's better," said Schroder as the younger man propped his elbows on the arms of his seat, and stared straight ahead. "Now you just sit here and listen, maybe learn something." He grinned and walked out of the courtroom.

Jenner felt his belly start to bubble again. An ulcer! That damn Schroder was giving him an ulcer, all over a case that was justifiable homicide if he ever saw one. He hoped Branson won because—he thought a minute—because he still didn't think the old guy did it. On the other hand, if Leroy *didn't* do it, he didn't want to have to hang around with Schroder until they found who did. He wished grown men were allowed to cry because he damn sure would.

"Call Rory Tinsdale," said Maximum Miller, standing and looking toward the double doors at the back of the courtroom. The bailiff walked to the doors, and repeated Tinsdale's name.

Jenner twisted around to watch for the DOE man. Tinsdale had been such a pest in the witness room that Elizabeth Thornton had told him to take himself somewhere else to wait. Jenner snickered to himself. Actually, she told him she'd kick him in the balls just to prove he didn't have any, and if he didn't want the truth known, he'd better get out of the witness room. Tinsdale had waited in lonely splendor in the hall outside the courtroom ever since.

Tinsdale pushed open the doors and hurried down the aisle to the witness chair. Sitting down, he straightened his tie, checked his cuffs, and crossed his legs. Jenner thought he looked like what he was: a prissy bureaucrat.

Judge Delaney looked at Tinsdale as if he were some rare species of imported cockroach, a species that needed exporting back to the point of origin. "Mr. Tinsdale, if you'll save your primping for another time, we'll get on with this trial. Mr. Miller, if you're ready."

"I am, Your Honor, but I thought I'd wait until Mr. Tinsdale checked his fly. It seems to be the only thing he missed." There were chuckles from the spectators.

"I don't have to listen to this abuse," said Tinsdale, unconsciously checking his fly.

"Of course, you don't," agreed the judge. He waggled a finger at the prosecutor. "Now, now, Mr. Miller, you mustn't be ugly to your witness."

"Yes, Your Honor, I'll remember that. Now Mr. Tinsdale, can you identify what has been marked State's Exhibits

23a and 23b?'' Miller held up the map with the containment area marked in blue, and the list of landowners.

Jenner tuned out the rest of Tinsdale's testimony. It was just a rehash of the statement he and Schroder had taken, except in polite courtroom language. He watched John Lloyd Branson instead. Not that there was any action going on there, either. Branson was sitting like a bump on a log doodling on a memo pad. Jenner wondered where the attorney's yellow legal pad was. He thought lawyers couldn't make it through the pearly gates without a yellow legal pad, much less a trial. He also wondered why the hell Branson wasn't making any objections. Strange behavior for a defense attorney.

"Mr. Tinsdale, was Mr. MacPhearson upset when he received a letter from Charlton Price-Leigh that his property was in the containment area and would be confiscated by the government?'' asked Maximum Miller.

"Purchased, not confiscated,'' said Tinsdale.

Miller rubbed his chin. "Purchased means that both buyer and seller have a choice, but it is my understanding that Mr. MacPhearson and the other landowners don't. Is that true?''

"The Department of Energy is obligated to pay a fair price,'' replied Tinsdale, beginning to squirm.

"But Mr. MacPhearson doesn't have a choice about whether to sell, does he? He can take your so-called fair price or the DOE will force him off the land?''

Tinsdale nervously pushed his glasses back up his nose. "The DOE can use the law of eminent domain if necessary.''

"Was Mr. MacPhearson upset when he discovered he was going to be forced to sell his land?'' Jenner noticed Judge Delaney examining Tinsdale. The judge looked as if he wished he had a can of bug spray.

"Yes. He told Price-Leigh that he would never live long enough to get his land.''

Jenner waited for Branson to object to that bit of testimony as hearsay, which it actually was. Branson checked his pocket watch and turned to look toward the courtroom doors instead. The lawyer was waiting for his luscious blonde clerk instead of keeping track of his business. Jenner shook his head in disbelief. Even the mighty John Lloyd Branson could be distracted by a woman.

"Your witness, Mr. Branson," said Miller, sitting down at his table.

John Lloyd stood up and the silence in the courtroom became absolute. Except for a faint sniffing sound coming from the custodian, now crawling around in back of the witness stand with his nose where the baseboards would be if the courhouse *had* baseboards.

"Mr. Tinsdale," he drawled, walking toward the witness. "I wonder, sir, if you might examine this document, conveniently labeled Defense Exhibit 1 for identification purposes?"

Jenner snickered. Branson was using a Southern drawl so thick, Jenner could smell shrimp creole and pecan pie just listening to it. He could hear three out-of-town reporters scribbling in their notebooks, and snickered again. If Branson suckered them into believing that Georgia peach drawl, they were going to be shocked as hell when he dropped it in favor of his .45 caliber voice when he was ready to shoot Tinsdale's pecker off during cross-examination.

Miller jumped up. "The State would like to see the document, Your Honor."

Judge Delaney nodded. "Mr. Branson."

John Lloyd bowed, and Jenner covered his mouth to hold in the laughter. "Certainly, Your Honor," said the lawyer. "I would be most honored to allow the worthy Mr. Miller to see our document."

Miller was breathing hard. "All right, Branson, you can drop the Confederate colonel act, and show this black boy what you *think* you're gonna whip his butt with."

Branson passed him the document. "Cleetus, I will do you the courtesy of allowing you to choose the number of lashes."

Judge Delaney pounded his gavel. "Gentlemen, I told you no histrionics!"

"Holy shit!" yelled Cleetus Miller.

The judge pounded the gavel again. "Mr. Miller, that will be a twenty-five-dollar fine for contempt of court. You know I don't permit profane language in my courtroom."

"Put it on my tab, Judge," said Miller, passing the document to Delaney.

"Holy shit!" yelled the judge after reading it, and pounded his gavel. The head separated from the handle and went sailing across the bench, past the court reporter's nose, to strike the custodian square on his posterior, catapulting him into Tinsdale's lap, then off onto the floor. The DOE man gave a high shriek, grabbed his crotch, fell beside the custodian, and rolled into a ball.

"Goddamn," exclaimed a reporter for the *Amarillo Globe-News* to Jenner while the bailiff was helping Tinsdale back into the witness box. "I wouldn't miss one of Branson's trials for a million bucks." Jenner decided he wouldn't either.

Judge Delaney passed the document to his court reporter. "Lillian, mark that for the defense, and give it to Mr. Tinsdale to examine. Let's see what he has to say."

Tinsdale looked as if he might have a hard time seeing the document, much less say anything about it. His eyes were still crossed behind his horn-rims and he was leaning over at a forty-five-degree angle. His face was white as the proverbial sheet and he kept emitting squeaks like a bat looking for a place to deposit some guano.

"Would you examine this document, Mr. Tinsdale, and tell the court what it appears to be?" asked John Lloyd, placing the piece of paper in the DOE manager's shaking hands.

Tinsdale blinked his eyes several times before he finally focused on the document. There was not a sound in the courtroom other than a few faint moans from the custodian, who was vigorously rubbing his behind. Tinsdale looked up and opened and closed his mouth several times. He cleared his throat and finally spoke. "It's a deed."

John Lloyd turned his back on the witness to face the spectators who all obligingly scooted forward to the edges of their seats. "A deed to what, Mr. Tinsdale?"

"Some land."

"Whose land?"

"Leroy MacPhearson's."

"The same land that DOE was planning to steal from him for their infamous containment area?" Branson's voice was a knife aimed for Tinsdale's belly.

"Not steal," began Tinsdale.

"Is it the same land?" Branson's voice was now a thunderclap.

"Yes," admitted Tinsdale.

"To whom is the land deeded?"

Tinsdale cleared his throat again. "To the state of Texas."

"For what purpose?"

Silence.

"For what purpose?" demanded John Lloyd, turning to face him. "You may read from the document if you are temporarily unable to formulate a sentence."

"To be designated a state historical landmark as the last existing example of native Panhandle grasslands, to be protected against all present or future environmental damage or risk of environmental damage, such damage to be determined and defined jointly by the Sierra Club and the Audubon Society. At no time, now or forevermore, may this land be designated for any purpose other than the stated one without the unanimous agreement of the above-mentioned Sierra Club, the Audubon Society, and the state of Texas. Signed and registered May 25, last year."

"So what Mr. MacPhearson actually meant by his superficially threatening statement to Price-Leigh was that no one would ever touch his land?"

"I guess so."

"I *know* so, Mr. Tinsdale. I drew up that deed."

"The Department of Energy can still confiscate the land."

John Lloyd smiled. "Not Texas public land, Mr. Tinsdale, and Texas is the *only* state in which that is true. Texas joined the union by treaty, not as a territory already owned by the United States. By that treaty, Texas owns absolutely all her public lands. They are not up for federal grabs."

He turned to Miller. "I told you Leroy MacPhearson had no motive for murder, Cleetus. None at all."

Jenner applauded, and one by one, the rest of the courtroom joined him. Judge Delaney searched for his gavel, found the broken handle, tossed it over his shoulder, and applauded, too.

The double doors slammed open as Schroder burst through. "John Lloyd, one of the D.A.'s secretaries just found Miss Fairchild unconscious in the elevator."

John Lloyd was halfway across the courtroom before Schroder finished talking. He vaulted the railing and was rushing toward the double doors when the custodian pointed his finger at Tinsdale. "Here he is, Your Honor. Stinks like a whorehouse."

John Lloyd stiffened and turned his head, his blank expression evolving into awareness. He whirled and started back toward Tinsdale, the deadliest look on his face Jenner had ever seen on a human being when Schroder stepped in front of him. "You're going the wrong way, Counselor," he said in as gentle a voice as Jenner had ever heard from the tough investigator. "You go on down and see about Miss Fairchild."

John Lloyd strained against Schroder's hold, his black eyes glittering as if diamonds were buried in their depths, while Tinsdale scampered around behind the judge's bench. Just like a cockroach, thought Jenner.

"Keep that madman away from me," squealed Tinsdale, grabbing the judge's sleeve, then scuttling toward the court reporter. An ominous ripping sound accompanied him as the judge's flowing judicial sleeve, still clutched tightly in Tinsdale's hand, parted company from the judge's flat fell seam.

Jenner thought that for a man who didn't cuss, Judge Delaney had a topflight vocabulary.

Schroder's head twisted almost completely around on his thick neck as he squinted at Judge Delaney hiking up his judicial robes and chasing Tinsdale around the witness box. The female bailiff, whose training courses had never covered a situation like the present one, sat frozen in her chair. Miller, whose head had swiveled between John Lloyd and Tinsdale like a compass needle seeking north, finally steadied on a course. Eyes fixed on Tinsdale, he screamed "Remember the Alamo," and launched himself over the counsel table, arms spread wide, head down, and butted the DOE manager in the chest. Tinsdale flew backward, slammed into the judge as he rounded the corner of the witness stand, and knocked them both against the jury box. Jenner's last view was of Delaney's and Tinsdale's legs as they both toppled over the railing into the jury box.

Miller reached over the railing, grasped Tinsdale by his collar and the seat of his pants, and heaved him out of the jury box. Dropping him on the floor, Miller placed a size-thirteen foot between Tinsdale's shoulder blades. He peered back over the railing. "You okay, Your Honor?"

The judge's voice reverberated against the ceiling and bounced off the curving walls of the courtroom. "That fucking little cockroach broke my fucking arm!"

CHAPTER
TWENTY

LYDIA SURVEYED HER FIVE FEET, TEN-PLUS INCHES AND made a mental list of the damages. One pair of panty hose with a fist-sized hole in one knee. One bloody scrape on that same knee. One silver dollar–sized grease spot on the hem of her powder-blue skirt. The rest of it was so dirty it looked like a mop rag. One bruised elbow, and a sprained wrist, expertly wrapped by one of the D.A.'s secretaries. One lump on the back of her head as big as a hen's egg, matching the one on her forehead where her face had hit the floor of the elevator.

Gingerly she opened one eye and peered into a small mirror she'd borrowed from the D.A.'s receptionist. Her blue eyes looked like bruises in her white face. The bump on her forehead was an interesting shade of purple. Actually, she decided it looked like a swollen caste mark. If she were from India, she might start a trend. She wasn't from India, however, and she merely looked as if she'd been scraped off the floor of an elevator.

She lay back down on the couch in the reception area of the District Attorney's office. At least she was in the right place. If anybody looked like a victim of violence, it was she. All she needed was a black eye.

The tall wooden doors to the D.A.'s suite slammed open and John Lloyd burst in. He looked awful, she thought. If anything, his face was whiter than hers, or maybe that was because his eyes were so black. And they were black, black and hard and glittery, and filled with foreboding. If he were anyone else, she would think he was scared.

She raised her taped hand. "Hey, John Lloyd, my skull's as thick as yours."

He knelt down, raised her hand to his mouth, and rested his lips against her wrist. She stared at the top of his gilded blond head, absently thinking how thick his hair was, and felt his hot breath against the inside of her wrist. God, she thought, if he's going to kiss me, I wish he wouldn't do it on the only taped spot on my body. Besides, his breath was going to melt the adhesive. It was already melting her bones. And was that drop of moisture she felt a tear? John Lloyd crying over her? Maybe there was a Santa Claus after all.

She touched his cheek with her other hand. "I'm okay, John Lloyd. Don't cry."

He jerked his head up. "Cry? My dear Miss Fairchild, I never cry. I was merely taking your pulse. It is fast, but not unduly so. Has a physician seen you?"

"Funniest way to take a pulse I ever saw," observed Jenner to the receptionist. Lydia saw him flinch when John Lloyd looked at him.

She pulled her hand back, and struggled to a sitting position. "No! I haven't seen a doctor. Why should I see a doctor?"

John Lloyd pushed himself up and collapsed on the couch beside her. "Miss Fairchild." His voice seemed to savor her name. "Miss Fairchild, being found unconscious on an elevator seems to call for some medical attention."

"I got it," said Lydia, picking up a sodden mound of paper towels. "I have an ice pack for the knot on the back of my head. That's all I need. I told you I have a hard head."

"Yes, and you are demonstrating it right now. You will see a physician." John Lloyd's voice held that imperial tone that made Lydia grind her teeth. Except this time her head hurt too badly to make the effort.

"I'll miss the trial," she protested.

"No, you won't, Miss Fairchild," said Jenner, sitting down on the other side of John Lloyd. "The judge ordered a medical recess."

She leaned across John Lloyd to look at him. "He didn't have to do that. I've been hurt worse than this in student protests."

John Lloyd focused his disapproving eyes on her, and she wished she hadn't mentioned the student protests. "It is not for your benefit, Miss Fairchild. There was a mishap in the courtroom."

"What kind of mishap?"

He told her, and she discovered that laughing made her head hurt. "Why was old Tinsdale afraid of you?"

"I was planning to assault him with the intent of doing grave bodily injury for his cowardly act."

"What cowardly act?"

"Miss Fairchild, not only did he strike you, but he did so when your back was turned." He frowned. "Of course, there is the possibility that he is intelligent enough to realize that a frontal attack would result in his being maimed."

Lydia's face went blank. "I never saw Tinsdale. I never saw anyone." She noticed Jenner moving closer with his notepad, and she suddenly remembered. "Oh, John Lloyd, I lost my briefcase with that lovely purple letter."

"No, you didn't, Miss Fairchild," said the receptionist. "One of the assistants found it stuffed in the trash in the men's room on the third floor." She handed it to Lydia, and gave John Lloyd a disapproving look that made Lydia snicker.

"You certainly have unusual clients, Mr. Branson. I've never smelled anything like that purple stationery in my life."

"The custodian has," he answered, an expression on his face that backed the receptionist up three steps. "And he smelled it on Rory Tinsdale."

"Tinsdale really hit her?" asked Jenner, looking a little furious himself.

"The only way he could smell like that is if he touched that purple letter, and the only way he could do that was to take it out of Miss Fairchild's briefcase. Either he hit her and took the briefcase, or he found her unconscious and stole the briefcase. It does not matter which. I shall deal with Mr. Tinsdale." He stood up and straightened his vest.

"No, sir. He's mine. I'm the cop," said Jenner, standing up and holding out his hands as if to stop traffic.

John Lloyd Branson was not traffic. He was more in the nature of a runaway freight train, thought Lydia. "Young man, you may be a very fine policeman, but I will take responsibility for my own actions in a just cause."

Jenner shook his head. "Leroy MacPhearson took responsibility in what he thought was a just cause, and he's sitting in a courtroom waiting to see if he's going to be tried for murder. I'm not going to let that happen to you. You're not going to touch a tentacle on that cockroach's head."

"Sit down, John Lloyd," said Lydia, grabbing his sleeve. "This isn't the wild West." She hoped she sounded convincing. Actually, there was something exciting about having a knight in shining armor (or embroidered silk vest) engage in combat on your behalf. But it really wasn't civilized. On the other hand . . .

"You both do me an injustice. I have no intention of physically harming Mr. Tinsdale. My behavior in the courtroom a few minutes ago is inexplicable to me. I pride myself on my logical, rather than emotional, response to such incidents . . ."

Her knight had tarnished armor. "Incident! Would you like to feel the lump on my head?" demanded Lydia.

". . . so I shall proceed in a perfectly legal manner by seeing to it that Mr. Tinsdale faces several serious charges at the conclusion of this case."

"But not simple assault, Branson," said Schroder as he and Miller walked through the door. "Tinsdale insists he found the briefcase in the men's john and opened your letter to see who it belonged to. Says he never saw Miss Fairchild."

"And you believe him, Sergeant?" asked John Lloyd, his eyes beginning to glitter again.

"Hell, no, but I don't know how to prove it."

"Hand me that letter, Miss Fairchild," said John Lloyd. "Perhaps if I had read it earlier, you would not have been assaulted."

Lydia picked it up by one corner and passed it to him as if it were a piece of particularly noxious trash. Which it was in her opinion. She noticed Jenner and Miller taking a hasty step backward as the scent of the stationery wafted past their nostrils.

John Lloyd unfolded the garish purple letter, read it, raised one eyebrow, and tossed it back in the open briefcase. He wiped his hands on his handkerchief. "What else was in there, Miss Fairchild?"

"A couple of legal pads. Who was the letter from?"

"Nothing to do with this case," John Lloyd replied in a puzzled tone.

"Are you sure you are able to continue, Miss Fairchild?" asked Judge Delaney in a solicitous tone of voice. "May I get you an aspirin? Or a soft drink? Bailiff, get the young lady a Coke."

"I'm fine, Your Honor. Fit as a fiddle. Top-rate. First-class."

"Miss Fairchild, you are babbling," said John Lloyd.

"Say thank you to the judge and sit down. I wish to finish this case by nightfall."

"Thank you, Your Honor," she obediently said, and sat down, wondering if she sounded as much like a parrot as she thought she did. She leaned over to speak to John Lloyd, and noticed he had switched from formulas to timetables. "Are you reconstructing the murder?" she asked in a stage whisper. Every reporter in the gallery moved to peer over John Lloyd's shoulder.

He glared at her and covered his notepad. "Miss Fairchild, when I want my tactics announced to the world, I shall hire the town crier."

"They went out of style at least a century ago."

He turned to glare at the reporters. "No, they did not. They merely went to work for the media." He went back to his notebook. "Now please be quiet."

Lydia was. Actually, her head hurt too badly to do otherwise. Her own voice was reverberating through her skull like a bass drum, and John Lloyd's kept fading out occasionally.

"Call Mrs. Aurora Silliphant," said Maximum Miller.

The poet floated in, though how a woman, a *short* woman, who must weigh two hundred pounds could float was beyond Lydia's comprehension. But float she did, in a purple chiffon garment that had no waist. Which was just as well, thought Lydia, since Aurora Silliphant wasn't blessed with a waist. She was altogether the most incredible woman Lydia had ever seen.

"It's *Ms.*," she said, patting Maximum Miller's cheek as she floated by. He stood with his mouth gaping open like a black bass darting for minnows.

Judge Delaney stood up and leaned over the bench. "I don't recall your being sworn in, Ms. Silliphant." His voice had a waspish sound to it. Possibly as a result of his broken left arm, now held immobile from shoulder to fingers by a plaster cast. Bent at the elbow, it jutted into the air as if he were perpetually swearing in a witness.

"I was late," said Ms. Silliphant, settling in the witness box with a flurry of chiffon. "Sweetie Poo was so distraught at my leaving that I just had to rock him a bit."

"A baby?" asked the judge.

She nodded. "My Pekingese."

Delaney whipped off his Ben Franklins to polish, realized he only had one unencumbered hand, and put them back on. "I see. If you would raise your right hand, please. Do you swear to tell the truth, the whole truth, and nothing but the truth, so help you God?"

"By the Great Universal Spirit, yes."

Delaney waved his left fingers. "That's close enough. Mr. Miller, you may proceed."

Miller stood and cleared his throat. "Ms. Silliphant, will you please tell the court where you were on August 25th of this year?"

"What time?"

"About ten-thirty in the evening."

Ms. Silliphant rearranged the cascading ruffles on her sleeves. "I was looking for Sweetie Poo. My baby."

"Where did you find your dog?"

She looked disapproving. "Sweetie Poo is not a dog. He is a kindred spirit."

Miller took another deep breath. Lydia imagined he was counting to ten. "Where did you find this kindred spirit?"

"In Charlton Price-Leigh's backyard."

"Did you see or hear anything when you went into the victim's backyard?"

"Oh, yes. I saw Charlton Price-Leigh and heard him say something to his visitor."

Miller turned to look at John Lloyd. "What did Price-Leigh say to his visitor, Ms. Silliphant?"

Lydia heard the question, but she didn't listen to the answer. There was no need. Ms. Silliphant was repeating her statement almost word for word. It was more interesting to try to decipher John Lloyd's latest doodles. Tilting her head, she studied two tiny triangles atop a small circle, which in turn was atop a larger circle.

". . . Sweetie Poo," she whispered. Miller grunted and suddenly looked toward Ms. Silliphant, his eyes bright and hard.

"Ms. Silliphant, I'll show you several photographs and ask if you can identify any of them as being a representation of the pickup you saw back into Price-Leigh's garage?"

Lydia nudged John Lloyd. "He hasn't laid a proper foundation to introduce those photographs."

John Lloyd smiled one his particularly nasty smiles. "It does not matter, Miss Fairchild. Her testimony is worthless."

"How?"

"All in good time."

Ms. Silliphant studied the photographs, holding them out at various distances, nodding to herself several times, then handed Miller one of them, laying the others on the witness box. "This one is the pickup I saw. It has the same dents, mudguards, that awful gun rack across the back window, everything."

Miller turned to face John Lloyd across the length of the courtroom. He smiled, and Lydia thought his smile was particularly nasty, too. "Let the record show"—his voice rolled out like a trumpet of doom—"that the witness has identified an aqua blue, 1983 Ford pickup belonging to the defendant, Leroy MacPhearson."

Lydia could feel the stares of the spectators, hear the hushed buzz of conversation, feel her palms begin to sweat and her stomach to tighten. It was true after all. Leroy MacPhearson was guilty. All the maneuvering and theorizing came to nothing. A big fat zero. She rubbed her hands on her skirt and wished she could lie down somewhere. She didn't want to hear John Lloyd's cross-examination. There wasn't any point. Aurora Silliphant had seen that pickup. The truth had a certain ring to it, like fine crystal, and Aurora

Silliphant's words had resounded with that ring. John Lloyd stood up, and Lydia composed her face into what she hoped was a supportive mask.

"Ms. Silliphant, I will try to be brief. I have had some experience with Pekingese, and I know they will suffer separation anxiety just as children do." John Lloyd's voice held a note of sympathy Lydia was prepared to swear was genuine.

Ms. Silliphant clasped her hands to her generous bosom and sighed. "That's so true. You must share your home with a Pekingese to understand so much about them."

"No, ma'am, I do not, but I understand helpless dependency of a pet, and the loving responsibility of the pet owner." Again Lydia thought she heard sincerity in his voice. Which was strange because John Lloyd didn't own a pet of any kind, and to her knowledge, had never owned one.

"Another peculiarity of small breeds and particularly of the Pekingese is their mischievousness. Is Sweetie Poo mischievous?"

"Objection, Your Honor. Is this a cross-examination, or a meeting of the American Kennel Club?" Miller tapped his fingers on the counsel table and chewed on a big black unlit cigar.

John Lloyd's eyes expressed innocent surprise. "But Mr. Miller, Sweetie Poo was the reason Ms. Silliphant was in Price-Leigh's backyard. I was merely trying to ascertain what Sweetie Poo was doing."

"Objection overruled," snapped Judge Delaney. "Witness may answer the question."

"But, Your Honor, I don't see what a dog's personality traits have to do with this case. Besides, Mr. Branson hasn't proved dogs have any personality."

Delaney's long nose twitched, and his encased fingers wiggled. "Mr. Miller, I have a Pekingese, and will testify that they *do* have personalities. Now sit down."

John Lloyd inclined his head in thanks, and turned to the

poet. "What was Sweetie Poo doing in Price-Leigh's back-yard?"

Ms. Silliphant ducked her head and looked at John Lloyd through her lashes, a coy gesture Lydia considered her twenty years and a hundred pounds too late to be attempting. "Sweetie Poo is so naughty. He just loves to tease. He'd scratch at Mr. Price-Leigh's back door, then run and dig up his bluebonnets. Not that there were really any bluebonnets in the flower bed. Oh, there were, but they weren't bloom-ing, and I told Charlton that the Panhandle had the wrong climate. But he wouldn't listen to me and got so mad at little Sweetie Poo. He wasn't a nice man sometimes."

John Lloyd nodded. "I believe you told Sergeant Schroder and Sergeant Jenner that Price-Leigh called him a mangy mutt?"

Ms. Silliphant's chins wobbled in indignation. "He was horrible."

"Was Price-Leigh wearing a shirt?"

"A shirt?"

"Was he bare-chested?"

"By heavens, no! Price-Leigh may have been a dog-hater, but he was proper." He was proper all right, thought Lydia. He was a proper pervert.

John Lloyd picked up his memo pad, made a note, looked up at Ms. Silliphant, and smiled. "Just a few more ques-tions, then you can return home to your pet. How long were you in your backyard before you saw the pickup?"

"Oh, I don't know. It's so difficult to keep track of time when I'm experiencing the moonlight. Perhaps ten minutes, fifteen minutes, or maybe even twenty."

John Lloyd tapped his chin with one lean forefinger. "Could we perhaps be a little more precise? What were you doing just before you went outside?"

Ms. Silliphant tapped her chin in imitation of John Lloyd. "I was emptying a vase of flowers, and composing a sonnet to the faded blossoms. Then I thought I needed more flowers, so I went outside to pick them." Her voice ended on a rising note as though she were asking John Lloyd if that were the course of events, instead of the other way around.

"What kind did you pick?"

"Roses," she said, with a beatific expression on her face. "Roses silvered by the moonlight are beautiful."

"I also enjoy roses," said John Lloyd. Lydia tried to remember if he had a rosebush in his yard. Maybe one, and the housekeeper tended it.

"Do you have some of those delicate yellow peace roses, the ones with such huge blooms?" he asked.

Ms. Silliphant looked disapproving again. "I don't believe in hybrids, only in the purest old-fashioned roses. They smell the sweetest."

"Could you estimate how long it takes you to pick each rose?"

"Perhaps a minute."

"And how many roses did you have when you noticed the pickup?"

She clapped her hands. "How clever. I never would've thought to mark minutes by roses. It's poetical."

"Your Honor." Miller's expression said he didn't think it poetical. "I've listened to questions about dogs, flower beds, and now roses. Is it possible for counsel to confine his questions to the subjects covered on direct examination?"

"Mr. Branson, how much longer on horticulture?" asked Judge Delaney, scratching futilely at his cast. The bailiff handed him a coat hanger straightened into a long piece of metal.

"I beg the court's indulgence . . ."

Judge Delaney made a snorting sound and pushed the coat hanger inside his cast and scratched. "You never begged anyone's indulgence in your life, Branson. How many more questions on horticulture?"

"One, Your Honor."

"Ask it." Delaney looked for his gavel, remembered its demise, and slapped his hand on the bench.

"How many roses, Ms. Silliphant?"

"A bouquet. That's about fifteen," she added.

"So you were outside about fifteen minutes?"

"That's right, Mr. Branson."

"Did you hear any sounds from the house during those fifteen minutes?"

She hesitated. "Yes, I heard a scream."

"What did you do then, Ms. Silliphant?"

"I picked up Sweetie Poo and ran into the house. I just knew something terrible had happened. I felt something in the atmosphere. I'm very sensitive to atmosphere. Most poets are, you know. Our art demands it of us."

"Can you estimate about what time this was, Ms. Silliphant?"

"I don't have to estimate, Mr. Branson. It was exactly twelve-forty-seven in the morning. I noticed the clock as I was rocking Sweetie Poo."

"No further questions," said John Lloyd abruptly, and sat down.

Leroy MacPhearson leaned over. "I know it looks bad for me, John Lloyd, but I didn't kill nobody. I swear to God I didn't," he whispered. "And if I ever do, it's going to be that no-good Tinsdale. He's asking for it."

"And Price-Leigh didn't?" asked Lydia.

Leroy's face closed up like a turtle retreating into its shell. "I don't have nothing to say about that."

"You must very soon, Leroy, or a murderer will go free," said John Lloyd, his voice matching his coldness of his eyes.

Leroy smiled. "Don't you worry about that, John Lloyd. No murderer's gonna go free. As for talking, the time ain't right yet."

"What are you waiting for?" demanded Lydia. "Armageddon?"

Leroy's smile vanished as if it had never been. "No, ma'am. I'm trying to prevent it." He folded his arms and closed his mouth for the rest of the trial.

CHAPTER
TWENTY-ONE

JUDGE DELANEY HAD A BEATIFIC EXPRESSION ON HIS FACE as if he had seen heaven. Jenner decided it was just a result of the judge being able to scratch where he itched, because it damn sure wasn't natural to him. Finally, Delaney extracted the coat hanger, and sighed. "Mr. Miller, call your next witness."

Maximum Miller stood up, a shit-eating grin on his face. "The State rests, Your Honor. It remains only for my misguided, time-wasting, hardheaded, bleeding-heart opposing counsel to present his pitiful reasons why this honorable court should release a cold-blooded killer to ravage society."

"Mr. Miller, this is not a melodrama or a political rally, although your dramatic outburst would do for both. A simple 'State rests' is sufficient. Mr. Branson, call your first witness, please." The judge grabbed his coat hanger again.

John Lloyd stood, and Jenner craned his neck to see the attorney's face. "Your Honor, the defense has no witnesses

236

to call, but wishes to recall Sergeant Schroder for cross-examination.''

Miller was on his feet. "What is this crap, Branson? Another question-and-answer session on roses and dogs?''

Judge Delaney slammed his hand on the bench. "No profanity in my courtroom, Mr. Miller.''

"I hardly think Sergeant Schroder is an expert on either subject, do you, Mr. Prosecutor?'' asked John Lloyd.

Miller waved both arms at the judge. "Your Honor, counsel is trying to waste this court's time. He admitted he's calling no witnesses, and he's only demanding to cross-examine Sergeant Schroder as a ploy to confuse the court.''

Judge Delaney stopped scratching and waved his plastered arm at Miller, the coat hanger sticking out of the shoulder end of the cast. "Are you implying the court, meaning me, is stupid enough to be confused by John Lloyd Branson?''

Miller hunched his head between his shoulders and snapped his mouth closed. For a split second Jenner knew the prosecutor had considered telling the judge yes. But even Maximum Miller knew better than that. "No, sir,'' he said. "But I still think he's trying to trick us.''

The judge looked at John Lloyd, who had remained standing with the innocent look of a choirboy who had just dropped a hairy caterpillar down the preacher's vestments. "Mr. Branson, you are planning to stick to relevant issues raised by the direct examination?''

"I plan to question Sergeant Schroder on certain items of physical evidence entered in the evidence log.'' He paused. "Of course, it will be necessary for the Sergeant to produce those items.''

Miller bounced to his feet. "I knew it, goddamn it! He's going on a fishing expedition, Your Honor, and he doesn't have a license.''

"Add twenty-five dollars to Mr. Miller's tab for using profane language in the courtroom,'' said Delaney to his court reporter. "Mr. Branson, what pieces of physical evidence are you requesting Sergeant Schroder to produce?"

"Item Number 325 on the evidence log."

"Item Number 325," repeated Miller, rummaging through his papers for a copy of his evidence log, which Jenner happened to know the prosecutor had given to Schroder during direct examination, and Schroder had forgotten to return. "What is it, and why the hell are you interested?"

"It proves Leroy MacPhearson is innocent of the murder of Charlton Price-Leigh."

The judge's eyes swept over the spectators. "Sergeant Jenner, go get that Item Number 325."

Jenner slammed out of the courtroom at a dead run.

Schroder grabbed his arm as he made a right turn down the hall. "Where the hell are you going? I told you I hadn't released your butt from Special Crimes."

"Special Crimes is where I'm going," replied Jenner, trying to jerk his arm out of Schroder's grip.

Schroder's grip tightened until Jenner wondered if his arm would fall off from lack of circulation. "Why?"

"Branson wants Item Number 325 on the evidence log."

"What is it?"

"Damn if I know! You've got the log."

Schroder stuck his hand in his sagging coat pocket, a feat of bravery that Jenner considered second only to rushing a machine gun nest. The investigator pulled out several sheets of paper folded into fourths. He meticulously unfolded them and found Item 325. He silently passed the list to Jenner.

Jenner looked at the description of Item 325, then to Schroder. "How's that gonna help Leroy MacPhearson?"

"I don't know, but you can bet it's the ace that bastard's been hiding up his sleeve since this trial started."

* * *

"Call Sergeant Ed Schroder," drawled John Lloyd after Jenner had passed the opened buff-colored envelope to the judge.

Jenner slid further down on his spine in the seat, and thought again that the chairs in the courtroom had not been designed with human behinds in mind. His own had begun to go numb the minute he'd sat down, and the run across the street and down the block from the Courts Building to the Special Crimes headquarters had merely made his butt tingle with returning circulation. He shifted lower in the seat until his head rested against its back. His knees stuck out like Ichabod Crane's, but at least he'd be comfortable. And he definitely wanted to be comfortable. This was the final act, and it was going to be better than *Perry Mason*.

The MacPhearson family, including Hap, sat behind him like some kind of fan club. Frances's seat creaked as she wiggled and squirmed. Her husband must have taken her bottle away, thought Jenner. Or maybe her butt was going numb, too. There was a young girl sitting by Elizabeth, not a bad looker either. Must be the niece with acne and boyfriend problems, come to root for Grandfather. He wondered if they knew about John Lloyd's bombshell. Somehow he didn't think so. The family all looked too scared.

Schroder ambled through the double doors like a bear roused from his long winter's nap. Jenner snickered, and Lydia Fairchild turned around and winked at him. Damn, but he wished he'd moved over behind the defense table sooner.

"Sergeant Schroder, can you identify this piece of evidence, carried on your evidence log as Item Number 325, and kindly marked as Defense Exhibit 2 by the court?"

Schroder took the envelope with the same reluctance he would express if John Lloyd had handed him a dirty postcard. He turned it over in his hands, looked closely at the postmark, sniffed it, and finally opened it. He cleared his throat several times. "It appears to be Charlton Price-Leigh's telephone bill."

"Appears to be?"

Schroder looked at Maximum Miller, scratched his chin, and cleared his throat again. "It is his telephone bill."

"Thank you, Sergeant," said John Lloyd. "If I may have the court's permission to approach the witness?"

"Yes! Yes! Yes!" snapped Delaney, turning his chair to watch Schroder's face, his hanger sticking out from the top of his cast like an antenna.

John Lloyd walked across the courtroom and leaned comfortably against the witness chair. "Sergeant, are there any long-distance calls listed on this bill?"

"Yes."

"Are the phone numbers to which calls are made listed on this bill?"

"Yes."

John Lloyd hooked his thumbs in his vest, and rested his elbows on the jury railing less than three feet from Schroder, his back pressed against the jury box. "I direct your attention to a call listed on page three of that bill, a call placed at eleven o'clock the evening of August 25th of this year. To what number was that call made?"

Schroder took his time running his finger down the page. He found the time and traced his fingers across the page. He stopped, frowned, and cleared his throat. That's what happens when you smoke four packs a day, thought Jenner.

"What is the number, Sergeant Schroder?"

"352-3889 in Amarillo."

"And do you happen to know whose number that is, Sergeant Schroder? The investigator was silent, and John Lloyd raised his voice. "Shall I ask the judge's secretary to call the telephone number company for that information?"

"It's Leroy MacPhearson's number."

"How many minutes did that call last?"

"Nine minutes, twenty-five seconds."

"Do you find another call made to that same number on the night of August 25th?"

Schroder rattled the bill. "Yes."

"At what time, Sergeant Schroder?"

"At twelve-fifteen on the morning of the 26th."

"And how many minutes did that call last?"

"Three minutes, five seconds."

"In other words, someone answered the phone at Leroy MacPhearson's home and spoke to Charlton Price-Leigh approximately fifteen minutes before he died?"

"Yes."

"How far is it from Leroy MacPhearson's home to the bloodstained bedroom belonging to Price-Leigh?"

"I don't know exactly."

"An approximate distance will be fine."

"Approximately twenty-five miles."

John Lloyd straightened and faced the judge. "Your Honor, the State wishes to charge a man with murder who had no motive, and who was twenty-five miles away from the scene at the time of the crime. We ask that the charges be dismissed."

CHAPTER
TWENTY-TWO

LYDIA HELD UP HER CAN OF COCA-COLA IN A SALUTE. "You were brilliant, John Lloyd, absolutely brilliant. Did you see Maximum Miller's face? Do you think the trial was too much of a strain on him?"

"I doubt it, Miss Fairchild."

"And did you hear the female bailiff apply for maternity leave? I congratulated her, but she said she wasn't pregnant yet, just needed nine months to recover from this trial, and decided she'd have a baby while she was out." Lydia swallowed a sip of soda. "She said morning sickness and labor would be a snap after what she'd been through today. I understand Judge Delaney's court reporter applied at the same time, but was denied. The judge can't do that, can he? That's discrimination."

"I believe Lillian had a hysterectomy last year."

"You can't blame her for trying, John Lloyd. Did you see Sergeant Jenner? I really believe he was glad Leroy was innocent. Speaking of Leroy, what did he say to you after the trial?''

"He told me he had an answering machine.''

Lydia dropped her Coke in her lap. She watched the sticky liquid soaking her skirt. Like blood staining that mattress, she thought, watching the soda seep out of the can. I wonder if the blood seeped out of Price-Leigh's heart as fast. "Oh, God, John Lloyd,'' she said, and heard her voice wobble. "That last call Price-Leigh made was answered by a machine. He never talked to Leroy at all.''

"If my theory is correct, Miss Fairchild, Leroy left his house shortly after the eleven o'clock call.''

"Then he's guilty after all.''

"He is a material witness who still refuses to tell what he knows. He is also an honest man. He felt it his duty to tell me the alibi I successfully used to get charges against him dismissed was a lie. That such a man participated in deceptions, and is continuing to do so, argues that his reason is just.''

"Like what?'' asked Lydia, looking in her shoulder bag for tissues to mop up her skirt.

"The dump.''

"The dump? Are you on that again? I thought you proved pretty conclusively that the dump wasn't a motive.'' She emptied her purse on the car seat.

"The dump issue obscured the real motive by altering everyone's behavior. Had it not been for the dump, Charlton Price-Leigh's murder would have been solved that same night. Had it not been for the dump, Leroy MacPhearson would not have entered into a series of deceptions all aimed at gaining time.''

"Time for what? It isn't to find the dirty pictures Price-Leigh took of Rachel because he evidently didn't take any.'' She began blotting her skirt.

Silence.

She looked over to see him staring at the contents she'd dumped out of her purse. "John Lloyd, what's wrong?"

He braked the car, for once not throwing her against the door, and pulled off the highway. Picking up a brown mailer with at least five dollars worth of stamps on it, he ripped it open. He glanced through the contents and leaned his head against the back of the seat. "Where has this been, Miss Fairchild?"

"In my purse."

"And before that?"

"Uh, in my briefcase. I took all the mail out when you told me to lock it up in the trunk." She frowned at his pensive look. "What is it, John Lloyd?"

He placed it back in her purse. "The reason Tinsdale assaulted you and stole your briefcase, the reason for many of the deceptions that have misled us, and the reason Leroy MacPhearson refused to speak ill of the dead."

He made a U-turn across the highway and drove west into the bloodred sunset. "I now can reconstruct all but the last fifteen minutes of Price-Leigh's life. For that I must talk to Leroy MacPhearson. Get on the phone, Miss Fairchild, and issue an invitation to all concerned parties, including our two sergeants and the admirable Mr. Miller. Tell the latter gentlemen to bring Mr. Tinsdale as their guest. The time has come to settle with that noxious insect. Tell them to meet us at MacPhearson's farm in two hours."

"Two hours? We can be there in fifteen minutes. We're only a few miles outside Amarillo."

"We have an errand we must do first, else many sacrifices will have been for naught. All in all, two hours should be enough to protect the innocent."

"Gentlemen, Miss Fairchild, and principals." John Lloyd stood in the center of Leroy MacPhearson's living room. Darkness pressed against the windows, and table lamps cast shadows on the plastered walls. The wheeze of the air-conditioner masked the sounds of the ten restless, shifting people gathered in the room.

Lydia crossed her legs nervously, flinched at the burning protest of her scraped knee, and tried to draw several deep breaths without hyperventilating. She felt as if she were watching a movie, one of those grainy black-and-white films made in the thirties. Close-up of John Lloyd's face with the background a blur of monochromatic shapes. Then the camera pulls back to frame the supporting actors: Maximum Miller, his skin a brilliant polished black; Schroder, face still, his ruddy color transformed into a pale gray; and Jenner, face tanned, and firm, a leading man miscast in a minor role. The camera moves back even further, and the audience sees the MacPhearson family as a montage of stiff, secretive faces.

The climax, the resolution of suspense—and Lydia felt only dread that made her hands shake and her chest tighten. She held onto the arm of the sofa with both hands. The thick yard of the afghan rubbed against her palms, and caught her nails in its loose fibers. She didn't want to stay to the end of this movie, didn't want to know the denouement, didn't want to see the truth stand exposed without passionate adornment. This wasn't a Thirties whodunit when the essential innocence of the times mandated a happy ending. This was a surrealistic Eighties production, which almost certainly meant tragedy.

John Lloyd tapped his cane with the imperial gesture of a king tapping his scepter. Not a modern limited monarch, bound by tradition and subject to law, but an absolute monarch who ruled by divine right, subject to no laws but his own conscience. And John Lloyd's conscience scared the hell out of her.

Some invisible director yelled *action*. The cameras rolled. The final scene began. And she was powerless to do more than watch and listen.

"In the beginning there was deception," began John

Lloyd, his voice deep, sonorous, and utterly without accent. The King's English, thought Lydia hysterically.

"The original deception," continued John Lloyd, "was the selection of Deaf Smith County as a site for the dump. From that deception sprang the others, each more dangerous than the preceeding one. What methodology was utilized by the site selection commitee? A scientific one, we are told. But memos dealing with that methodology were shredded and staff correspondence obtained under the Freedom of Information Act heavily sanitized. Deception. Deaf Smith County was classified as having 'no significant agricultural production.' Deception. Deaf Smith County is the tenth most productive county in the United States. The DOE only needs nine square miles for the dump. Deception. DOE will take another six square miles for what they term a containment area. But what of the Ogallala Aquifer? Will it be safe? The repository will be built below the aquifer. There is no danger of contamination. Deception." John Lloyd's eyes were blacker than ebony and as hard. "It was over the issue of water that Charlton Price-Leigh died."

Maximum Miller shook himself out of his daze, and Lydia envisioned the imaginary camera focusing on his face. "Just a minute, Branson. What in the hell are you talking about? If water was the motive, then damn near anybody in an eight-state area could be guilty, and that's a pile of crap."

John Lloyd lifted his cane and pointed it at Miller. "Sit down, Mr. Prosecutor. Do not interrupt the storyteller."

Lydia held her breath as Miller slowly sat down, elbowing a place on the couch between Schroder and Jenner. The younger sergeant smiled an apology as he squeezed Lydia against the arm of the couch. Four crows on a fence, she thought with a giggle, that old journalistic phrase used to describe four people posing in line to be photographed.

John Lloyd inclined his head in acknowledgment of Miller's obedience and continued. "The root cause of Price-Leigh's death was water. The issue set in motion a series of events to which he reacted according to his individual personality traits. His behavior culminated in his death. But the deceptions involved blinded us to the root cause. Let us examine those deceptions.''

He took a step forward, and the effect was a 3-D projection into their midst although he was only a few inches closer. ''Water is the Achilles' heel of the DOE. If we can prove that the dump will threaten the primary underground water source of the area, the site must be abandoned. If that occurs, then the original deception will be exposed, that the selection of Deaf Smith County was not a scientific decision, but a political one. The head-hunting and bloodletting by congressional committees would be on such a scale that Watergate would recede to the level of a minor dispute. At the very least, those involved would be fired.''

John Lloyd smiled at Tinsdale, who watched him rather like a hypnotized rabbit watching a snake. ''But the contamination of the aquifer by nuclear waste isn't the immediate danger, is it, Mr. Tinsdale? It is the reverse. The contamination of the nuclear waste is more dangerous than can be imagined. Certainly more dangerous than bureaucrats can imagine. Uncontrolled water leaking into hot nuclear waste results in boiling water, and we all know what boiling water produces. Even the DOE knows, doesn't it, Mr. Tinsdale? Steam, ladies and gentlemen. Every cook who's ever used a pressure cooker knows that steam must be vented or the resulting explosion will spread the evening's dinner all over the kitchen ceiling. But we're not speaking harmless roast and potatoes. We are speaking radioactive steam and debris venting itself into the atmosphere. Impossible? Not at all. Remember the two shafts to be drilled by the DOE in order to gain access to the dump area. Two huge vent holes, or chimneys, emitting a deadly smoke that will kill and kill and kill. Over how great an area, Mr. Tinsdale? Have you produced one of your famous worst possible scenarios for this probability?''

Tinsdale's face was wet, and Lydia knew without touching him that the sweat droplets would be ice-cold. The DOE man's tongue flicked out like a lizard's to lick thin bloodless lips. "We certainly haven't. The chances of such an accident are infinitesimal."

John Lloyd smiled again, and Lydia clutched her shaking hands. John Lloyd was deadly when he smiled like that, deadly and merciless.

"Oh, Mr. Tinsdale, the time for deception is past. The game is over. You see, I have Price-Leigh's papers, the ones you believed to be in Miss Fairchild's briefcase. You should have stolen her purse instead."

Tinsdale rose to a crouch, like an animal ready to spring. "Those papers prove nothing. The man was morally corrupt and mad. No one will pay any attention to his conclusions."

Schroder lumbered to his feet, and grabbed a handful of Tinsdale's shirt. He lifted the DOE project manager until Tinsdale's toes barely brushed the floor. "Sit down and shut up before I gag you."

"You can't! Freedom of speech is my constitutional right," squawked the other man.

Maximum Miller crossed one foot over the other and leaned back against the couch. "I believe that Justice Black, or maybe it was Justice Holmes, once said that freedom of speech didn't include the right to yell fire in a crowded theatre." The prosecutor sniffed the air. "I don't smell any smoke, so shut up."

Schroder extended his arm and dropped Tinsdale into a chair. He nodded at John Lloyd. "You've got the floor again, Branson."

"My apologies, Sergeant Schroder. I had not fully appreciated your usefulness until now." He turned his attention back to the others. "There was another man whose virtues I did not appreciate, and to whom I can no longer apologize because he is dead. I refer, of course, to Charlton Price-Leigh, bureaucrat extraordinaire, a man nurtured on DOE deceptions. Like most spokesmen for most entities, he professed to believing the deceptions. Until he moved to Hereford and something happened to him. He joined the ranks of others who see beyond the desolation of this land. He saw beauty in vastness. He felt his soul expand to meet the horizon because, for the first time in his life, he could see the horizon uncluttered by the artificial creations of man. He covered his walls with Panhandle landscapes, filled his bookcases with poetry and Texas history. He was a man in ecstasy. He was also a man in agony. He loved this land, but he was its destroyer. To save it, he also turned to deception. His left hand did not know what his right hand was doing. In the vernacular of espionage, Price-Leigh had become a mole.''

He paused, waiting for his audience to refocus their image of the dead man, then continued. ''Using his own financial resources, he secretly began drilling boreholes in playa lakes. After months of work, months of living a personal deception, he had his raw data, data that proves the Permian salt beds, the very salt beds in which DOE plans to bury seventy million metric tons of nuclear waste are in a state of active dissolution. Water from the playa lakes is infiltrating the salt beds, producing brine, which will produce steam, which in turn must be vented or it will produce an explosion. It did not require higher mathematics for Price-Leigh to realize that the steam generated by saltwater heated by *seventy million metric tons* will require more vents than merely two pitiful shafts and what minuscule boreholes may be left over from a century of drilling for water. It requires a gigantic vent, a vent the dump will provide for itself. Underground nuclear waste explosion, Elizabeth. Price-Leigh tried to tell you. My witness misunderstood the words he yelled as you and Hap left his house. My witness repeated them as 'Remember you-alls.' Actually what Price-Leigh said was 'Remember the Urals.' ''

"Oh, my God, John Lloyd!" said Elizabeth Thornton, her voice more subdued than Lydia had ever heard.

"What about the Urals?" asked Miller. "What does Russia have to do with the dump?"

"A defecting Soviet scientist brought word of an underground nuclear waste explosion in the Ural Mountains in Russia in the 1950s, an explosion that rendered 450 square miles uninhabitable, and killed thousands of people. That explosion did not involve nearly the amount of waste as the DOE is planning to bury in the Panhandle. An explosion of our dump would render hundreds of thousands of square miles uninhabitable."

His eyes focused on Tinsdale. "The publication of Price-Leigh's data and his conclusions meant the end of your project, Mr. Tinsdale. End of the deception."

"Price-Leigh was a crazy, perverted psychotic," Tinsdale burst out.

"Was he really, Mr. Tinsdale, or was that another deception?" asked John Lloyd.

"The proof was all over his bedroom," argued Tinsdale.

"Cameras with no film, sexual paraphernalia that had never been used, pornographic photographs available in any adult bookstore, a fountain that had been placed in the room so recently that when Miss Fairchild accidentally moved it, the carpet underneath was not even crushed. Remove the mirrored tiles from the ceiling and the suspicious lighting simply becomes indirect lighting common to many homes."

"You're crazy!" screamed Tinsdale.

"What the hell are you getting at, Branson?" demanded Maximum Miller, pulling a large cigar out of his pocket and sticking it, unlit, in his mouth.

"Deception, Mr. Miller. A setup, as Miss Fairchild would call it."

"You have no proof of anything. You're just concocting wild theories like you always do at the public hearings." Tinsdale's hair was limp with sweat.

Then John Lloyd slowly shifted his body toward Leroy MacPhearson, who was sitting like a carved statue in his rocking chair. "Leroy, it is time. All will be well, I promise you, but only if you answer my questions. Will you?"

Leroy exchanged glances with John Lloyd, and Lydia felt she was witnessing an oath of fealty. Leroy MacPhearson was pledging this trust in exchange for—what? Protection? The transfer of responsibility from Leroy to John Lloyd? Lydia shook her head in puzzlement. Out of the corner of her eye she caught a speculative expression on Schroder's face. Be careful, John Lloyd, she silently implored.

"Ask your questions, Lawyer Branson," said Leroy, beginning to rock.

"Did Price-Leigh's bedroom have a mirrored ceiling and a fountain consisting of an entwined couple involved in questionable sexual practices?"

Leroy grinned, an incongruous expression in the dramatic circumstances. "I ain't sure what questionable sexual practices means, but there wasn't any fountain in that bedroom, and no mirrors on the ceiling either."

"He's lying!" screamed Tinsdale, springing to his feet.

Schroder pushed him back down in his chair. "Don't interrupt your betters, Tinsdale."

John Lloyd smiled that ugly smile again, and Lydia knew the snake was about to swallow the rabbit whole. "Sergeant Schroder, I would suggest that Special Crimes check the *underside* of those mirrored tiles for fingerprints."

"Where'd all that shit come from, Branson? Suppose you tell me that," demanded Maximum Miller, chewing on his unlit cigar.

John Lloyd smiled. "Mr. Tinsdale's car was filled with empty boxes the day Sergeant Schroder apprehended him in Price-Leigh's house. We assumed they were to be packed with cameras and other items embarrassing to the victim, and thus to DOE. That was another deception, one that led me to waste a great deal of time on an unproductive line of inquiry. I believe those boxes had just been unpacked of those same cameras and other items. In Miss Fairchild's colorful vocabulary, evidence was not removed from the crime scene, but planted there to reflect a false image of the victim's character. Is that not true, Mr. Tinsdale? You needed to defame Price-Leigh's character in order to cast doubt on the validity of his research, thus saving your project, and protecting the original deception.''

"What about it, you weasely son of a bitch?" asked Miller.

Tinsdale's laugh was high-pitched. "And I suppose Mr. Branson will also claim I put up a mirrored ceiling and carried in a fountain in the length of time between Schroder's call and his arrival. You've lost, Branson. You and all these ignorant peasants.''

John Lloyd appeared not to hear Tinsdale's insults. He took another step forward, and Lydia noticed his limp was pronounced. "You are saying, then, Mr. Tinsdale, that you only learned of Price-Leigh's death when Sergeant Schroder called you?''

"Yes! I thought he was out of town as his note said. The note your *client*"—he spat out the word—"left on my desk.''

"Yes, of course, the note," said John Lloyd. "We only have your word that such a note ever existed, just as we only have your word that Leroy MacPhearson ever threatened Price-Leigh. We seem to have taken your word about a number of things. Let me pose a hypothetical situation, Mr. Tinsdale. Suppose there was no note. Suppose you drove by Price-Leigh's house for your usual round of golf. There was no answer to your knock. But you had a key to the door. Or was it a key you used? Was it rather an electric garage door opener that allowed you to enter the house unseen by the curious little boys who seemed to have the annoying habit of watching Price-Leigh's habitation? You entered the house, found a bloodstained mattress, and remembered the body found on Leroy MacPhearson's property. This was your opportunity to discredit Price-Leigh.''

"You're wrong," said Tinsdale, folding his arms across his chest.

John Lloyd studied the man, then slowly nodded. "You are correct, Mr. Tinsdale. I am wrong. Perhaps I should restate my scenario. Leroy," he said without moving his eyes from Tinsdale. "Whom did you threaten?"

Leroy stopped rocking and frowned. "Like you said in court, I didn't rightly *threaten* anybody. I just told Tinsdale that he wouldn't live long enough to take my land."

"You told *Tinsdale*?" asked John Lloyd.

"Yeah. Price-Leigh was there, but I was talking to both of them. I sure am glad I can tell this. I was pretty mad that Tinsdale made it sound like he wasn't involved."

John Lloyd smiled that dangerous, deadly smile again. "You were unaware that Price-Leigh had sent letters to the landowners until Leroy MacPhearson's visit the day of the murder, weren't you, Mr. Tinsdale?"

"We had not intended to notify them yet. Procedures have not been formulated for the acquisition of land. I was puzzled by Charlton's action."

"More than puzzled. You were suspicious. You are a bureaucrat, Mr. Tinsdale. Deception is meat and drink to you. You immediately assumed that Price-Leigh was misleading you for some reason of his own. You were correct. Price-Leigh *was* misleading you. *And* DOE."

John Lloyd shifted his weight, and Lydia knew his leg must be aching. "But Price-Leigh faced the classic difficulty of any agent who must cross over to the other side. He must make contact with his new allies without arousing the suspicions of his old ones. The letters were his method, letters that only were sent to landowners who were on the committee of STAD. Only two letters were sent, and the method failed. MacPhearson confronted him in the presence of Tinsdale. There was no opportunity to persuade Leroy of his trustworthiness.''

''Why didn't he just pick up the phone and say, 'Boy, do I have a sweet deal for you'?'' asked Miller. The prosecutor was still chewing on his unlit cigar.

John Lloyd clasped his hands over the head of his cane. ''Charlton Price-Leigh was still a bureaucrat. The direct approach did not come easy for him.''

''That's why he said in his letter that he wanted to discuss my opinions,'' said Elizabeth. Her voice was still subdued, and her face was drawn. For the first time since Lydia had met her, she looked every year her age. ''But he waffled around like he didn't have good sense, and I didn't understand a thing he said. I don't think Hap did either.''

Maximum Miller catapulted off the couch. ''Where is that redheaded son of a bitch?''

Silence. Finally John Lloyd nodded at MacPhearson.

''Gone,'' said the man, gripping the arms of his rocking chair like a man preparing to withstand a blow.

Miller dropped his cigar as his mouth flew open. He stood speechless for a moment as he swung his head from side to side, looking first at MacPhearson, then at John Lloyd, as if he couldn't make up his mind which one he wanted to maim first.

He made his decision and advanced on John Lloyd, teeth bared and fists clenched. ''Branson, you bastard. You've been flapping your mouth like some sleazy used-car dealer trying to sell us a repossessed heap with the speedometer turned back, while a murderer takes a hike. I'll have your license for this, you crooked . . .'' He stopped, mouth working soundlessly as he hunted for a suitable epithet.

''Deceitful?'' suggested Lydia.

''Miss Fairchild, I believe Mr. Miller is articulate enough without your suggestions,'' said John Lloyd in a cold voice Lydia thought might possibly be above freezing, but not by much.

"At least you got a partner who sees through you, Branson," said Miller. "The bar association'll want to talk to her."

"Miss Fairchild must return to her classes without the somewhat dubious honor of discussing my behavior with the local bar," drawled John Lloyd. "Besides, Hap is not the murderer." The drawl was gone again, and so was the glint of humor in his black eyes. "Although he is not innocent of wrongdoing, he has not taken a life. He did not even lie in his statement. He said he checked on Elizabeth and Rachel at twelve, could do nothing, and left. He did exactly what he said. He left. He met Leroy and drove with him to Price-Leigh's house. It was he who so sanitized the murder scene that Special Crimes found almost no fingerprints at all, except a few isolated ones having no reference to the crime. It was he who burglarized the drilling company, again leaving no fingerprints, looking for copies of Price-Leigh's data. Is that not true, Leroy?" he asked, whirling on the old farmer.

MacPhearson hesitated a moment. "Yeah, that's right."

"He did so not to conceal a murderer's identity, but to conceal his own and that of an innocent person who cared nothing for the dump, or DOE, or any of the issues involved, cared only for Price-Leigh."

"Who?" demanded Miller.

"It is not necessary for you to know. You have my word on that."

"I wouldn't take your damn word that the sun was shining without looking out the window first. Whose fingerprints did Hap rub out? I want a goddamn name."

"Mine." The voice was quiet, young, and trembling.

"Oh, my God," screamed Frances.

"Shut up, Frances," said Elizabeth, her voice sounding tired and resigned. "Let's get the whole story out. You were wrong. I was wrong. The least we can do is explain ourselves and hope Rachel understands someday."

"Rachel?" asked Miller, his eyes searching the room and finding the girl's trembling figure crouched on the floor behind John Lloyd.

"I was in love with Charlton, and he was in love with me; I don't care what my mother says. If she and Aunt Elizabeth hadn't held me a prisoner, I would've been with him that night, and maybe he wouldn't have been murdered."

"Don't be melodramatic, Rachel," said Elizabeth. "You'd have just been killed, too."

"No," said John Lloyd, trying to look at Rachel. His voice was deep and kind. "It is possible she is right. By being prevented from seeing you, Price-Leigh was isolated from human warmth. However, it is equally true that your presence would only have worsened an already tense situation, and perhaps changed the resolution not at all. As you have reminded me, you are not a child. One of the most unpleasant features of not being a child is learning to live with uncertainty."

"Why did Hap conceal his own identity?" asked Miller, his chin thrust forward until Lydia wondered how he kept from dislocating it.

John Lloyd was silent, and Lydia knew he was prepared to protect Hap if it meant going to prison.

"Come on, Branson, why?" demanded Miller. "Who is he? An AWOL soldier, an escaped prisoner, a goddamn terrorist?"

"He was here. He influenced these events. And now he is gone. I respect his need to remain . . ." he hesitated— "unknown, to expiate whatever sin he feels he has committed."

"Texas has a great little facility down in Huntsville for expiating sins," snapped Miller. "If I ever catch him, I'll ask the warden to put him in the cell right next to yours."

"Leroy, did Hap murder Charlton Price-Leigh?" asked John Lloyd.

"Nope," said the old man, and began rocking again.

"I thought not," said John Lloyd.

"I don't give a goose's fart in a high wind what you think, Branson." Cleetus Miller's skin had a purple tinge.

"Now, Cleetus, remember your blood pressure." Schroder's voice rumbled out of his square frame like sand over gravel. "Let's hear the rest of Branson's story."

"An excellent suggestion, Sergeant Schroder." John Lloyd tapped one finger against his chin. "I think I was interrupted after ascertaining that Elizabeth and Hap were unsympathetic to Price-Leigh's attempt to explain himself. They left, according to my informants, just before dark, which is about eight-thirty this season of the year. So at eight-thirty in the evening, on the last day of his life, Charlton Price-Leigh was understood by no one, believed by no one, trusted by no one."

CHAPTER
TWENTY-THREE

THE HAIRS STOOD UP ON JENNER'S ARMS AND HE SMOOTHED
them down. Damn, if that overdressed undertaker of a lawyer
didn't sound like some TV documentary on the last hours of
Lincoln, or Christ, or some other doomed saint. Branson
almost made him feel sorry for Price-Leigh. Almost, hell,
Jenner thought. He did feel sorry for the poor bastard. There
he was, sitting on proof that would sink the DOE ship, and
no one would listen to him. Jenner imagined him sitting in
his living room, maybe staring at that big painting of the old
cowboy riding fence while cars zipped by on a highway just
a few feet away from his horse's hooves. What had Price-
Leigh been thinking about those last few hours before someone stuck a knife in his chest?

"What Price-Leigh did between the hours of eight-thirty
and eleven when he made his phone call to Leroy Mac-
Phearson will always be in shadow."

The lawyer's voice was almost hypnotic, thought Jenner.
He almost made you believe that whatever he was describing

actually happened. Even when you knew for sure that he had to be making up part of it. No one could really know. Except the murderer.

"But we may surmise certain things about that shadow time," continued John Lloyd. "For instance, we may be certain that Mr. Tinsdale visited Price-Leigh during that period."

Tinsdale's face lost all color, and his breath made a wheezing sound in the hushed room. "You can't prove that, Branson," he whispered.

The lawyer lifted one hand, palm up, in a gesture of agreement. "Perhaps not. I do not intend to try. That is Sergeant Schroder's province, and I suspect that he will not only try, but succeed . . ."—he paused for the space of a heartbeat—"with my help. Your wreck with Frances Whitley was a very suspicious coincidence, so suspicious that I suspect it was not a coincidence at all. Frances, how long had you been following Mr. Tinsdale?"

Frances moaned, and twisted in her chair. Willis patted her shoulder. "Answer the question, hon."

Hon's face was sulky, and Jenner suspected she didn't want to talk at all, but it took a stronger person than a drunk not to answer John Lloyd Branson. "I followed him from Price-Leigh's house. I saw this big fancy car pull out of his garage. It looked like the kind of car a man who chased little girls would drive. I didn't know I was following the wrong person until the wreck."

"It is gratifying to have a supposition proved," said John Lloyd.

"Supposition, shit," said Miller, rolling his cigar between his fingers. "Why don't you call it a guess?"

"Because it is not a guess. Each murder case has a certain rhythm, a certain pattern of events, that reveals itself quite clearly when the psychology of all the participants is known."

He slowly took a step forward. "Your profile, Mr. Tinsdale, that of a suspicious bureaucrat, dictated that you must know why Price-Leigh sent those letters. I am sure you spent the early evening hours searching his office only to find nothing. So you went to his house as a friend and colleague to see what, if any, hints you might gather from casual conversation. It was during that visit, when you found Price-Leigh depressed and desperate, that you learned what he had done. Did he attempt to persuade you of the error of your ways, Tinsdale? Or did he speak of his findings?''

John Lloyd nodded as Tinsdale turned even whiter. ''Yes, I think in view of your subsequent behavior, he did tell you. Otherwise, why attempt to blacken his character, and fix the blame for murder on MacPhearson? And you did both. You discovered the bloodstained bedroom sometime after the Saturday news reported a body on MacPhearson's farm. There was never any note, and you had nearly a week to enter the house by way of the garage, and alter an ordinary bedroom into a den of iniquity. But you left the map and the list until Sergeant Schroder called, then allowed yourself to be caught with them. What better way to draw attention to their importance than to be caught trying to hide them.''

Tinsdale put his hands over his face, and swayed back and forth on the chair. ''I want a lawyer.''

His voice was muffled by his hands, and Schroder levered them away from his face. ''What did you say, Tinsdale?''

''I want a lawyer,'' repeated the DOE project manager. ''I have a constitutional right to a lawyer.''

''He's gonna quote you the Miranda warning, Schroder,'' said Jenner, leaning forward on the couch. ''Branson must have hit him where it hurts.''

''Not in the balls,'' said Maximum Miller, looking like he had a bad taste in his mouth. ''Little fucker got 'em mashed flat today.''

John Lloyd stepped closer to Tinsdale's cowering figure. Jenner watched the attorney's shadow cast on the wall, completely enveloping Tinsdale's. ''Had you not made that last visit," said John Lloyd in a deep, slow voice, "Charlton Price-Leigh might be alive today."

"Mirandize him, Schroder," said Miller, springing up from the couch and rubbing his hands together in anticipation. "We got ourselves a murderer."

"No!" John Lloyd's voice would have stopped God himself, thought Jenner, as Cleetus Miller dropped back on the couch and stuck another cigar in his mouth. "Tinsdale did not murder Charlton Price-Leigh. He was gone by eleven o'clock when Price-Leigh called Leroy MacPhearson. At eleven o'clock, Charlton Price-Leigh had approximately an hour and a half to live."

Tinsdale sagged back against his chair.

"Damn it, Branson, you just accused him of murder," said Cleetus, chomping on his cigar. "I was getting curious about how the little shit set up his alibi." Jenner noticed that the prosecutor was almost as good as Schroder at talking out of one side of his mouth.

John Lloyd wore an impatient expression, as if he were tired of interruptions. Jenner decided he'd keep his comments to himself. A tired John Lloyd Branson was a mean mother.

"You misunderstood. Tinsdale undoubtedly threatened Price-Leigh with DOE retaliation for his actions. He increased Price-Leigh's feelings of isolation and desperation, but he pushed too hard. He became the enemy and was either verbally or physically ejected from the house."

John Lloyd's voice deepened, took on a funereal tone, and Jenner felt he was listening to a eulogy. "At that point, the die was cast. Unable to convince Tinsdale, Price-Leigh was committed to making a heroic gesture. There was no way back. He had to contact STAD immediately in order to save the Panhandle. At eleven o'clock, he picked up the phone and dialed Leroy MacPhearson's number."

Jenner looked at MacPhearson. The old man was resting his head against the back of the rocking chair, and his eyes were closed. His mouth gaped open and for the first time, Jenner noticed that he wore dentures. His skin was rough, and weathered to the consistency of shoe leather, worn shoe leather. Leroy MacPhearson was a tired old man who'd carried guilty knowledge longer than his body could stand.

MacPhearson opened his eyes and gazed at the ceiling. "He wasn't making too much sense at first, and he woke me up, so I didn't have my mind working too well either. And I was mad when I realized who it was. Frances had called all upset about him and Rachel, and I wasn't too quick to be cordial to the man. But he kept repeating salt dissolution, and saying he could prove it. I didn't much believe him, and didn't trust him at all, but I finally listened. He sounded desperate, like John Lloyd said, and frustrated, like he was about to explode. I finally told him I was too old to be taken in by a cock-and-bull story by some government thief who didn't have the decency to keep his hands off little girls. I wish I hadn't told him he wasn't decent. That's weighed on my mind since he died. He told me to come to his house, and he'd prove he was sincere. I kind of put him off and hung up."

The old man stopped and rolled his head to one side to look at John Lloyd. The lawyer nodded. "Thank you, Leroy. That's enough for now."

Jenner thought at first he was imagining the quiet sobbing coming from the corner of the room behind John Lloyd until he felt Lydia Fairchild's silk shirt shiver against his arm as she rose from the couch. The lamplight glinted on her blonde hair as she knelt by young Rachel and held her like a child.

The lamps cast islands of light on the listeners. Tinsdale huddled as far from the light as possible. Just like a cockroach, thought Jenner. He noticed Leroy MacPhearson shifting his rocker closer to the light as if he were cold. Jenner shivered himself. If the old man wasn't cold, he ought to be. John Lloyd Branson's story was enough to freeze the blood. Or maybe the air temperature was dropping. Maybe there were cold spots forming in the room like all good ghost stories described. Maybe Charlton Price-Leigh's spirit was hovering just outside the lamplight, listening to the account of his own last hours.

John Lloyd turned back, and Jenner felt the hair on his arms stiffen again. There was something about the lawyer's eyes, something sad. "It is now approximately eleven-thirty and Charlton Price-Leigh has an hour to live. I do not know all of what he did during that hour, but I do know that he walked to the mailbox on the corner, less than twenty yards away, and mailed a package containing all of his data and his interpretation of it, to me. I was the only member of STAD who was not a landowner. I was his last hope. It is now eleven-forty-five, and he has another forty-five minutes to live."

"Please, John Lloyd," said Lydia. "I'm getting the shivers with your counting down his last minutes."

Jenner thought for a second that he saw the attorney's eyes soften. Trick of the light, he decided in the following second, because John Lloyd Branson's eyes looked like his idea of God's right before the almighty sent the flood.

"To celebrate the last hours of the only meaningful time in his life is the least I can do, Miss Fairchild," said John Lloyd, his voice sounding stern and loud. "Perhaps he dreamed of a hero's sacrifice during those thirty minutes before his last visitors came. Perhaps he had a drink, proposed a toast to the land, dreamed he was riding side by side with that old cowboy in the largest of his paintings. He read poetry, after all. It is not unreasonable to believe he might have sought refuge in some romantic daydreams. I pray that he did. I pray that those last minutes were sweet. It is now approximately twelve-fifteen, and he has fifteen minutes to live."

John Lloyd stepped backward until he stood just outside the circle of light cast by MacPhearson's lamp. "Leroy," he said, his voice quiet. "Leroy, it is time now. You know that, do you not?"

The couch sagged next to Jenner as Maximum Miller shifted his weight forward, then sat motionless.

Leroy MacPhearson rested his arms on his knees and rubbed his hands together. Jenner frowned as he tried to remember where he'd seen that same action performed. He dismissed the worry as MacPhearson looked up at John Lloyd. "I called Hap after I hung up on Price-Leigh, and we had a confab. I reckon I didn't believe Price-Leigh and Hap didn't either. But we couldn't be sure, don't you see. That's why we decided to go talk to him. We thought those letters meant the government was getting ready to make a move. I had them stopped on the containment area, but that didn't mean they still wouldn't put the dump in. We were ready to grab at anything to make Congress listen to us, even talk to Price-Leigh in the middle of the night."

MacPhearson was silent for a minute while he rubbed his hands together and drew a breath that lifted his shoulders, a runner exhausting his strength for one last effort. "If a man believes in something enough to die for it, then maybe it's time to take a second look. Trouble was, we didn't know where to look. Price-Leigh never told us who he sent his research to. I didn't know what to do. Hap and me was standing in a room with a dead man and all I could think about was that he didn't have no socks on."

MacPhearson looked down at his left foot in its thick-soled shoe. "I don't never let anybody see my naked feet, and I didn't want him laying there without his socks either. Hap was pretty shook, too, but his head was clearer than mine. Anyway, Hap said we had to hide the body, give that research time to be delivered and be made public. Otherwise, the police would confiscate it as evidence, and it might be months before we could get it to the right people. I saw what Hap was getting at, but it wasn't decent to leave a good man's body lying around where the varmints could chew on it. Hap argued with me, but I said we were going to leave the body where it'd be found quick and get a decent burial. It was the least we could do. Hap argued about that, said everybody in STAD would be a suspect, and the research would still be confiscated. Well, he had me there. I didn't want the police hassling my friends."

He drew another deep breath and when he exhaled it, Jenner thought he looked more shrunken and old than even a few minutes ago. "I told Hap not to worry 'cause Price-Leigh was gonna be found in my field, and I'd be the only suspect. Hap acted like a crazy man at that idea, but I wasn't gonna change my mind. Finally, he kinda settled down and said if we couldn't hide the body, we'd hide the identity. That's when Hap came up with his idea."

"What idea?" demanded Miller.

MacPhearson squeezed his lips together and looked at John Lloyd. "Deception, Mr. Miller." John Lloyd's voice sounded matter-of-fact, a nineteenth-century professor explaining a theorem to a class of not very bright scholars. "It was the first deception perpetrated by the side you loosely call the defense. If Leroy would not permit the body to be hidden, then at least the identity could be. It was at that point that Hap"—he raised his eyebrow in inquiry, then continued as MacPhearson nodded—"stripped and shaved the body."

"Jesus Christ!" exclaimed Miller.

John Lloyd raised an eyebrow again. "We can only hope that He understands and sympathizes with the defense's dilemma. Leroy did, after all, place himself in jeopardy in order to insure that Mr. Price-Leigh's mortal remains might receive a speedy and *decent* burial. He also protected Mr. Price-Leigh's reputation at some risk to his own."

"Jesus Christ!" repeated Miller. "Now you're saying MacPhearson's a hero?"

"And why not? Leroy MacPhearson sacrificed his own welfare that others might be safe. Price-Leigh also sacrificed much, his job, old friends, if losing Tinsdale might be considered a sacrifice, but in the end it was not enough.''

"It sure wasn't, was it? Somebody knifed him in his chest for his troubles,'' said Miller.

"I think it is necessary to hear an account of Price-Leigh's last quarter hour on earth.''

"That would be real nice, Branson,'' said Miller. "We've had a damn diary of his whole day, including what happened after his lights went out, but we haven't heard about the instant somebody flipped his switch.''

"Has no one ever told you that patience is a virtue?'' asked John Lloyd.

Miller growled, and Jenner scooted away. If Maximum Miller started biting, he wanted to be out of the kill zone.

John Lloyd touched Leroy on the shoulder. "I could recount the events, but I was not there. This is no time for speculation.''

Miller growled again and lumbered to his feet. "Just a goddamn minute, Branson. You proved this afternoon that MacPhearson wasn't at Price-Leigh's house.''

"Your refer to the phone call made to Leroy's number just prior to the time of death? The phone call that was answered?''

Jenner thought Miller just might add foaming at the mouth to growling. The prosecutor looked mad enough to handle doing both. "Yes!'' Miller spat out the word, and Jenner was definitely glad he was out of spitting range.

"The call was made, and it was answered by that technological irritant know as an answering machine.''

"That does it!'' exclaimed Miller. "Sergeant Schroder, arrest that man for murder.''

"Do not be precipitate, Mr. Prosecutor, or I will direct my client to say nothing further, and this case will remain forever unsolved. All that you have heard thus far will be ruled hearsay and inadmissible in court because no one received a Miranda warning. My desire to see justice done to

a dead man does not extend to having an innocent man un-
justly charged. What is your decision, Mr. Miller? Will you
call for a new deal, or play this hand out?''

Jenner held his breath. No one would ever accuse John
Lloyd Branson of being afraid to gamble. Of course, knowing Branson, he probably had another ace up his sleeve.

Miller sat down and wiped his glistening forehead. ''I'll
play these cards, Branson, but the next deal's mine. You understand? Pull a joker on me, and I'll close your game
down.''

John Lloyd nodded. He squeezed MacPhearson's shoulder
and stepped back out of the light, a darker shadow among
the shadows.

''Price-Leigh wasn't surprised when Hap and me got
there,'' began Leroy. ''He wasn't happy either. In fact, he
wasn't anything, except maybe resigned. He asked if we believed him, and I said not exactly, but we'd look at his proof.
That's when he laughed. Only heard one other man laugh
like that. It was like a buddy of mine who fought in every
battle in Europe in the Second World War. Made it home
without a scratch, then fell off his porch and broke his back.
I went to see him in the hospital, and he was laughing just
like Price-Leigh.''

MacPhearson rubbed his hands against his pants legs, and
cleared his throat as if what he was about to say next was
harder than anything he'd said before. ''Price-Leigh said he
didn't have the proof anymore, that he'd sent it to his last
hope. We didn't know he was talking about John Lloyd. I
got mad. Here I drove down in the middle of the night to
find some crazy man talking about last hope. I called him a
liar and a few other names I had handy.''

MacPhearson drew another one of those shuddering
breaths. ''That's when he pulled open his shirt and pointed
to his heart. 'I am sincere,' he said real solemnlike. 'I'm
willing to prove it.' I said I might believe him on his deathbed
and not before, then Hap and I started out the door and

slammed it behind us. I heard him cuss, then I didn't hear nothing else until Hap and me was almost out to the pickup I'd parked in front of his house. We heard a scream that raised our hackles. We turned around and ran back into that house like the devil himself was on our heels. We found him laying on the floor with a little fancy-handled knife sticking out of his chest. We picked him up and carried him into the bedroom. He looked at us and asked, 'Do you believe me now?' The blood bubbled out of his mouth and ran into his beard and he died.''

MacPhearson looked over at Maximum Miller. ''It was an honor to lay him out on my land.''

EPILOGUE

MAXIMUM MILLER BRACED HIMSELF AGAINST THE HOOD OF his parked Suburban and looked at MacPhearson's farmhouse, still another unlit cigar in his mouth. "That's the damnedest story I ever heard in my life, Branson. A man'd have to be crazy to believe a word of it. Tampering with evidence, committing perjury, a murder that turns out to be suicide, and that ain't the most unbelievable thing. You know what is? That a DOE man would change his spots. I can't buy that. But I'll give you credit for the best goddamn cover-up since Watergate. Hell, Nixon should've hired you, and the son of a bitch'd *still* be president."

"It is your deal, Mr. Prosecutor," said John Lloyd quietly. "What will the ante be?"

"Who's Hap?"

"That is the ante?"

Miller clamped his teeth together. Like a bulldog, thought Lydia. "I don't like witnesses taking a hike, Branson."

John Lloyd looked toward the west, his eyes focused, as

if he didn't really see the horizon. "He lived on Love Canal in a home built over the worst part of the toxic dump. His infant daughter died of leukemia, and his wife committed suicide, a very public suicide that changed nothing. Perhaps that was why Hap was so determined that Price-Leigh's death accomplish its goal."

"What's the rest of the story, Branson? What you've told so far is no reason for a man to run."

"Hap was an executive of one of the chemical companies involved in dumping toxic waste in Love Canal."

Maximum Miller turned his head to look across the plowed fields toward the skyline of Amarillo. The moonlight turned tiny sweat beads on his forehead into iridescent pearls. "What did you do with that stuff Price-Leigh sent you, Branson?"

John Lloyd smiled. "Miss Fairchild, please enlighten Mr. Miller."

Lydia cleared her throat, clasped her hands, and hoped the prosecutor was a big supporter of the anti-dump movement. Otherwise, she and John Lloyd might be cellmates of Tinsdale's. "A printer is making enough copies to send one to every representative and every senator in the United States Congress. We're also sending a copy to each editor of a major U.S. newspaper, magazine, and to the television networks, of course. The original is locked up in a safety deposit box to which John Lloyd holds the only key." She glanced at him. "He said the key was safest with him because he was impervious to pressure."

Cleetus Miller nodded. "Then I suspect I'd better have a copy for my press conference tomorrow when I announce Price-Leigh committed suicide. Gotta cover my ass, you know."

"Then you believe Mr. MacPhearson?" asked Lydia.

"About like I believe in Santa Claus, Miss Fairchild." He opened his car door, put one foot on the runner, then turned to John Lloyd. "I just want to know one more thing, Branson. Why the hell did MacPhearson put socks on the corpse?''

John Lloyd touched his cane. "We always project our own infirmities on others. I would have left on the victim's trousers. Leroy MacPhearson has a mutilated left foot. He would find bare feet totally unacceptable.''

"But a pink and yellow sock?''

"Leroy is not color-blind. However, I must conclude that Hap was, and Leroy didn't know it until he actually laid out the body in his field. I recall Sergeant Schroder mentioning in his original incident report that Leroy seemed upset about the color of those socks.''

"And the knife?''

"Another way to direct suspicion upon himself while knowing that the autopsy would prove a much smaller blade was actually the murder weapon. Leroy may be a hero, but he is not a fool. Leaving the murder weapon in Price-Leigh's chest would have made it almost impossible for me to argue persuasively for an examining trial.''

"Now that I can believe,'' Miller said as he sat down and slammed his door. Immediately he rolled down his window and stuck his head out. "Schroder, what the hell's taking you and the Hardy boy so long? Get Tinsdale in your car, take him back to Amarillo, and book him for tampering with evidence.''

Schroder kept his grip on Tinsdale's arms as Jenner opened MacPhearsons's yard gate. "We already charged him with that, Cleetus.'' Schroder's voice didn't so much float on the evening air as bounce like a gravel-filled beach ball.

Cleetus Miller tapped his fingers on the car door. "Charge him with failure to identify himself as a witness to a crime. We ain't charged the son of a bitch with that yet.''

There was a high-pitched squeal like a defective microphone, then a series of grunts, as if someone were trying to scream and couldn't—until finally Lydia began to sort out words: ". . . damn, mangy, misbegotten dog! I'll kill it! Let go of me so I can kill that dog."

"What the hell's going on over there, Schroder?" yelled Miller at the burly investigator who was holding onto Tinsdale as he hopped around like a man afflicted with St. Vitus' Dance.

"It's nothing sir," replied Sergeant Jenner. "A dog . . ." His voice began to shake, then broke altogether into the loudest guffaws Lydia had ever heard.

"A dog what?" demanded Miller, leaning out of his window and peering at the group struggling twenty feet away alongside Schroder's dilapidated car.

"One of Mr. MacPhearson's dogs just pissed all over Tinsdale's leg, Cleetus," said Schroder. "He'll be all right. He can strip off his pants in the backseat. I got a blanket he can wrap up in."

The last Lydia heard from Tinsdale was a loud wail as Schroder's car careened down MacPhearson's driveway toward Soncy Road.

Cleetus Miller turned on his ignition and put his Suburban in gear. "Branson, how about sharing the pot on this one. I don't buy your client's story, or at least not all of it, but I don't think you do either, so let's call this one a draw."

Miller stuck his hand out the window to John Lloyd. "Sometimes I think you skate so close to the edge of the law, you'll fall off, Branson, but damn if you don't liven things up."

He shook hands with John Lloyd, then offered his hand to Lydia. "You ever want to work on God's side, Miss Fairchild, you just come on down to the Potter County's District Attorney's office and hire on."

Lydia shook hands with the black assistant, then clasped John Lloyd's arm. "Thanks, Mr. Miller, but I'll stay with the last hope."

"Miss Fairchild, the correct term is last *best* hope," remarked John Lloyd.

Cleetus Miller grinned and raised his hand in fare-well. "Until the next time, Branson. Keep your powder dry and your pecker primed."

Lydia stood watching Miller's car until its taillights disappeared into the stream of traffic on Soncy Road. "What really happened in that house, John Lloyd?"

"Shall we get into the car, Miss Fairchild? I believe one of Mr. MacPhearson's dogs is studying your leg with a great deal of interest."

"That dog is more interested in your car's front tire," retorted Lydia. "Quit changing the subject."

John Lloyd glared at a brown-and-white hound until it lowered its leg and slunk away with its tail between its legs.

"Well," demanded Lydia.

He leaned against the car. "I think Leroy MacPhearson told the truth as he knew it. Whether it is the whole truth or not is immaterial. The legend will say that Charlton Price-Leigh committed suicide in a last desperate effort to draw attention to his research. When forced to choose between the truth and the legend, pick the legend."

Lydia tucked her arm in the crook of his. "So what's the truth, John Lloyd? Who killed Price-Leigh?"

John Lloyd blew a smoke ring and watched it float away. "Are you aware of how extraordinarly difficult it would be to commit suicide by stabbing oneself in the heart? At the first tremor of pain, one would automatically let go of the knife. Yet if we believe Leroy MacPhearson, only the hilt was showing. I believe Price-Leigh intended some dramatic gesture such as pricking himself in the chest. However, fate intervened. You remember from this afternoon's testimony that Price-Leigh had a dislocated toe?"

Lydia nodded. "So what?"

John Lloyd tilted his head back to look at the stars. "I believe, Miss Fairchild, that Carlton Price-Leigh stubbed his toe, stumbled, and fell on his knife. He turned an accident into suicide, which was construed as murder. Deception to the last.''

''You're incredible, John Lloyd,'' said Lydia. ''You're just as guilty of deception as anyone in this case.''

He took her arm and led her toward the car. ''I have never denied being devious on occasion. For a good cause. Shall we go home, Miss Fairchild? Someone is sending prostitutes invitations to join a heavenly choir. One such soiled dove has applied to me for help.''

''The purple letter!'' exclaimed Lydia.

''It promises to be a most interesting case. I shall count on your assistance.''

''But I have to go back to school.''

''That is unfortunate. Ah, well, perhaps something interesting will occur in time for Thanksgiving.''

Lydia tilted her head back to look at him. ''You could have a relapse.''

He stood without moving for a few seconds, then reached in his pocket. He withdrew his car keys and dropped them in her outstretched hand. ''Would you please drive home, Miss Fairchild? I seem to be feeling quite ill.''

POSTSCRIPT

ON DECEMBER 22, 1987, PRESIDENT RONALD REAGAN signed into law a bill designating Yucca Mountain, Nevada, as the only dumpsite to be tested for suitability. Should Yucca Mountain prove unsuitable, the Department of Energy must return to Congress for further orders.

The DOE was given ninety days to get out of the Panhandle.

Occasionally one can fight City Hall and win.

About the Author

D. R. MEREDITH's first John Lloyd Branson mystery, *Murder by Impulse*, was published by Ballantine in 1988. That novel and the sequel, *Murder by Deception*, were Anthony Award nominees. Subsequent installments in the series include *Murder by Masquerade*, *Murder by Reference*, and the forthcoming *Murder by Sacrilege*. Ms. Meredith, who lives in Amarillo, Texas, with her husband and their two children, has also written four mysteries featuring Sheriff Charles Matthews: *The Sheriff and the Panhandle Murders*, *The Sheriff and the Branding Iron Murders*, *The Sheriff and the Folsom Man Murders*, and *The Sheriff and the Pheasant Hunt Murders*.

EDWARD MATHIS

A DAN ROMAN TE★AS MYSTERY